You Make It Feel
Like Christmas

You Make It Feel Like Christmas

DONNA HILL
AND FRANCIS RAY

ST. MARTIN'S GRIFFIN
NEW YORK

Published in the United States by St. Martin's Griffin, an imprint of St. Martin's Publishing Group

YOU MAKE IT FEEL LIKE CHRISTMAS: ROCKIN' AROUND THAT CHRISTMAS TREE. Copyright © 2003 by Donna Hill and Francis Ray. THE WISH. Copyright © 2002 by Francis Ray. All rights reserved. Printed in the United States of America. For information, address St. Martin's Publishing Group, 120 Broadway, New York, NY 10271.

www.stmartins.com

Designed by Gabriel Guma

The Library of Congress Cataloging-in-Publication Data is available upon request.

ISBN 978-1-250-81856-0 (trade paperback)
ISBN 978-1-250-81857-7 (ebook)

Our books may be purchased in bulk for promotional, educational, or business use. Please contact your local bookseller or the Macmillan Corporate and Premium Sales Department at 1-800-221-7945, extension 5442, or by email at MacmillanSpecialMarkets@macmillan.com.

Rockin' Around That Christmas Tree first published by St. Martin's Press

The Wish first published in *Gettin' Merry* by St. Martin's Paperbacks

First Edition: 2021

10 9 8 7 6 5 4 3 2 1

Rockin' Around That Christmas Tree

DONNA HILL AND FRANCIS RAY

We lovingly dedicate this book to all of our loyal fans who have supported us through the years, and welcome the new ones. May your holiday season and all the days that follow bring you joy, peace, and happiness.

We deeply thank our ever-creative editor, Monique Patterson, who told us we could do this, believed in us, and made sure we got this done!

DENISE'S TEA CAKES

2 cups sugar
¾ cup solid shortening
2 eggs
1 teaspoon baking soda
1 teaspoon vanilla extract
2–3 cups sifted flour
½ cup buttermilk

Preheat oven to 375 degrees Fahrenheit. Cream sugar and solid shortening in a large mixing bowl. Add eggs and stir until smooth. Combine baking soda with ¼ cup flour, then add to ingredients in mixing bowl. Mix well. Add vanilla and stir. Alternate flour and buttermilk until buttermilk is incorporated. Continue adding flour until dough is firm. Cover bowl with waxed paper and refrigerate for 3–4 hours. Roll out dough, cut into desired shapes. Bake for 8–12 minutes (depending on thickness of cookie). Lift with spatula onto cooling rack. Or just eat hot. Enjoy.

ONE

Denise Morrison could have cheerfully strangled her husband, Edward, a man she'd loved for more than half her life. *Enough was enough.* Minutes earlier, she'd been elbow deep in dishwater and he'd asked her to refill his coffee cup while he leisurely read the *Atlanta Journal* before going to work. The only reason he wasn't trying to wrestle her apron from around his neck was that he'd said "please."

Men! They had the sensitivity and the single-mindedness of an ant.

"Good coffee," Edward mumbled.

Denise rolled her eyes as she continued to wash the breakfast dishes. Once they'd had so much to talk about, to plan. Those days had somehow slipped by and in their place was complacency.

Denise paused to stare out the window of their rambling two-story home on an oversize lot in the Atlanta suburbs. The large, well-manicured yard was still green with rye grass in late November. The four seven-foot oak trees they'd raised blisters on their hands to plant now towered forty feet and gave shade to the winter-hardy petunias and the hammock that hadn't been used in years. The trees and grass thrived, but their marriage had lost its magic. The knowledge hurt deep inside her. Love like theirs should have lasted a lifetime instead of twenty-seven years. They had accomplished so much and now seemed to share so little.

"I went shopping for the kids yesterday," Edward said.

Denise glanced around at Edward sitting across the room at the dining table instead of at the end of the island directly behind her. He used to sit there to be closer to her when they'd first built the house twenty years ago. She tried to remember the last time he had eaten his meal on the island while she worked in the kitchen, or the last time they had sat side by side on the two stools on the end, arms and hips, hearts and minds touching—and couldn't.

"Denise, did you hear me?" Edward asked, his gaze still on the business section of the newspaper. His dark head tilted to one side to pitch his voice in her direction. She wasn't even important enough to take his attention from the newspaper.

"I heard."

He nodded and turned the page, then put the newspaper down and swiveled toward her. His handsome chocolate-hued face was animated as always when he spoke of their two children. "I got the diamond earrings Christine has been hinting at and Anthony the newest Palm Pilot. They're wrapped, so you won't have to worry about it. We're finished with their big gifts."

For a moment Denise was at a loss as to what to say. "I thought we were going shopping for them together?"

Edward turned back to the newspaper. "Christine called yesterday to say hello and mentioned she had seen the earrings on sale. I didn't want them to sell out since she had her heart set on them. There was an electronics store across the street, so I decided to take care of Anthony's as well."

Denise placed the plate in the drying rack and reached for the skillet. He took care of too many things. The sad thing was, he wasn't doing it maliciously. He'd been brought up to take care of his family. He was, in her grandmother's words, a man's man.

"It will be great having them home for Thanksgiving," he continued. "Aunt Etta and Uncle Eddie will be here too. I left you some extra money on the dresser to get anything you need. I want the dinner to be the best ever. This will be the first Thanksgiving with the children here since Christine got married and Anthony moved into his own place."

Denise's slim fingers tightened around the skillet handle. So, now she was needed! She could cook for the family, but her help wasn't needed to help pick out her own children's Christmas presents. For one wild moment she thought of seeing if the skillet could sail like a Frisbee. "I went grocery shopping last week," she said evenly, keeping her temper in check.

"Good." He stood, shoving the ladder-backed chair beneath the round oak table. "And another thing, you know I don't like you sewing for other people. I hope that wedding dress you were working on last night is the end of it."

She spun around. Dishwater dripped from her hands onto the spotless hardwood floor. Sewing was the only thing she did that was strictly *her* accomplishment. "I like sewing. People are beginning to call me."

He paused in pulling on his black baseball cap with the name of his construction company emblazoned in gold lettering. "I hope you told them no. You have a family and a house to care for. And you certainly don't need the money."

I need to be needed, she almost said. "Is it so bad that I want to earn my own money, to want to be able to buy you or the children something without first going to you?"

Impatient lines radiated across Edward's strong forehead. "I take care of my family, Denise. If you need money, all you have to do is ask or write a check."

"I'd rather have my own," she said with an unconscious tilt of her chin.

"It *is* your money," he told her with a brisk jerk of his cap. "I can't see why you'd think otherwise. Have I ever said anything about how you spend money or asked you about a check you'd written?"

"No, but you write the checks for all the bills and the expenses."

"So you won't have to worry about it," he told her. "I do it for you."

She shook her head. "But remember how I wanted to buy a new sewing machine after people started asking me about making clothes for them, when they saw how beautiful the dresses I designed and made for Christine and her wedding attendants were? You said no."

"You shouldn't be sewing for people. They just want to get it cheap because they know you won't charge them full price," he said, picking up the insulated lunch Thermos she always prepared for him when he planned to work in his office.

"That may be true, but it also gives me the chance to do something I love," she said, trying to make him understand. "You and the children certainly don't need me sewing for you. I completely redid the house before the wedding. Sewing helps fill the day."

"With the holidays coming, you'll be busy enough," he said, a hint of exasperation in his deep voice. "I don't want my wife sewing for people and being taken advantage of."

Edward always had enough pride for two men and was more stubborn than a mule when he'd made up his mind. "They're not taking advantage of me," Denise replied. "I get the pleasure out of seeing my ideas come alive, and they get a beautiful dress. The customer and I both win."

His brown eyes narrowed. "If you want to sew, then sew for yourself or Aunt Etta."

"Neither one of us needs a wedding gown nor any of the other designs I've been thinking about lately," she told him, her hands pressed against the cool ceramic tile on top of the island, trying to tease him back into his usual good humor. It didn't work. His mouth remained in a thin, disapproving line.

Unwilling to give up, she tried another tack. "Sewing makes me feel the same way you feel when a design for one of your projects is finished."

He tsked dismissively. "You can't compare what we do."

Denise realized it would be useless to continue. He didn't think what she did was important. She looked at him and wanted to snatch the lunch Thermos out of his hand. He was almost a stranger. He used to listen to her, even if he always made the final decision. Perhaps it was her fault for always being a follower instead of being more assertive. If she had been, perhaps he would treat her as an equal in their marriage.

"What am I supposed to do with my time while your behind is glued to that ugly orange chair watching TV?" she asked with growing irritation. Not for love or money would he let her get rid of or reupholster the bulky lounger that was covered with an atrocious bright orange tweed. "We haven't gone out to dinner or to a movie in months."

"My chair is not ugly and I'm tired when I get home. I've never forced or stopped you from doing anything, have I?" he challenged.

"No, but you made it so obvious that you didn't want me to do it that I felt uncomfortable."

He gave the baseball cap another impatient jerk. "I'm just trying to look out for your best interests. You didn't come up as rough as I did. You don't know how harsh the world can be, and I don't intend for you to find out. You have a nice home, all the bills are paid, a new car. I work hard to give you everything you want."

Everything but the freedom to make my own decisions and run my own life, she thought silently. She was no longer a teenage bride, unsure of herself and looking to him for guidance and approval. She was a grown woman who needed to live her own life and make her own mistakes if necessary.

"Denise."

The unyielding way he said her name was a command for her to fall in line as always. She could argue, but she'd promised herself long ago that she'd never get into the screaming matches her parents had while she was growing up. Edward wasn't being mean; he was just doing as he always had, taking care of his family by handling all the finances and solving all the problems. He didn't seem to understand that making all the important decisions made her feel like a bystander in her own home.

Her shoulders slumped, and when she spoke, her voice was barely above a whisper. "All right, Edward."

He nodded his head in satisfaction. "If you get any more calls about sewing, just tell them no. You'll be too busy preparing for the holidays. I'll start putting up the Christmas lights tonight so Anthony can throw the switch after Thanksgiving dinner." He stuck the business section of the newspaper under his arm. "I won't be home until late. Good-bye."

Denise watched him walk out of the kitchen toward the front of the house where his SUV was parked. No good-bye kiss, no hug, nothing, just instructions to make Thanksgiving dinner the best ever and not to sew for anyone. She had the childish urge to stick her tongue out at his broad back. She was his wife, not his housekeeper.

It used to be that they couldn't be in the same room without touching. Now they seldom touched unless it was in bed, and then they'd burn up the sheets. But she needed—wanted—that same loving feeling when her feet were planted firmly on the floor. Her mouth quirked as she thought, *With my clothes on.*

They'd met when she was seventeen and he'd come as a carpenter's helper to repair her grandmother's wooden back porch. She'd answered the door, seen Edward with a two-by-four on his broad shoulder, and fallen hard. Deeply muscled and lean-hipped, he'd made her body shiver and her heart pound.

She'd made excuses to go outside while he was working. No matter how busy he was, he always stopped to get the back screen door for her. She'd heard the other worker teasing him, but he hadn't seemed to mind. That night he had called and they'd started going out. For her, there had never been anyone else.

Their closeness was cemented even more when he helped her during her parents' messy divorce. After years of making each other and everyone around them miserable, her parents had finally decided to move on. Denise had been sent to Atlanta to live with her maternal grandmother because her mother worked at night and her father was moving to another city. She had looked at the move as a punishment until she'd met Edward.

Walking over to the table, she picked up his coffee cup and took it back to the sink. He had always been so sure of himself, so assertive. Since she had lacked those qualities, she had admired them in him. But Edward had to accept that she was capable of making her own decisions, of running her life. She desperately wanted to do both.

The phone on the counter rang and she picked up the receiver without much enthusiasm. "Hello."

"Good morning, Mama."

A smile blossomed on Denise's face on hearing her daughter and eldest child's voice. "Good morning, Christine. How's Reese?" The happy laughter she usually heard when she mentioned her daughter's husband of five months didn't materialize. A frown worked its way across Denise's brow. "Is everything all right?"

"Sure, Mama," Christine quickly said, but the words sounded forced. "It's just that since Reese started his second-year residency at the hospital, he's been spending a lot of extra hours there. I miss him."

Denise tried to relax, but couldn't. If there was a problem, would her daughter tell her? Both Christine and her brother, Anthony, sought the counsel of their father more than hers. An-

other area over which Edward thought he should have domin-
ion.

Christine bubbled over with life and the men she'd dated were
usually the same way. Denise had been surprised when she first
met Reese, a first-year surgical resident at Atlanta General. He
was a tall, lean, good-looking young man with a serious face
and a disposition to match. They'd met when Christine, a social
worker for the city, had gone to the hospital to visit a child in
her caseload and Reese had been the attending physician. "All
marriages go through a period of adjustment. Reese is a wonderful man and he loves you," Denise said.

"I know. Is Daddy around?"

"No, he just left. Can I help?"

"Thanks, but I need to talk with him."

Denise tapped her fingernails on the countertop. "If it's about
the furniture you and Reese have stored in the garage, it's not
in the way."

"It's not that. Daddy already said we could leave it there until we decide what we want to do with it," Christine told her,
sounding a bit distracted.

Denise might have known. Daddy had decided, therefore the
opinion of her mother didn't matter. She continued to tap out
an agitated tattoo. *Typical,* she thought. *Just typical.*

"I gotta run. Bye, Mama. I'll see you in a couple of days for
Thanksgiving. I can't wait for some of your broccoli and cheese
casserole." She smacked her lips.

"Hmm," Denise murmured. She could cook, but not help
with anything else.

"We're going to see Reese's parents this weekend," Christine continued, unaware of her mother's growing irritation. "She's a terrible cook." Christine giggled. "Even Reese says so, but she's a wonderful woman."

Denise couldn't recall Christine ever calling her wonderful except in terms of her cooking or sewing. Her initial happy mood on hearing her daughter's voice declined sharply. She knew she had to get off the phone before it came through in her voice. "The roads will be heavy with holiday traffic. You two drive carefully."

"We will. Bye, Mama."

Denise hung up the phone. For a long moment, her hand stayed on the receiver as she tried to push away the recurring thoughts that had plagued her these past months. Her family loved her, but they didn't need her.

She looked around the bright lemon-yellow kitchen with blue accents. The yellow ceramic tile on the countertop gleamed, as did the hardwood floor extending to the family room to her right. A competent housekeeper could replace her and no one would probably notice.

Tired of her own unhappy thoughts, Denise made her way out of the kitchen, up the stairs to the second floor, then farther to the attic. The large room was as scrupulously clean as the rest of the house. In the very center beneath track lighting and between two elongated windows was her grandmother's old Singer sewing machine on which Denise had learned to sew, and continued to use. A few feet away was the scarred oak kitchen table upon which she and her grandmother had shared so many wonderful meals and good times. The table was now used as a cutting surface for Denise's designs.

Usually, when she was in this room, along with her grandmother's two most prized possessions, Denise felt her nearness and her unconditional love. Today was different. She felt every one of her forty-five years, and then some. She felt old and tired; even worse, useless.

On a dress mannequin was the wedding gown she was sewing for the daughter of a friend. The young woman and her mother had been by yesterday for her final fitting and were scheduled to pick up the dress that afternoon. The bride-to-be had glowed with happiness.

Denise absently fingered the floor-length skirt of heavy white satin. People had said the same thing about her when her wedding day approached. She had just finished high school and Edward had completed his freshman year at Grambling. Neither wanted to wait to get married. They couldn't keep their hands off each other and had been so in love, so sure of themselves and their happily ever after.

When had the glow begun to dim?

Was it when Edward had to drop out his junior year to get a full-time job after her unplanned pregnancy with Christine? Or was it her planned, but complicated, pregnancy with Anthony, a math wizard, two years later? Or had it begun later when Edward's construction business started taking off and he was more and more often gone from home?

Or did the cause really matter? The outcome was the same. The magic was gone from their marriage. That thought brought a pang to Denise's heart and carried her to the old trunk on the other side of the attic.

Kneeling, Denise lifted the lid. Inside were the treasured quilts her grandmother had sewn by hand, the first dress Denise had made by herself, the table linen for the first tiny apartment she and Edward shared, Christine's and Anthony's christening gowns. So many warm memories were wrapped carefully in tissue paper, and that was exactly where her life would remain if she let things continue the way they were.

Edward saw her as a wife and mother, not as the independent woman and partner to him she yearned to be. Part of the problem, she knew, was that the few jobs she'd held before she became pregnant with Christine were a way of making ends meet and had nothing to do with establishing a career. After her daughter was born, Denise had never gone back to work. Taking care of her family became her focus and goal in life.

But now that her children were grown and Edward was successful, she had begun to think about how she might focus her time and energy. After receiving so many compliments on Christine's and her attendants' dresses, Denise had realized what she wanted to do.

Only Edward refused to listen. He knew very well other women had successful, fulfilling lives outside the home, but he wanted her chained to the house with a spatula in one hand and a vacuum cleaner in the other. Even their daughter had a career she enjoyed and could look at what she did with pride.

Edward might not see her sewing as measuring up to what he did, but Denise did. She loved Edward, but she didn't want to continue going through the motions of marriage. She wanted the juice, the fire, back in their marriage; she wanted what they'd shared when they were fiercely in love and stood side by side.

Edward needed a wake-up call. He needed to understand that he couldn't run her life or take her for granted. If she thought the knothead didn't love her, she'd have packed his bag and sent him to live with his eccentric aunt and uncle. That would get his attention.

She paused as the thought swirled around in her head. What if he really thought she wanted out of their marriage? Would it shock him enough to make him really listen to what she was saying? She swallowed. Was she courageous enough to jeopardize her marriage? Despite everything, she loved Edward and couldn't imagine life without him.

Her teeth clamped down on her bottom lip. She'd never been a gambler, but did she have a choice if she wanted Edward to see her as a partner and not as a cook and housekeeper, if she wanted their marriage to be what it had once been?

Her arms drew the quilts and christening gowns to her chest. She really *didn't* have a choice. Tonight, when Edward came home, she was going to shake things up. She was going to ask for a divorce.

TWO

Edward stepped outside to an unusually brisk Atlanta morning. Gazing across his lawn, then out onto the quiet, tree-lined street, he smiled with pride at all that he'd accomplished.

Everyone in this upper-middle-class development was a blend of old family money and new economics—those who'd made their mark during the wave of financial prosperity in the eighties. His neighbors owned their two cars and their homes, and their children all went to good schools. Husbands went to work every day, some of them owning their businesses. They made the money that paid for the houses, the cars, the manicured lawns, and the better education. The wives took care of the family. *She* was the thread that held everything together in the home. And they certainly didn't take in "day work" to make ends meet or to fill some need.

"Hey, Jeff. How's it going?" Edward called out to his neighbor next door.

"Wife's due any minute now," he said with a chuckle. "Have to put in some extra time at the office."

"I hear ya. Take it easy," Edward said as Jeff hopped behind the wheel of his Benz and pulled out of his driveway.

Edward pulled up the collar of his jacket as a cold breeze slid around his neck and down his back. He took a quick look at the overcast sky. "Rain," he muttered as he quickly slid into his Escalade and revved the engine.

He'd come a long way from the poverty, illiteracy, and family strife of his early days in Alabama, he mused as he glided by the photo-perfect homes along Morningside Lane. He'd seen up close what working on one's hands and knees had done to his mother. He'd witnessed the shame and regret that etched permanent lines of sorrow on his father's weather-beaten face because he couldn't support his family, and the total exhaustion that turned down the corners of his mother's mouth and curved her back. Then one day his father just couldn't take it anymore, couldn't take looking at himself in the mirror and not seeing the man he believed he should be. Rather than be a burden, yet another mouth to feed, he walked out one summer afternoon and never came back. His mother quietly passed away the following winter, right on the bathroom floor of her employer's home—bristle brush and a bar of lye soap in her hands.

Edward swallowed the knot of pain that periodically rose to his throat at the memories of days gone by and flipped on the windshield wipers as the first drops splattered angrily against the glass. He'd gone to live with his Uncle Eddie and Aunt Etta in Marietta, Georgia, until he graduated from high school. They'd done their best by him, but they were not much better off than his folks had been. They had plenty of love to give, but not much else. The life he'd lived as a boy was not what he wanted for his family. Not one day would they have to do without, or see him as being less than a man, a provider, someone they would be proud to call Dad. When he lucked out and secured an athletic scholarship to Grambling, he made a vow that he would never see his family struggle or want for anything. They would be looked up to and not down on by their neighbors. And whatever it took to make that happen, he would do, even if it meant saying no to his wife.

Edward reached for the radio dial and tuned in to his favorite jazz station. "Body and Soul," one of his favorite John Coltrane tunes, filled the confines of the plush leather interior. He smiled. *Body and soul,* that's what his wife was to him. He knew he didn't always tell her how much she meant to him, but he tried to show her with the things he did for her and the kids. He wanted her to always know that she could depend on him, no matter what.

He eased into the turning lane and made the quick left that would take him to his office. He could see the sign from the expressway—MORRISON DESIGN AND CONSTRUCTION. Yeah, it was all his. He'd built his business from a little storefront with a desk and four chairs to a two-story, 8,000-square-foot spread with a staff of twenty.

Edward pulled into the parking lot and eased into the space marked RESERVED/OWNER. Although the front door was mere feet away, he was in for a drenching. The rain was coming down in blinding sheets by the time he'd turned off the ignition. As he jogged to the entrance, he seriously contemplated adding an underground garage for days just like this one.

"Morning, Mr. Morrison," he heard one after another say as he double-stepped down the corridor, anxious to get out of his wet clothes. He smiled and waved along the way. He had to admit he had a great staff, some of the most talented contractors and designers in the state. It wasn't luck and it wasn't affirmative action that landed his team one major development job after another—it was talent. It was drive. It was pride in what they did, and it was a willingness to be the best.

"Hey, Ed, look a little wet there, brotha," William Henry said with a chuckle as he caught up with Edward moments before he entered his office.

"I'm seriously thinking about underground parking," Edward said as he took off his jacket and shook it like a wet dog. He hung it on the hook behind his door, then looked down at his pants and wondered if Denise had remembered to have his extra work pants delivered from the cleaners. "What's up, man? Everything cool with the Davidson project?" he asked as he opened the closet on the far wall and found his slacks hanging neatly beneath plastic. He smiled. *Denise.*

"Yeah, yeah," William said, nodding as he took a seat. "I just wanted to run some things by you before we signed off on the shopping complex blueprints."

"Sure. Can you hang on a minute? Let me get out of these wet pants."

William nodded and began looking over his notes while Edward stepped into the adjoining bathroom—which was only a toilet and sink—and changed his slacks. Refreshed and dry, he stepped out and pulled up a chair next to William rather than sit behind his desk. "Shoot. What's on your mind?" Edward slid on his glasses and scanned the plans and notes that William spread out on his desk.

"I was going over the schematics for the plaza level . . ."

The two men talked for nearly forty-five minutes for what

could have been a ten-minute conversation, but Edward was in-terrupted at least a dozen times with twice as many emergen-cies and inquiries to respond to.

Finally, William stood. "Thanks. I'll work out the details with the suits over at Davidson and meet with our team."

"This project is too big to let anything fall between the cracks," Edward said. "It and this company have been in the papers at least once a month for the past year. Everyone has their eye on us, waiting for us to slip up so they can slide in. There is a ton of money, prestige, and manpower involved. When we pull this off—and we will—Morrison Design and Construction will be engraved on the map."

William grinned broadly. "I know, man. We won't let you down."

Edward slapped William on the back as he walked him to the door. "I know you won't."

Edward pulled in a long breath. The Davidson contract was one that designers and contractors dreamed of. It had taken hard work and long hours at the negotiating table, but he'd won the bid. Now, it was time for show and tell. He had to be on his mark and not let anything distract him from what needed to be done. One of the reasons why his company was so successful was that he prided himself at being a hands-on boss. There was nothing that went on in his company that he didn't know about down to the last detail; from signing off on supply orders to working shoulder to shoulder, pouring foundation. He would never be accused of being the kind of owner who was ignorant to what went on in his company. He was the same way at home. A man had to be responsible. That was his motto.

He took off his glasses and walked around to his desk, all set to dive into the mound of paperwork that awaited him, just as his private line rang.

"Morrison," he said by rote.

"Hey, Dad, you don't have to sound so formal," Christine said, her voice light and teasing.

A smile spread across his mouth at the sound of his daughter's voice.

"Hey, baby girl. And to what do I owe this early morning pleasure?"

"I tried to catch you at home, but Mom said you'd already left for work."

"Gotta make an honest dollar to ensure that my family lives in the style they've grown accustomed to," he joked.

"You've always taken good care of us, Daddy. No one can ever say otherwise. And Reese is the same way."

"How is he, anyway? Hope he's not leaving you alone too much."

"He's fine. He's been putting in extra hours at the hospital with all the cutbacks, but . . . makes it up to me every chance he gets," she added, practically singing.

"Well, doll, I think that's more information than your dear old dad needs to hear." He smiled at her laughter on the other end. "So, what can I do for you? You just name it and it's yours."

"I was really calling to find out what you think would be the perfect gift for Mom. I swear she has everything. And I'm at a total loss. I'm taking the next few days off from work and I want to get my holiday shopping done."

"Hmmm. You're right about her having everything. Maybe a watch?"

"I got her a watch for her birthday, remember?"

He didn't really, but agreed anyway.

"How about something for her sewing clients? She seems to really—"

"No, forget it. Your mother and I talked about that and after she finishes this gown—which she promised she'd do— she won't be taking in work anymore."

"Really?" Christine frowned. "If you say so," she murmured. "Anyway, I guess I will have to figure something out on my own. Have you talked to Anthony lately?"

"Not in a few days. I guess he's all tied up with his girlfriend. The last time I talked to him, he said he was going to bring her for Thanksgiving dinner. So it must be serious."

"Who would have thought that Mr. Playboy would get his date card pulled?" They both laughed.

"I know what you mean. I was pretty sure Tony was going to teach courses in being a professional bachelor. But I'm glad to see that he's finally taking life seriously and settling down. Having a good woman in your life only makes you a better man," he said.

"Do you feel that way about Mom?" she asked softly.

"I wouldn't be where I am today without her. She's been in my corner from day one, taking care of you and your brother, me, the house. She's one incredible woman," he added wistfully.

"That's really nice to hear, Dad, especially when so many marriages are falling apart. I only hope that Reese and I will stay as happy as you and Mom."

"It takes two to make a marriage work. Always remember that."

"I will. Listen, I have to run. See you for Thanksgiving. Mom promised she was going to make her famous casserole and I can't wait!"

Edward laughed. "That's one thing about your mom; she can burn, as you young folks would say."

"And so would you," she said, laughing. "Take care, Dad."

"You too, baby girl." He hung up the phone and smiled. Yes, he had a great life.

The rest of Edward's day continued at a rapid clip, with the usual amount of headaches and successes, and by six o'clock he was more than ready to head home to a good meal and a hot bath.

When he got home, the house was strangely quiet. If he didn't know better, he'd swear his wife wasn't home. But that was impossible. For the past twenty-seven years of their marriage there had not been one day that he'd come in from work or from a business trip and Denise had not been there to greet him.

"Denise! I'm home." He hung up his coat and walked into the living room. "Denise!" The room was empty. He headed for the kitchen and looked around, growing more perplexed when he noticed that the stove was bare of pots and not a scent of food was in the air.

His heart started to pound. Something was wrong. He took the stairs two at a time and flung open the bedroom door, certain that he would find his wife asleep—the only reason he could come up with to explain the unexplainable.

But when he stepped inside, he found that room empty, just like the rest of the house. For several moments, he simply stood there, totally mystified. Where was Denise? He looked on the dresser for a note and found none. He checked his cell phone to see if he'd perhaps missed a message from her and again, nothing.

He sat on the side of the bed. His first instinct was to reach for the phone and call the police. He tried to recall all the *Law & Order* shows he'd watched. The police would want information: the last time he saw her, height, weight, what she was wearing. And suddenly, for the life of him, he couldn't remember if Denise's hair was dark brown or black.

The phone rang and he nearly jumped out of his skin. He snatched it from the receiver.

"Denise!" he shouted.

"Keep your shirt on, boy, this is your Uncle Eddie. What's wrong, can't keep up with your wife?" He chuckled. "Told you a hundred times, boy, you gotta keep 'em happy like I do with your Aunt Etta and you won't have to worry about where they are. A little James Brown, some Wild Irish Rose, and good lovin' will keep a smile on their face."

"Uncle Eddie, I really can't talk to you right now."

"You tellin' me you can't make time for your old uncle, the man that used to wipe your butt and your nose?"

"Uncle Eddie, I was a teenager when I came to live with you. I really don't think you were wiping my butt or my nose."

"Humph . . . you know what I mean. And don't sass me, boy. You're not too big for a whipping. This old man still has a few good ones left in him." He coughed a smoker's cough. "You having trouble with your woman? 'Cause if you are, you've come to the right place."

Edward shook his head, not knowing whether to laugh or scream. "Everything is fine, Uncle Eddie."

"So, where's the little lady?"

"She . . . went out."

"Hmmm, really?"

"Yes, really," he said, pacing the floor as he talked and wishing his uncle would just hang up. He needed to find his wife.

"If you say so. But just remember this one thing."

"What's that, Uncle Eddie?"

"I ain't no fool. So don't be trying to fool your old uncle. Just remember that. Hang on, your Aunt Etta wants to talk to ya."

"Uncle . . ."

"Etta! Etta! Come talk to this boy. Sounds like he can't find his wife."

Edward rolled his eyes to the heavens. He knew his aunt and uncle meant well, but they drove him crazy. Nutty as fruitcakes, Anthony always joked.

"Well, where in the dickens did he lose her?" Etta was saying as she came to the phone. "What you do to that woman?" Etta demanded of her nephew. "Did you run her off with those James Brown records your uncle gave you? Eddie, I told you not to give that boy those records. They done drove Denise right out of that pretty house. How come you can't build me a house?"

"Ouch!" he heard his uncle yelp. "Whatcha go and do that for? Same spot you hit me on just before dinner. Lawd, woman. You wanna knock all the sense outta me?"

"You ain't got no sense to knock out."

"That's 'cause you done knocked it all out yesterday."

"Wouldn't have to if you didn't give that boy those records and run off his wife."

Edward quietly hung up the phone as they continued to bicker about the value of James Brown on a marriage and headed back downstairs before calling the police in the hope that perhaps he'd missed a note somewhere. He'd hate to sound like a fool on the phone only to find out that his wife was at the supermarket.

Just as he reached the bottom, the front door opened and Denise walked in.

Relief flooded through him and he almost rushed to her and swept her up in his arms. But he didn't.

"Where have you been, Denise? I was worried sick. This isn't like you to just run off without a word," he chastised her, like a parent scolding a child.

Denise walked past him without a word of acknowledgment, opened the closet door and hung up her jacket, then set her purse on the top shelf. She closed the closet door and walked into the kitchen.

For several moments, Edward stood rooted to the spot with his mouth open. He shook his head and followed her.

"Did you hear what I said?" he asked, storming into the kitchen.

Denise took a teacup from the hook beneath the sink, filled it with water, and stuck it in the microwave. She pressed the numbers, hit start, folded her arms, and waited.

"Denise, I'm talking to you," he said, growing more frustrated by the minute. What had gotten into her? *Must be those talk shows,* he concluded.

The bell chimed on the microwave and Denise removed the cup, added a teabag and some sugar, walked right by him again, and went upstairs.

Edward followed her, determined to get some answers. He didn't know what was on his wife's mind, but he damned well was going to find out. The instant he crossed the threshold of the room, Denise looked up at him from the bed and his whole world came to a grinding halt.

"Edward, I want a divorce."

THREE

For a moment all Edward could do was stand there. Divorce! All those years of working with drills on the construction sites had definitely affected his hearing, because he was certain he could not have heard her right. That had to be the reason why he felt as if someone had just kicked him in the head; his hearing was going bad. He shook his head to clear it and hopefully when he looked at Denise again, she would turn back into the same dependable, loving woman he'd married. But then his mind and his vision cleared and what he saw in front of him was a woman he barely recognized, from the firm line of her usually soft, pouty mouth, to the ramrod-straight back, to the look of resoluteness in her eyes that gave him a chill. He quickly donned his king-of-the-castle cape and stepped fully into the room.

"This is not a time for games, Denise," he said in his best no-nonsense voice.

"I'm not playing," she responded calmly, reaching for the nail file from the nightstand and holding it up in front of her. She stared at the point, then at him.

Reflexively, Edward took a step back as the tiny file seemed to grow to lethal proportions in front of his eyes. He'd watched enough Lifetime Channel episodes to know that the women always seemed to have a justifiable reason why they did away with the men in their lives. *Too much television, Edward,* he inwardly scolded himself. *You are not afraid of your wife.* He cleared his throat. "Fine. You're not playing and neither am I. I asked you a simple question and you give me some ridiculous response."

Suddenly Denise sprang up from her perch on the side of the bed, the nail file pointing menacingly at her husband. "Did you say ridiculous? You think divorce is ridiculous? Well, I'm glad you do, because I don't," she said, her words coming so hot and fast they stumbled over each other on their way out. "I can't take it anymore, Edward." She began to pace in front of him.

"Take what anymore?" he asked, truly baffled.

She halted midstep and whirled toward him, throwing her arms into the air. "Everything!"

His head snapped back, his nose missing the tip of the deadly file by mere inches. "Everything? What in the world are you talking about?" he asked, wondering if he should wrestle her for the file. If those things were now banned from airplanes, they should certainly be banned from bedrooms.

Denise planted her fists on her hips. "That's just it, Edward, it would take the rest of my life to try to explain. I've spent the past twenty-seven years living for everyone except myself. I've put my needs and wants on hold for you and the kids. What I want has never factored into anyone's thinking. Just that Mom will be there to cook, clean, and say yes to everyone. Well, the kids are grown now, Edward. They're on their own. You have a thriving business. It's been clear for quite some time that none of you really need me. I'm like an old shoe—comfortable. Not anymore. I want to be a stiletto!"

A stiletto?

"I've sat on the sidelines while everyone around me built a life. Now it's my turn, and I'm taking it—without you." She tossed the file on the bed and walked toward the window, turning her back to him.

Edward breathed a sigh of relief. "Denise, you can't be serious. Divorce is not something you do on a whim."

She laughed harshly. "Typical response. What makes you believe that I haven't thought about it?"

Slowly she turned to face him and he saw the depth of her pain swimming in her eyes. *This was real.*

"You really don't know me at all, do you? After all these years," she whispered. "Everyone has grown, except me, or so you thought. I'm not the same young, impressionable girl you met all those years ago. Somewhere along the way you let go of my hand and moved on without me. You may have been here in body, but not in spirit. Not really. This hasn't been a real marriage for years. It's been an arrangement. And now I'm making arrangements to change all of that."

Gingerly he moved toward her. He knew that if he could just touch her, hold her close to his heart and let her hear the terror that beat there, she would say it was all a mistake. That she was just upset, that her hormones had gone out of control. Something, anything but what she was telling him now.

He reached for her and she stepped away, knowing that if she inhaled his scent, felt his hands on her body, her resolve would crumble as it had so many times in the past.

Stung by her reaction, he stepped back, dropping his hands to his sides. "Denise, baby, please listen to me. I know you're upset."

"Do you really, Edward? Or are you just concerned that your dinner isn't cooked?"

"That's not fair, Denise."

"Fair hasn't been a part of the equation in our marriage for a very long time."

A sudden sense of desperation seized him. He had to try another tack, some way to reach her. "Don't you love me anymore?"

Denise's body tensed. She should have known that he would toss love into the mix. "What's love got to do with it? This is not about loving you, Edward, it's about loving me." She poked her finger at her chest.

"This isn't making sense. What can I do? What *did* I do? You don't just decide to get a divorce after twenty-seven years of marriage. We have to talk about this, Denise," he pleaded. "Haven't I been a good husband, a good father, a solid provider? Have I ever cheated on you?"

"That's just it. *You've* been this entire marriage, and every now and then I get to participate." She lowered her head. "And I'm tired. I want to see what I can do for Denise before it's too late."

"Look, we just need some time to think this through. Whatever it is, we can work it out. I know we can."

She refused to look at him. "I think you should sleep in Anthony's old room tonight." She turned away. "I want to be alone."

Edward's entire body went cold. "Anthony's room?" he croaked in disbelief. "Are you telling me to get out of our bedroom?" he asked, the words coming out slowly and painfully.

"Yes," she said emphatically. "I am." She breezed by him and placed her hand on the open door—waiting.

Edward stared at this stranger who had taken his wife's place.

It was surreal, like the movie *Invasion of the Body Snatchers,* he thought, completely dazed by what had transpired. He had the overwhelming urge to peek under the bed for pods.

He drew in a breath. Fine, if this is what she thought she wanted, he'd go along with it for a minute. He was pretty damned sure that after a good night's sleep without him, she'd change her mind. *What if she didn't?* He strode toward the door with not as much pep in his step as he would have liked, but he refused to beg. "Good night, Denise," he said through his teeth.

She pursed her lips, waited for him to cross the threshold, and closed the door behind him.

Somehow, Edward found his way to his son's old bedroom. He stood in the doorway and looked at the single bed, the trophies on the shelf, and the wall plastered with his favorite sports heroes: Michael Jordan and Magic Johnson. His son hadn't used this room since he'd moved out, but Denise didn't have the heart to change it.

"I want it to be just like he left it for those times when he comes home. It's comforting to know there is somewhere you can go where things are the same—familiar. Don't you think so?" she'd asked him as they'd both stood in the doorway on the day of Anthony's departure.

He'd draped his arm around her shoulder, hearing the hitch in her voice. "He's all grown up now, Dee, and so is Christine. When they come back it will only be for holidays and short visits. They have lives of their own now. They've moved on. It's just me and you."

A tear slid down her cheek. "I know," she'd whispered. "Just us." She'd eased away from his hold and walked away.

As Edward stepped into Anthony's room, he wondered now if Denise had been sad because the children were gone or because all that was left was the two of them. Was he that awful to live with? A knot filled his gut. He looked down the hallway to the closed door of his bedroom. He took two steps in that direction, but stopped. No. He wasn't going to plead. He wasn't going to ask for forgiveness for something he hadn't done. What they both needed was some sleep, some time to think. Thanksgiving was in two days. The whole family would converge on the house, filling it with love and good cheer, and Denise would see for herself what she was throwing away. He'd give her the time and space she needed. But one thing he was certain of: He was getting back in his bedroom with his wife. A sudden frightening image of his aunt and uncle flashed before his eyes. If they ever found out . . . He didn't want to think about it. This mess had to be fixed before they arrived on Thanksgiving morning.

Reluctantly, Edward closed the door and crossed the room to the narrow bed. He pulled back the quilt and slid between the cool cotton sheets. He had to get some sleep. Tomorrow was a big day with the executives from the Davidson project—the ground-breaking ceremony. The press would be there in droves. He had to be sharp. He squeezed his eyes shut and prayed for sleep.

More than an hour later he was still wide awake, staring up at the ceiling. He turned over too quickly and almost fell out of the bed. "Dammit!" he sputtered, catching himself before he hit the floor, and wondered how on earth his six-foot, one-hundred-and-eighty-pound son had ever slept in this make-believe bed.

Truly annoyed, he pulled the covers up to his chin and tried to get comfortable. He missed the warmth of Denise next to him, the sound of her soft snore, the feel of her body nestled against his.

Tossing the covers aside, he got up. "This is ridiculous," he muttered as he pulled the door open and strode down the hall-way toward *his* bedroom. He turned the knob and pushed. He frowned. The door wouldn't open. *It must be stuck,* he thought, and tried again. It wouldn't budge. And then it dawned on him. She'd locked him out! She'd actually locked him out. He couldn't believe it and was so stunned he couldn't move or think. His wife had lost her natural mind. That was the only explanation.

He raised his fist, but stopped. He wouldn't reduce himself to knocking on his own bedroom door. This was his house, his bedroom, and his wife. *Then why am I standing on the outside of a locked door?*

"Denise," he whispered timidly, the humiliation so intense he could barely get her name to cross his lips. He listened for any sound—and then he knew he'd just entered the Twilight Zone, and this was all some bizarre nightmare episode.

Coming from the other side of the door was a wail from the Godfather of Soul, James Brown, singing "I Feel Good."

Edward whirled away and stormed back down the hallway, slamming the door behind him. Everyone had gone completely mad!

FOUR

Safely inside their bedroom, Denise breathed a little easier. She'd done it!

Yet, for a split second, she'd almost caved in as she'd done so many times. She loved him so desperately. She'd grabbed the fingernail file to keep from grabbing him and to give her a reason to look away. Seeing him in pain and knowing she caused it was like slicing into her own body. The only reason she hadn't given in was that she was aware that if she did, nothing would change. She'd go back to being a housekeeper and cook instead of a wife and partner.

This was for both of them.

With a click of the stereo's remote control, the rambunctious sounds of James Brown singing "I Feel Good" increased in volume. In her off-key voice, Denise joined in, doing a little spin and slide in a good imitation of James. If she didn't think she'd injure herself, she'd try a split. *I do feel good.* She'd passed the first hurdle.

Initially she'd turned on the stereo because she'd been afraid she might cry and hadn't wanted Edward to know how much

asking for the divorce, even make-believe, had torn her up inside. If he had sensed any weakness, he would have pushed her
or taken her into his arms, and she would have lost the will to
fight.

He had always been aware of the power he had over her. Her
grandmother had once said if Edward led her off a cliff, she'd
happily follow. Her grandmother had been right. Every time
Edward picked her up, her grandmother would stare both of
them in the eye and tell them to be careful. She wasn't talking
about Edward driving his old Ford Pinto.

At no other time is love so desperate—and the need to express that love so intense—as when you're a teenager. She'd
fallen in love with Edward on their second date when she'd cried
in his arms after pouring out her heart to him about her parents'
impending divorce.

"Letting go is hard, but if it helps, I'm here," he'd said, his
strong arms around her as they sat in his car. It had.

From then on, they'd spent as much time as possible together.
Her grandmother teased him about charging rent because he
was at her house so much. His comeback was that the only reason he was there so much was for her wonderful cooking. His
response never failed to cause her grandmother to blush and
make Denise think how lucky she was and how much she loved
him.

Loving Edward had been easy. He was fun to be with, intelligent, handsome. He shared his dreams with her, held her
when she was sad, and helped her adjust and make new friends
in Atlanta. To express that love she let Edward go further, let
him touch her in places no other man ever had. Three months
after they'd started dating, he'd gone from being her best friend,

to her boyfriend, to her lover on a beautiful summer afternoon while on a picnic.

She'd been scared. He'd been gentle and patient. "I promise, Dee, I'll love you forever."

He had kept that promise, but now he had to let her live her own life.

Denise awoke on Edward's side of the bed. Instinctively her body had sought the comfort of his. She ran her hand over the cold sheet next to her. She missed him and just hoped she'd shaken him up enough to make him realize he had to let her be a partner in their marriage and have her say in her own life. Last night had probably been as difficult for him as it had been for her.

A wicked smile curved her lips as she envisioned ways of making it up to him. She just hoped it didn't take him too long to come to his senses.

Yesterday she'd broken the tradition of being at home when he arrived to prove a point: A change had come. Time for round two.

Finally opening her eyes, she stared at the digital dial of the clock radio: 7:03 A.M. *I overslept and it feels wonderful.* Her internal clock usually went off around 6:30 A.M. Edward's alarm clock went off at 6:40 A.M. A heavy sleeper, he often ignored the alarm and she had to wake him up. A dreamy smile lit her face as she remembered that on many of those occasions, he'd draw her into his arms and make love to her. Sighing with regret that she wasn't getting any of that good loving today, she rolled out of bed and headed for the shower.

Taking off her nightgown, she dropped it into the dirty clothes hamper, trying not to think of just a few days ago when Edward had joined her in the glass enclosure and they'd steamed up the shower with their own heat. It was futile.

His large, calloused hands had roamed freely over her body, building passion and need. That man of hers knew just where to touch her. She hadn't cared one bit that her shower cap had come off and her chemically processed hair was getting wet. Her cries of fulfillment had filled the enclosure. Afterward, when their breathing had almost returned to normal, he'd grinned at her and said it was nice not having to worry about the kids hearing them.

Resolutely, Denise turned and went to the sunken tub across the room. She could fight herself, Edward, and memories, but not all three at the same time.

Fifteen minutes later, Denise walked into the kitchen, expecting Edward to be making his usual mess. A couple of years ago she'd had the flu and he'd been completely inept. She'd wanted to cry when she'd come downstairs after he'd left for work and seen the wreck he'd made of her beautiful kitchen. He'd been so pleased with the hard scrambled eggs and overcooked pan sausage he'd brought on a tray. At least the toast hadn't been burned. He could be the most thoughtful man in the world, or the most stubborn.

Her brows bunched when she didn't see him. He was probably getting dressed for his big meeting today. Continuing across the room, she went to the refrigerator and began pulling out sausage and eggs. She was hungry. Edward, as she had told him, was on his own.

In a short time, breakfast was ready and still Edward hadn't arrived. Denise frowned. It wasn't likely he'd left without talking to her. She'd heard him try the locked door last night. That had to have made him angry. He'd gone back to Anthony's room, as she'd suspected he would, but he'd be back. He was relentless when he wanted something. And he wanted his life back the way it was.

Picking up a plate, Denise filled it with grits, soft scrambled eggs, perfect sausage patties, and light, fluffy biscuits, then took a seat at the end of the island. He'd soon learn that it was no longer what he wanted, but what *she* intended to get.

FIVE

Edward was jerked awake when his two-hundred-pound body hit the floor. He groaned and rubbed his hip, then his shoulder. "What the . . . ?" He looked around through half-opened lids. It took him a couple of minutes to orient himself as the room slowly came into focus, then the night before. His pulse picked up a beat. *Denise locked me out. I spent the night in my son's bedroom. I am forty-seven years old and I just fell out of bed.* If it wasn't so horrible, it could almost be funny.

He held his watch up to his face and squinted. 8:45 A.M. He struggled to his feet, using the side of the bed for leverage. Then it hit him: 8:45! His meeting started in just over an hour, followed by the ground-breaking. Was Denise that upset with him that she wouldn't even wake him up? She woke him every morning. He depended on her. She knew how hard he slept. At least he pretended to sleep hard. He liked to watch her from the corner of his eyes as she moved around the bedroom in the morning and then tiptoe over to whisper in his ear, "Time to wake up, baby." Ooh, how he loved that. Her warm breath right up against his ear would raise his testosterone level to mammoth heights. Just thinking about her made his juices rise. He looked down at the tent in his shorts and thought about all the ways Denise made it go away. Then reality bit him. *Denise wants a divorce.*

Edward darted out of the bedroom and half limped, half sprinted down the hallway, determined that if the door was locked, he was breaking it down with his good hip and shoulder.

He turned the knob and the door sprang open. His gaze zeroed in on the bed, which was neatly made and empty. Where was Denise? The clock on the nightstand read 8:50. As much as he wanted to deal with the crisis at hand, he would certainly have a mega one brewing if this Davidson project fell apart. He had a staff and their families that he was responsible for. He wouldn't let them down. This mess between him and Denise would be settled tonight once and for all. And then maybe life could get back to normal.

Showered, shaved, and decked out in the new suit Denise had insisted that he purchase, Edward adjusted his tie in the mirror and had to admit that the midnight blue Armani suit fit as if it were made for him. He remembered the conversation he and Denise had about his wardrobe. "If you are going to be successful, then look the part," she'd admonished as she dragged him through the men's department of Saks. "You can't go on television or turn up on the front page of the *Atlanta Journal* with jeans and chambray shirts all the time. You've come a long way from the storefront, honey."

He *had* come a long way, he admitted as he dabbed on some cologne and clipped his cell phone to the waistband of his pants. As a businessman his abilities were unquestionable, and until last night he would have thought the same of himself as a husband.

Taking a deep breath, he pulled away from his reflection and headed downstairs, hoping to at least grab a cup of coffee before he hit the road. Hopefully, Denise would have been kind enough to put a pot on, even though the aroma of freshly brewed coffee was not in the air.

She heard him grumbling before she saw him. Even impeccably dressed, he looked as miserable as she felt.

When he entered the kitchen, he was surprised to find Denise sitting at the kitchen table, sipping a cup of tea with a plate of half-eaten food in front of her. If he didn't know better, he'd swear she looked totally rested and relaxed, as if last night hadn't happened.

"Good morning," he murmured, testing the waters.

She barely looked up. "Morning," she said, and snapped open the newspaper.

"Uh, the big ground-breaking is this morning. I should have been at the office already," he said, hoping that normalcy had returned.

"Oh . . . is that today? I forgot." She sighed, took a sip of her tea, and continued reading the paper. "Good luck," she added over the top of the page, barely looking up. "I'm sure it will be fine." She turned toward the window. "Radio said we're expecting a major storm today. Hurricane watch. Don't forget your umbrella." She went back to reading.

He swallowed, suddenly unsure of how to talk to her, how to reach this woman he'd loved and lived with most of his life. His heart ached with a kind of emptiness that he couldn't explain. He wanted to tell her how scared he was, but he didn't know how and wasn't sure if she would listen. But he had to try.

"Denise . . . about last night . . . you really didn't mean what you said. Did you? You were just upset. If you would only tell me what's wrong, I'll fix it."

"It's too late to fix it, Edward. And sometimes, whether you believe it or not, *you* can't fix everything. That's part of the problem. Our marriage is not one of your construction projects. I've thought about it, thought about us. It's not working and hasn't for a very long time. You and the kids have your life and I want to have mine."

"Why are you so dead set into believing that we can't have the life you want together? Is divorce the only answer?" he asked, his frustration mounting.

"It's the only answer for me. Do you really think I'm taking all of this lightly? I'm not. This marriage has been all about you, what you want, how you want it. I can't even have a conversation with the kids without them making sure it's okay with you first. What kind of marriage is that? What kind of relationship is that to have with your children? I don't want this to turn into something ugly, Edward. I won't wind up like my parents—at each other's throats, bickering and fighting, unwilling to let go."

"I can't let you do this," he said, instinctively returning to the self he knew best—take-charge.

She laughed harshly. "Do you hear yourself?" She shook her head. "I'm sure you don't. You never have." She took a sip of her tea, then absently stirred the grits with her fork. "You'll miss your big event if you don't hurry," she added, her voice devoid of emotion.

He glanced at the clock, then at his wife, torn between his

responsibilities. For the first time in his life, he felt totally incapable, inept, and unable to put the pieces together. The realization left him confused and reeling.

"Take your umbrella," she reminded him again.

"We're going to talk this out when I get home tonight, Denise. I don't want another night like last night. No matter what you might think or believe, I missed you."

Denise finally turned to look at him and for a split second he saw the same misery swimming in her eyes that was in his. His hopes rose. Maybe, just maybe, she was feeling as bad about this as he was.

She pressed her lips together, took a deep breath, and looked him straight in the eye. "I want to sell the house." With that, she rose from her seat and walked out, leaving him with his mouth open.

For several moments he stood there in stunned silence, until finally he heard the door to their bedroom slam shut. He blinked and somehow found his way to the front door and outside to his SUV. His eyes burned and his stomach rolled dangerously. It was all he could do to stick the key in the ignition.

Behind the wheel of his Escalade, Edward could barely keep his attention focused on the road. His thoughts jumped around like jackrabbits in a meadow. One minute he was thinking about the unbelievable twist in what he thought was his stable marriage; the next he was thinking about what to say in front of the camera. Then his thoughts would swing back to the look in Denise's eyes and the emptiness in her voice. And her final statement—"I want to sell the house." *The house that I built for them.* He was so stunned he still couldn't respond. His whole life was coming apart at the seams and he had no idea how to put it back together.

The clock on the dash read 9:40 A.M. His meeting started in twenty minutes and he still had at least another forty before he would arrive at his office. He slammed his palm against the steering wheel. His well-ordered life was falling apart. What was happening?

SIX

Edward found his way to work by pure instinct. By the time he arrived, the meeting was already in session in the company's conference room. William Henry, sitting at the head of the table, jumped up and met Edward at the door.

"Hey, man, everything okay? We were getting worried and the suits from Davidson were getting pissed. The press is here too, champing at the bit. But I held everyone off with my incredible charm." He chuckled.

Edward tried to focus, put his mind on the task at hand and not the drama that was happening in his household. He'd always prided himself on being able to separate business from his home life, but today he didn't know if he had what it took to get through the rest of the day.

"Yeah, fine. Sorry I'm late. Car wouldn't start," he offered up as an excuse.

William patted him on the back. "Well, now that you're here, let's get this party started. Did you have to get it towed or just a boost?"

Edward looked at him curiously. "What?"

"The car. Did you get it started or did it need to be towed?"

"Oh. Uh, hey, I got a boost," he lied.

"You sure you're okay? You look like you haven't slept."

The previous night ran through his head like a bad movie. "I'm cool. Let's do this. I don't want to keep them waiting any longer than I already have."

After making his apologies, the balance of the meeting went smoothly. The heads of the Davidson group were pleased with the proposal and signed off on all the documents to the flash of the news media's cameras. They all posed for the standard grin-and-grip shot, then piled into cars for the official ground-breaking ceremony on the other side of town.

By the time the groups arrived at the site, the skies had turned a dangerous gray. Rolls of thunder could be heard in the background even as the legion of speakers took their turns at the microphone.

The mayor of Atlanta stepped up to the mic and they all instinctively knew that with it being an election year, whatever the good mayor had to say was going to be long.

"I'm honored to stand before you today on such a momentous occasion for the citizens of Atlanta . . ."

William leaned over and whispered to Edward, "The sky is going to open up any minute, and I don't think this tent is going to do us much good."

"Hmmm," Edward murmured, just willing the day to be over so that he could get back home. He needed to speak to his wife. Their life together was coming apart and he was clueless as to the reason why. It seemed that overnight his wife had turned into someone that he no longer knew: an unhappy woman who, according to the little Denise divulged, had been unhappy for a long time. How could he not have known? Had he been so involved in his own life, building a life for them, that he'd missed all the cues?

"Look, I don't want to get in your business, but is everything okay at home?" William asked, cutting into Edward's thoughts. "I know we have things locked down here. But I've never seen you so distracted, especially with something this major going on."

Edward turned to his friend of more than ten years. William had been there with him from the early days of his storefront. He'd helped him build the business from the ground up. Edward had been the best man at William's wedding, and they'd spent many a weekend sharing a beer over a sports game. There was a part of him that desperately needed to bare his soul, to share his angst, fear, and confusion. Yet there was that other part, that "gotta be a man" part, that dictated he keep his own counsel, fight his own battles. And that realization made him feel so very alone.

"Everything is fine at home. You know, the usual stuff, getting ready for the holidays, bills, the kids."

"Kids okay?"

"Yes." At least that much was true. "Christine and Reese are settling into his work routine and Anthony seems to be hot and heavy with his new girlfriend. She's supposed to drop by for Thanksgiving after she visits her folks."

William chuckled. "Anthony? Serious about a girl? Who would have thought it?"

Edward smiled, thinking of his son and how he'd matured over the past two years. He had a good job, a decent apartment, was a respectful young man, and now might be on the brink of settling down. He was proud of Anthony. They'd done a good job raising him and his sister. *They*. It had taken two of them to raise the children. Two of them to build a life, a family, security. How could Denise ever believe that she was not part of the process?

The drone of the mayor's speech filtered into Edward's thoughts. He checked his watch. There were at least two more hours of this back-patting to go and then he could head home. But suddenly, as if someone had hit a switch, all the power went out; the microphones sputtered and died and the huge lighting lamps flashed and went dark. The sky turned pitch black and the heavens opened in a torrent of blinding rain. Everyone outside the tent ran for cover, followed by those beneath as a mighty gust of wind ripped the tent from its stakes, sending it flying across the field.

"Run for the car, man!" William called out over the roar of wind and rain.

"Right behind you."

Edward ran against the wind, trying to get to his car, when one of the speakers that was perched on a platform was thrown through the air, knocking William to the ground. Edward darted around fallen debris to his friend's side.

"Will, Will . . ."

William groaned and slowly pulled himself to his knees.

Rain and wind whipped around them, making it impossible to see.

"Can you get up?"

"I think so."

"Let me help you." He put his arm around William and pulled him to his feet. With all the strength he could summon, he half walked, half dragged William to his SUV.

Though he was barely able to see out of the window, Edward could still make out the devastation. He shook his head in disbelief. Denise mentioned rain, but no umbrella made by man could have helped today.

"Bad storm," William murmured.

"Let me see if I can get the news." He reached toward the dial on the radio and after long moments of static, he was finally able to locate a news station. And the news was not good. Roads were washed out and flash flood conditions were in effect across the state, with dangerous lightning and power outages. Hurricane warnings were in effect through the night.

"Oh, man," Edward said. "I've got to get home."

"There's no way we can make that trip," William said, rubbing the knot on the back of his head. "Maybe we can make it to the office and hole up there."

Edward peered out of the window and was able to make out the headlights of the vehicles as they slowly eased their way out of the field.

"You're right. We can't stay here. It's too dangerous. I need to call home and make sure Denise is okay." He reached for his cell phone, but it was gone. He slapped his hand against the dashboard. "You have your cell with you?"

"It's in my car back at the office. I left it in the charger."

"How's your head?" Edward asked as he put the car in gear.

"Feels like I've been hit in the head with a speaker." He tried to laugh, but groaned instead.

"As soon as we get back to the office, we'll get some ice on that knot."

What should have been a twenty-minute drive turned into a two-hour marathon of slow going through blinding rain, dodging downed trees and power lines and being rerouted through flooded areas. Finally, they pulled into the parking lot and made it into the building.

Edward's secretary Lena jumped up from her desk the moment they entered.

"Mr. Morrison, Mr. Henry, thank goodness. We were all so worried." Then she took a look at William and her hand flew to her mouth in alarm. "Oh, no, Mr. Henry, you've been hurt. Let me get you some ice." She darted off before they could say a word.

"I'm going to my office and stretching out on the couch," William said, holding a handkerchief to his forehead.

"I'll check on you in a few," Edward said just as the lights blinked off and then on again. "The generator must have kicked on. I better try to call Denise."

He went to Lena's desk and called home. The phone barely rang once before it was picked up by Christine.

"Christine?"

"Dad. We were worried. Are you okay?"

"Yes. I'm fine, sweetheart. What are you doing there? Is your mother all right?"

"She's fine. I took today off and when I heard the weather report I decided to come over today. Anthony and Aunt Etta and Uncle Eddie are here too. I guess they thought the same thing. No one wanted to miss Mom's Thanksgiving dinner."

"Is your mom around?"

"I'll get her. How long do you think you'll be?"

"I don't know, sweetheart. All the roads are either closed or flooded. And it doesn't look like the rain is going to let up."

"Oh no," she moaned. "Let me get Mom."

Edward waited with his heart in his throat. He had no idea what kind of reception he would receive from Denise.

"Hello. Ed?"

"Hi. I just wanted to make sure you were all right."

"I'm okay. The kids are here, and your aunt and uncle. Will you be able to make it home?"

"I don't know. It looks like I might have to wait it out. But the minute they give the all-clear, I'll head home."

A long moment of silence hung between them.

"Guess I should have taken my umbrella, huh?" He tried to laugh.

"You just be careful, Ed," she said softly. "Call if you can't make it tonight."

"I will," he said, matching her tone, and hoping that the concern he heard in her voice was real and not his imagination. "Denise . . . about last night, and this morning . . ."

She lowered her voice. "I don't think this is a good time to talk, Ed."

He swallowed. "I guess you're right. But we have to. I need you to help me understand why you don't want to be married to me anymore."

"Mom!" Christine called out in the background. "Aunt Etta is in the pots," she singsonged.

"We'll talk, Ed. But I'd better go before Etta adds some of her special ingredients to my gravy."

"Sure. I'll call later."

"Bye."

Slowly he hung up the phone and wondered for the hundredth time how he was going to fix what was wrong with his marriage.

SEVEN

Edward found it hard to imagine that any night could have been more difficult than the one before, but this night took the cake. Not only was he not in bed with his wife, or at the very least banished to his son's old bedroom, he was knotted up on a love seat in his office, stuck until morning. Instead of the gentle, soft snore of his wife, he was rocked and rolled by the inhumane rumbling of William, who'd decided to camp out on the leather recliner.

"I'm gonna stay in here with you, man," William had announced once it was determined that travel for the night was out of the question. "I heard that if you had a head injury you needed to be monitored in case you slip into a coma. You got my back, right?"

"Sure. I'll keep an ear out for you. But I'm pretty sure you're fine. I've seen enough episodes of *ER* where the patients had head injuries. There've been no signs of dizziness or nausea," Edward said with authority.

"You sure know your stuff," William said as he made himself comfortable in the chair.

But now, hours later, eyeing William with bleary, sleep-deprived eyes, as much as Edward cared about him, he would pay big money to *put* him in a coma, anything to shut up the herd of buffalo that William expelled every time he breathed. Morning couldn't get there fast enough. He would rather stay mystified by his wife's totally bizarre behavior than spend another night in the same room with William Henry. The only conclusion he could come to was that he was paying for some misdeed in a prior life. He closed his eyes and prayed for deliverance.

The light tap on his office door stirred him from a fitful sleep. Slowly, he opened his eyes. He looked around. It was the same nightmare. He groaned as he tried to unravel his body and sit up. On stiff legs and with an aching back, he made his way to the door.

"Morning, Mr. Morrison," Lena murmured. "The news report says that the roads are open. Thought you'd want to know."

"Thanks, Lena." He rubbed his eyes and yawned.

Lena peered around him. "What's that noise?" she asked, looking very concerned.

Edward looked over his shoulder and twisted his mouth into a grimace. "The creature from the black lagoon," he said, and meant it.

Lena giggled. "Anyway . . . I'm going to head home. The staff that were stuck here are heading out as well."

He rotated his neck. "Drive safely."

"You too, sir. And happy Thanksgiving. Give my best to your family."

"I will. You do the same."

"Enjoy your day." She turned and left.

Enjoy my day. He had no idea what awaited him at home, but whatever it was, he would be prepared. At least he hoped so.

B y the time he arrived at home, tired, gritty, and in desperate need of a hot shower, Thanksgiving at the Morrison household was in full swing. He could hear music and laughter the moment he entered the door, with Uncle Eddie having everyone in stitches doing his version of the James Brown slide.

When Edward walked into the living room, Uncle Eddie had donned an old blanket and thrown it over his shoulders as a cape. He was hunched over, singing "Please, Please, Please." Anthony played the famous sidekick Maceo by replacing the cape each time Eddie threw it off in the throes of his performance.

Edward couldn't help but laugh at the scene and he had to admit that the old man was pretty good, right down to the pressed, shoulder-length hair and platform shoes. Aunt Etta was beaming like a schoolgirl as she sipped what he knew was not iced tea, unless the iced tea was being refilled from the flask in her purse. And even Denise had a smile on her face and the old sparkle was back in her eyes. If he didn't know better, he'd bet money that all was as it should be. But he knew better.

"Happy Thanksgiving, everybody!" he greeted, stepping into the room.

All eyes turned in his direction. Christine was the first one at his side and in his arms.

"Dad," she greeted effusively, giving him a big kiss on the cheek. "Uncle Eddie was keeping us entertained until dinner."

"So I see," he said with a chuckle. "How are you, baby girl, and where is that son-in-law of mine?"

Christine's expression darkened. "Working. He tried to get out of it," she offered in his defense. "But the new residents always have to pull the holiday and graveyard shifts."

"Hang in there, baby girl." He gently patted her back and looked at Denise. "It will all work out. Don't you think so, Dee?"

"Reese is a good man. I'm sure he and Christine will get through this rough time," Denise offered, deftly sidestepping Edward's real question.

"Hey, Dad," Anthony said, stepping up to his father and giving him the one-fisted hug. "You look a little worse for wear."

"Thanks, son, always the bearer of good cheer." Edward chuckled. "Is your lady friend going to be able to join us?"

Anthony shrugged. "I hope so. I may have to go and pick her up. Depends on when her folks finish up dinner. I really do want you all to meet her. She's hot!" He rubbed his hands together.

"Anthony!" Denise mildly reprimanded. "Is that how you describe your girlfriend?"

Anthony chuckled. "Absolutely!"

"Thatta boy," Uncle Eddie said. "As long as they stays hot, you can have fun putting out the fire! Ain't that right, Etta?"

"You old fool." She popped him in the head with a pillow. "Sit down and stop filling that boy's head with your foolishness."

"Foolishness! You didn't say that last night." He howled with laughter.

Anthony looked from his great-uncle to his great-aunt. "How old are you two anyway?" he asked, totally unable to believe that they could possibly have any spark left in the tank.

"Old enough to teach you a thing or two, boy. Ask your daddy, taught that boy everything he knows. Ask your mama. She'll verify it. Ain't that right, Dee?"

Denise put her hand over her mouth to keep from bursting out laughing. "I think it's time for dinner. Let's adjourn to the dining room," she replied instead.

The troupe happily filed into the dining room, animatedly discussing the validity of Uncle Eddie's claims, leaving Denise and Edward alone.

She turned to Edward. "Why don't you go shower and change while I get the food out on the table?"

"Can't I even get a hello?" he whispered. "Didn't you miss me just a little bit?"

Denise opened her mouth to speak, just as Etta's voice rose from the kitchen in concert with the banging sounds of pots.

"I know what I'm doing! If you need to heat up the food, put the gas on high! Pass me the hot sauce."

"You better go tend to *your* aunt," Edward murmured, knowing how Denise maintained complete domain over the kitchen.

"*My* aunt! That's *your* bloodline. We're only related by marriage," she tossed over her shoulder as she hurried into the kitchen, panic etched on her face.

"But for how long?" he whispered as he headed upstairs to shower and change.

EIGHT

Your father and I have decided to get a divorce," Denise announced, and watched shock spread around the table. For the first time, Aunt Etta actually appeared at a loss for words. Uncle Eddie looked at his nephew as if expecting him to say it was all a joke.

Denise hadn't planned on making the announcement at dinner, but after seeing Edward's desolate expression when he returned and worrying half the night that he was injured, she'd been afraid of weakening. Even now, she had to clench her hands to keep from walking over and touching him to reassure herself that he was unharmed. But it was the shocked faces of her children that wrenched Denise's heart and almost caused her to forget the whole idea.

Anthony simply stared as her as if he couldn't get his mind to reconcile with what she'd just said. Christine had no such difficulty. She was as volatile in her reaction as Denise had expected.

"No! You can't!" Her frantic gaze snapped from one parent to the other, finally resting on her father, the person she had always gone to when she was hurt or in need of advice or just a hug. "Daddy?"

Edward, who had glanced down at his barely touched plate of food when Denise had begun talking, raised his head, but instead of looking at his daughter he looked at her. Denise clenched her hands so tightly her nails dug into her palms. She refused to be swayed by the pain in his tired, bleary eyes. She simply couldn't go on as they had before. He had succeeded in his business while she was not even allowed to try.

She deeply regretted she wasn't able to confide in her children, but knowing how much they loved their father, she hadn't been sure they wouldn't have told him the whole thing was a hoax. Reese's absence also created a problem. She had counted on him being there with Christine.

Finally, Edward's gaze swung to Christine's and for the first time Denise wondered if he would paint her in a bad light to her children. He could, if he wanted. They had always loved him the best.

"Your mother and I are having some problems," he said as if each word were being ripped from his heart.

"You work through problems," Anthony blurted, his boyishly handsome face pinched with concern. "You don't get a divorce."

"He's right, Eddie," Aunt Etta said, jabbing her fork in the direction of her nephew. "You got the children and too much invested in this house and each other."

"We're selling the house," Denise said calmly, although her nerves were jumpy. Edward had to believe this was real. She was determined to find out exactly how much she and their marriage meant to him.

"What?" Christine came to her feet. "Daddy built this house! We grew up here."

Denise expected the outburst and her daughter's first thoughts to be of her father. "It's settled. The house is too big for either of us to maintain on our own."

"Daddy?" Christine said. Her voice sounded frightened, the way it had when she was scared of monsters in the dark and her father had to go in her room to scare them away.

Denise's hand felt numb she held them so tightly. She was sorry she had to put her children through this, but she couldn't back down now.

"We discussed selling the house," he repeated dully.

"I've already contacted a realtor," Denise said calmly, picking up her glass of iced tea.

The flatness in Edward's dark brown eyes vanished. They blazed as he leaned forward in his seat. "You called them already?"

She wouldn't shrink from his anger or feel bad that she had finally taken a step without his permission. "I saw no reason to wait."

"Just like you saw no reason to at least wait until dinner was finished," he accused her, with just enough bite in his tone to raise Denise's own temper.

"Dinner *was* finished. All that was left was clearing the table and since I'm always left to do that alone, as well as wash all the dishes by myself, I decided to tell them now," she shot back.

Edward started, then he said, "We help."

Denise tsked. She was not even going to dignify that out-and-out lie with a reply. They ran from the kitchen like a stampeding herd of wildebeests being chased by a lion to watch football on the TV.

"What about Christmas when we all get together?" Anthony almost whined.

Looking in her son's lost eyes, the pressure in Denise's chest increased and she almost gave in, but she stiffened her back once again. Perhaps he needed a wake-up call as well. She still did his laundry and picked up his dry cleaning. "I'm not sure where I'll be, but you're welcome to come over."

"But it won't be the same," Anthony said, looking at his father. "So that's why there weren't any lights on the house or on the lawn?"

"I just didn't see the point," Edward said, his attention on Denise again. The gazes of the children followed.

Christine was the first to say what was on everyone's mind. "Who asked for the divorce?"

Denise and Edward stared across the end of the table at each other.

"Daddy works like a dog to give Mama everything she wants," Anthony said.

"Mama, you've always been there for us," Christine said.

"He treats her like a queen," Aunt Etta said.

Uncle Eddie nodded in agreement with his wife.

"The boy never even looked at another woman. Don't know why he should 'cause she treats him like a king."

"Mama, Daddy, what were you thinking?" Christine cried. "You can't sell the only home Anthony and I remember. You're ruining the holidays for all of us!"

Denise stared at the accusing faces and rose regally to her feet. "I've spent the past twenty-seven years giving to everyone except myself. For the most part, none of you have ever noticed me unless it was time for dinner or you needed something sewn. You wouldn't be upset now if this weren't interfering with your plans for the holidays. Well, I suggest you make other arrangements." She tossed her napkin on the table. "This queen is abdicating her throne."

Denise's righteous anger carried her to the attic, where she flung herself into a chair. Pressing her arm across her eyes, she wondered if she might have gone a bit too far and how long she could keep up the charade.

NINE

Edward went through his dresser drawer and shoved his necessities into an overnight bag. He went to the closet and pulled out his pressed shirts, a sports jacket, two pairs of slacks, and two ties. He took his shaving kit from the bathroom and dumped that in the bag as well. He had enough supplies to last at least two days. Enough time for Denise to come to her senses and beg for him to come back. *Let's just see how long she manages without me.* Two could play at this game, he concluded. As much as he dreaded spending a minute more than was necessary with his aunt and uncle, he took them up on their offer to stay with them.

After Denise's pronouncement at the dinner table, Uncle Eddie had pulled him to the side and whispered his version of sage advice.

"You know how women have those spells," he said, looking around to be sure Etta was out of earshot.

"Spells?" Edward asked, perplexed.

"Yeah, you know what I mean, boy. PBS."

Edward tried not to laugh. "You mean PMS, Uncle Eddie?"

"Whatever. That thing that makes 'em crazy. Well, I done discovered the cure."

"Really?" He tried to contain his humor. "And what might that be, Uncle Eddie?"

"Head for the hills, boy, until they come back to themselves. When you come home, they'll be just as loving as a newborn baby. Works like a charm." He lowered his voice and looked around again. "And believe me, I know all about those spells. You come stay with me and Etta till Denise's spell passes."

"You and Aunt Etta?" he said, alarm raising his voice. Nothing could be that bad. But the truth was, maybe Uncle Eddie was right, in a way. A few nights out of the house may be just the thing Denise needed to snap out of it. All he'd have to do was sleep there. He wouldn't have to deal with them for any length of time. Besides, he was confident he'd be back home in a heartbeat.

"All right. But just for a night or two," he finally agreed.

"Thatta boy." Uncle Eddie slapped him on the back. "What you really need is a man-to-man talk. And I'm just the one to give it to you. Grab some things. We'll be outside." Uncle Eddie ambled off to the beck and call of his wife.

"Man-to-man talk," he groaned. Just what he needed. *What have I agreed to?* he thought as he zipped his bag and headed downstairs.

His daughter and son were at the bottom of the landing, looking up at him as he came down the stairs.

"Oh, Daddy," Christine said sadly, wrapping her arms around him. She pressed her head against his chest. "You're not really going to stay with Aunt Etta and Uncle Eddie, are you?" she whispered. "You know they drive you up the wall."

"It will be fine," he assured her, and kissed the top of her head. "Call me if you need anything. Me and Mom will work this out. We just need some time away from each other."

She stepped back and looked into his eyes. "But Aunt Etta and Uncle Eddie?"

Edward's stomach knotted at the prospect, but it was too late to back out now. He certainly wasn't going to move in with the newlyweds, and Anthony's lifestyle was a little too risqué for him. The less he knew, the better. And another night on the love seat in his office was out of the question. "They go to bed early and I get home late," he finally said.

"Does this mean I come from a broken home?" Anthony asked, half in jest.

"You're a little old to come from a broken home, silly," Christine admonished. "Can't you be serious for one minute?"

"I'm sorry, O great big sister. But I just find it too hard to believe." He slung his hands in his pockets.

"Well, believe it. You heard Mom."

"Okay, cut it out. You both sound like two little bickering kids," Edward warned. "We don't need you two at each other's throats too."

"Sorry," they murmured in unison.

"I'm going to go home with Eddie and Etta. You two are going home. Your mother and I will work it out."

"Do you really think so, Dad?" Christine asked.

"Of course. Haven't I always been able to fix things around here? Have I ever let you or your brother down?"

Christine and Anthony shook their heads.

"All right then. Go on home, get some rest, and before you know it, everything will be back to normal." He hugged his daughter and son, took one last look around his home, then headed out to the waiting car.

The last time he'd lived under the same roof with his aunt and uncle, he'd been nineteen years old. Unfortunately, nothing had changed. The instant he crossed their threshold, he was no longer a forty-seven-year-old man with a wife, kids, house, and a thriving business, but a teenage boy who was instructed on what to do, from making sure he brushed his teeth to being informed that he was not to bring any of his friends home without one of them being there.

He looked around at the small but neatly furnished room. At least it had a full-size bed, he thought, consoling himself. He sat on the side and wondered how things could have gotten so bad. He was still in shock that Denise would make that kind of announcement at the dinner table. This was serious. And serious situations required serious measures. He would approach this the same way he approached a new project: lay out all of the possibilities and take the best course of action.

"It's after nine o'clock, Edward," his aunt called out from the other side of the door. "Time for bed. You need your rest."

Edward lowered his head, shook it, and groaned. "Yes, Aunt Etta."

"All right, now. Don't make me have to come in there."

He heard her shuffle down the hall in the same ratty slippers she'd worn when he was sixteen. Some things never change, he mused, a wry grin curving his mouth.

He was just about to take off his shoes when there was a stealthy tap on the door.

"Yes?"

"Sssshhh," Uncle Eddie whispered before tiptoeing inside. "I just wanted to tell you . . . don't pay attention to any noise you might hear during the night."

"Noise?"

"Yeah, you know . . ." he said with a wink.

Edward's eyebrows rose in understanding. "Sure, Uncle Eddie. Don't worry about me."

Eddie patted him on the back. "See you in the morning." He tiptoed back out, closing the door quietly behind him.

Edward undressed and slid beneath the covers. As soon as he'd closed his eyes, he heard the distinct sounds of his aunt and uncle's bed doing the two-step. He put the pillow over his head to drown out his aunt's wails of ecstasy. How old were they anyway? No wonder his aunt wanted him to go to sleep early. It was an old trick he and Denise used on their own kids.

He missed her. Desperately. And he would do whatever was necessary to get their marriage back on track. If only he could figure out where they'd gone so wrong.

"Oh, *James*!" Etta cried.

Edward burrowed further beneath the blanket. Maybe there was something to this James Brown thing.

TEN

Christine bit her lip to keep from crying as she rode the elevator to the third floor of Community Hospital. The shiny red garland strung around a glass-enclosed bulletin board made her think all the more how this Christmas holiday was going to be the worst ever. She had to see Reese. She had never felt so helpless nor so lost as she had on seeing her father drive off behind Aunt Etta and Uncle Eddie. He loved his father's youngest brother and his wife, but he couldn't handle them.

Christine sniffed. Her father had looked so pitiful coming down the stairs with his bag. He didn't say so, but Christine had seen him come out of Anthony's old room before dinner. Her mother had put him out of her bed *and* her life. How could she have done that to a wonderful man like her father? Her mother has always been so dependable . . . so quiet. What had happened to make them want to end what Christine thought was a perfect marriage and disrupt all their lives? Including hers.

The elevator door slid open on the medical-surgical floor and Christine stepped out, then went directly to the nurses' station. More red garlands mixed with green hung from the waist-high partition. Several silver cardboard snowflakes hung from the ceiling. Everyone was gearing up for the holidays. She had been too . . . until her mother's announcement. It was almost 9:00, visiting hours were over, and the hospital was eerily quiet. "I'm Mrs. Evans, Dr. Reese Evans's wife. Is he on the floor?"

The eyes of a woman in surgical scrubs, whose name tag identified her as a registered nurse, widened for a fraction. Then she glanced uneasily behind her to another woman dressed the same way. The other woman smirked, then said, "He's in the lounge two doors down."

"Thank you," Christine said and left, dismissing the strange attitude of the women until she pushed open the door to the lounge and saw her husband standing very close to a woman. Reese's back was to her and he didn't see Christine. The woman saw her, smiled, then slid her arms around his neck, pressing her body to his in one practiced move.

"Reese!" Christine shrieked. Shock and anger locked her in her tracks.

Reese sprang back, pulling the clinging woman's arms from around his neck. He blinked behind his wire-rimmed glasses.

"Honey." Reese gulped, then stepped away from the other woman. "It's not what you think. I was just trying to help Loretta feel better after Swanson jumped all over her for nothing." Frowning, he threw a confused glance at the silent woman beside him. "I don't know how it happened."

Christine did. She recognized Loretta immediately. This wasn't the first time she had seen the brazen woman in her husband's face. The smug expression the woman wore said it wouldn't be the last. Christine took a deep, calming breath. Snatching her weave out by the roots might be satisfying, but it was more important to speak with Reese. He had always been able to ground her, to steady her. Outside of her father, he was the most honest, dependable man she knew. Which was probably another reason hair wasn't scattered all over the lounge.

"Reese, I need to talk with you."

"Sure, honey," he said and started toward her.

"Wait," Loretta said with a girlish giggle. "You can't go anyplace with my lipstick on your shirt collar." Planting herself in front of him, she ineffectually brushed at the red smear on the white collar Christine had ironed that morning.

Christine spun on her heel. If she stayed one more second—

"Christine," Reese called, catching up with her outside the lounge and swinging her around. "I swear it didn't mean anything!"

Christine stared at her husband and wondered how any man who had always been in the top one percent of his class since grade school could be so dense. "That woman is after you."

He blinked, then smiled boyishly at her. It was the same smile that always went straight to her heart; because he was usually so serious, the smiles were so precious. He leaned over to kiss her and Christine pulled back. "Honey, she's just an old friend. You got this all wrong."

Before Christine could speak, the door behind them opened and Loretta came out. Christine considered sticking her foot out to trip the wanton nurse, then dismissed the idea because Reese would rush to her aid and once again, he'd have his hands on her . . . exactly where the hussy wanted them. "She wants more than friendship. She hugged you after she saw me. She wanted to make trouble."

Reese had the audacity to smile. "Loretta isn't that type of woman. We've known each other since my first year in med school. I was trying to comfort her and must have finally gotten her to see that she's a wonderful staff nurse when you walked in." He shrugged. "In any case, it's over and it doesn't matter."

Christine felt steam rise through the top of her head. "It doesn't matter, huh?" She glanced around and saw a surgical resident on Reese's rotation. "What if I went over there and sought a little comfort from Dr. Blair?"

"That's not funny," Reese said, his hands tightening on her arms.

Christine was too hot to take comfort in his jealousy. "It wasn't meant to be. If you want me to believe you, then don't let yourself be caught in that woman's clutches again."

Reese's dark eyebrows lifted. "She's one of the best nurses on this floor. I depend on her for my patients' care. You're getting all worked up over nothing."

Christine barely kept from sputtering, she was so incensed. "Perhaps because my life is in turmoil, perhaps I need a little comfort, but first I have to push another woman out of the way," she said, her voice trembling.

His concern was immediate. "Honey, what's the matter?" he asked, bending down to stare into her face.

"Would you care?" Christine sniffed, feeling the tears she had held at bay so long building in her eyes and clogging her throat.

"Dr. Evans. Emergency room, stat. Dr. Evans. Emergency room, stat."

"Damn," he muttered. "I have to go. I love you. I'll call you as soon as I take care of this." With a quick peck on her cheek, he was racing to the elevator. It opened almost immediately. He waved, and then the door closed and he was gone.

She's after him. I just know it and he won't listen," Christine cried, reaching for another tissue on the coffee table in the family room of her parents' home. She'd thought of going to see her father, but she hadn't wanted to deal with Uncle Eddie and Aunt Etta. Instead she'd driven to her mother.

"I can't believe he actually thought he could kiss me after having that . . . that . . ." Christine's lips clamped together before the word she wanted to call Loretta slipped out. "I should have snatched her bald."

Denise continued the relentless sweep of her hand up and down Christine's rigid back. There was nothing else she could think of doing to help. It had taken thirty minutes to calm her hot-tempered daughter down enough for her to explain what had upset her. The incident with Reese couldn't have happened at a worse time. Christine had enough to contend with.

"Reese loves you," Denise said.

"That may be, but that's not stopping that woman from trying to take him from me."

After hearing her daughter's account of what had happened, Denise was inclined to agree with her daughter. "Christine, if this woman is—"

"*If!*" Christine cried. "Weren't you listening?"

Since Denise knew exactly how it felt when your marriage was threatened, she didn't reprimand her daughter for her tone. Instead, she closed her hand over her daughter's, clamped tightly in her lap. "Please, let me finish. If she is after Reese, and I believe she is, by letting your temper do the talking for you, you left the door wide open for her."

"If he really loved me, no matter what that woman did, he wouldn't look at her twice." Christine turned on the sofa to face her mother. "Daddy would never cheat on you or you on him. Whatever problems you are having, infidelity isn't one of them."

With difficulty Denise kept her hand and voice steady. "We aren't discussing your father's and my problems."

"He loves you."

Not enough or too much, the results are the same. He wants me dependent on him. "Christine."

"All right, but he does."

Denise almost smiled. Christine was loyal to a fault. "It's after twelve. You're not driving home. Call Reese and tell him where you are so he won't worry."

"He won't miss me with Loretta there," Christine said bitterly, but she reached for the phone on the end table by the couch and dialed Reese's cell.

"Dr. Evans," answered a too-sweet female voice.

Christine shot to her feet. "What are you doing answering my husband's phone?" she asked, then seconds later, slammed the receiver down. "I should have snatched her bald!"

Denise rose to place a comforting hand on her daughter's rigid arm. "What is it?"

"*She* answered the phone," Christine explained, folding her arms defensively around her stomach. "She said he had lost his cell, but he's too conscientious, I tease him all the time about being surgically attached to it. He never takes it off until he's ready for bed and always puts it back on when he puts his pants back . . ." Her voice trailed off as the implication of her words sank in. "Mama."

Denise pulled her daughter into her arms. "Don't borrow trouble. Wait until you hear what Reese has to say."

Christine shook her head, her shoulders shaking from the force of her tears.

Denise thought of Edward. Maybe he could help. "Christine, do—"

The phone interrupted her. "That's probably Reese," Denise said, helping Christine to retake a seat on the sofa before picking up the phone. "Hello." Her gaze swung to her daughter, her arms wrapped once again around her stomach. "Reese, yes, she's here. Christine?"

She shook her head.

"She doesn't want to talk. Maybe in the morning," Denise said, feeling sorry for the desperation in Reese's voice and wishing he were a little more perceptive about women. "Reese, we both know how stubborn she can be . . . All right." Denise put the phone to her daughter's ear.

Moments later, more tears coursed down Christine's smooth brown cheeks, then she was up and heading for the stairs. Denise brought the receiver back to her face. "Reese, I have to go." Hanging up the phone, Denise followed and found Christine in her old room in her bed, crying her heart out. Denise had kept both the rooms as they'd been if the children ever wanted to spend the night.

Sitting beside her daughter, she stroked Christine's shoulder-length black hair.

"He said he'd die without me," Christine cried, curled into a knot.

Denise continued stroking her daughter's hair. "Don't give up, Christine."

"What if I don't have a choice? What if he's given up on me?"

For herself Denise knew what the answer was, but this was her child, her only daughter.

"You fight to get him back."

Christine rolled over on her back and looked up at her mother through tear-stained eyes. "Are you going to fight?"

"That's what I'm doing," she said softly, then went on to explain and finished by saying, "Your father has to let me make my own decisions and to stop taking me for granted."

Christine bit her lower lip. "I think we all did."

"I let you because I loved you so much, but I did us all a disservice." Denise's expression hardened. "It stops now."

Christine gazed at her mother with new appreciation. "Mama, I've never seen you like this."

A smile touched Denise's lips. "Neither have I, and to quote Mr. Brown, I feel good."

ELEVEN

Friday afternoon Denise answered the front door with a smile on her face and laughter flowing from her mauve-colored lips. She'd seen Edward coming up the walk. His timing was perfect. Round three was about to begin.

Edward's gaze locked on her, then zeroed in on the ruggedly handsome man coming down the stairs and continuing into the family room. "Who's that?" he demanded, trying to brush pass Denise.

A sweetly innocent smile on her face, Denise continued to hold the doorknob, effectively blocking his path. "Did you forget something?"

He scowled down at her. "Who's that man?"

Since his left eyelid had begun to twitch, Denise thought it best to answer him, although she was positive he wasn't going to like hearing what she had to say. "Come inside and I'll introduce you."

Edward stalked inside as soon as she stepped back. Quickly shoving the door closed, she hurried after him. She'd forgotten how possessive and jealous Edward had been when they were dating. The man rose from the sofa in the family room, a smile on his darkly handsome face. Denise gave him points for smiling instead of running for the nearest exit as Edward headed for him.

"Edward, this is Paul Carter, the wonderful man who is going to sell our house."

Edward stopped on a dime and whirled toward her. Denise thought it prudent to take a couple of steps back. Edward had never been violent, but he'd never had a tic before either. "Paul, this is my husband, Edward."

Either Paul loved living dangerously or he was used to dealing with angry men. Edward outweighed him by thirty pounds and had more muscles. Paul extended his hand and kept his smile in place. "Glad to meet you, Mr. Morrison. Your wife showed me around your beautiful home already. You've got yourself a very nice place here."

Finally, Edward looked at the realtor instead of her. Grateful for the reprieve, Denise took a seat on the navy blue leather sofa and gracefully crossed her long legs, which Edward had always had a thing for. If and when Edward stopped glowering and took a seat across from her, she wanted him to notice she wore a cranberry-colored, figure-flattering knit dress.

"This house shouldn't stay on the market very long," Paul said, sitting beside her. "It's even lovelier and more appealing on the inside than on the outside."

"Thank you," Denise said, thinking it was fortuitous that Christine had a realtor friend who didn't mind helping with Denise's plan. "It's nice of you to come out so quickly. I just called Wednesday."

Paul flashed her a set of perfect white teeth. She thought she heard Edward growl. "Your home is in a very desirable area.

Peachtree Crossing has excellent schools, is near the express-way and, despite the growth of the surrounding area, has man-aged to keep the close-knit neighborhood feel." His manicured hand gestured around the living area. She caught the flash of his gold Rolex. "Buyers will snap this one up fast. You have so much space and the house is so well laid out."

"My husband built the house," Denise commented, the pride coming through in her voice as she looked at the high-ceilinged room with crown molding and inserts, the hardwood floors, the bay window that was repeated in the separate dining room across the hall. They'd planned the house for years before they actually had the money to build and by then, they'd had a box-ful of ideas.

"*We* built this house," Edward stated with pointed emphasis.

Her gaze met his. He wasn't looking at her with anger any longer. In his face she saw traces of the loving, wonderful man she had begun falling in love with the instant she'd first seen him.

Paul nodded, then made a notation in his notebook. "You did a marvelous job. The house flows beautifully and is picture-perfect. Did you have a decorator?"

"I did everything myself," Denise said, picking up a pillow covered in pale blue damask that exactly matched the covering of the Queen Anne side chair. "Of course, I had nothing to do with *that* chair."

The realtor's gaze followed the direction of Denise's. His ex-pression became pained as he stared at the orange tweed chair. He cleared his throat. "You might consider placing it in the ga-rage. It throws off the aesthetic flow and beauty of the room."

"Nobody touches my chair," Edward snarled.

Paul blinked, drawing his notebook closer to his chest. Perhaps he wasn't as immune to Edward as she had thought.

"I'll certainly take your suggestion into consideration," Denise placated, urging the realtor to continue.

Paul nodded, then glanced around again and made another notation. "I assume you plan to leave the custom draperies throughout the house?"

"Of course." She'd spent countless hours searching for the right fabric in the right colors at the right price, then more hours sewing. She'd wanted to make their home a place her family could be proud of. She'd succeeded in that, if not in making her family proud of her.

Once again, her gaze fell on the side chair that a stiff Edward sat even more stiffly in. It had been a garage sale find they had refinished and she'd reupholstered. She'd been so scared of wasting the fabric she'd caught on sale at a fraction of the original price, but Edward had said if anybody could do it, she could. He'd always been supportive of whatever she did in the house, but when it came to the children or their finances, he always made the final decisions.

Her short, oval nails dug into the pillow. He had no confidence in her if she wasn't cooking or sewing.

"Excellent." Putting the notebook aside, the realtor then pulled a clipboard with a form attached from his briefcase. "Now, all I need is both of your signatures on this sales agreement. I plan to put your house on our website and feature it prominently. We should get hits right away."

"I'm not signing," Edward said, his voice defiant.

Denise paused in reaching for the clipboard. She studied her husband's hard expression for a moment, then turned to Paul.

"Why don't you leave the papers and you can pick them up when they're signed?"

Paul needed no further urging. He practically threw the sales agreement at Denise as he gathered his things and made a hasty retreat to the front door. "Thank you, again."

Feeling Edward's gaze boring a hole in the middle of her back, Denise said, "Thank you for coming."

"My pleasure." Paul glanced at the crystal chandelier above in the vaulted ceiling, then back at Denise. "And please rest assured that Homestead Realtors prides itself on only bringing serious clients to see properties. We respect our clients' privacy, which is another reason we don't put up signs in the yards."

"I appreciate that." Denise was glad she had thought of that potential problem. She had a couple of nosy neighbors who would be all in her affairs if they had a hint of what was going on. This was family business.

"Good-bye. I hope to have a prospective buyer out within the week, and when you're ready to look for a place of your own, I'm at your disposal. I have some simply gorgeous condos in my listings."

Denise heard that growl again. She discreetly shooed Paul out the door. "Good-bye."

"Good-bye." After a friendly nod, he went down the curved walk to the gleaming black Mercedes sports utility vehicle parked by the curb. Denise waited until he got inside the car before turning and facing her angry husband.

"I can't believe you'd really sell the house!"

"It's too big for either of us to care for alone," she said, brushing by him and going to the kitchen for a glass of water. She wished she could add an aspirin for the headache that was building, but that might be too revealing. In the past, she'd always shied away from confrontations.

Opening the oak cabinet and seeing the jumble of glasses increased the pain in her head. Edward and the children—she doubted his aunt and uncle had helped—had washed the dishes and cleaned up the kitchen last night. Since they never helped, they had stuck things where there was room and not where they went. It had taken her ten minutes this morning to find the skillet to fix Christine's breakfast.

She was annoyed enough to turn and glare at her husband. "Look what you did!"

He blinked. "What are you talking about?"

"This." She gestured wildly toward the glasses. "My cabinets below are even worse."

He crept closer as if he expected something to jump out and bite him. He peered at the glasses, then back at her. "What?"

Denise bit back a frustrated scream and started pulling glasses out. "They're supposed to be grouped by design and size."

"Oh," he mumbled.

Denise continued until she felt his warm hand on her arm. Startled, she glanced up at him.

"I messed it up. I'll do it."

She simply stared at him. If her family wasn't eating, they didn't want to be anywhere near the kitchen.

He stared back. "I can do it."

"Be my guest," she said and went to the refrigerator. If Christine returned after work, Denise wanted dinner ready. Hopefully, she'd eat this time. She'd picked over her favorite breakfast of strawberry waffles.

Denise hoped Christine had followed her advice to talk to

Reese again, and try to listen without losing her temper. The thought of her daughter going through what she was experiencing made her entire body ache.

Last night had been the worst in her life. She hadn't been able to go to sleep until almost dawn. She and Edward had always slept cuddled together. They wouldn't start that way, but always, always, before the night was over, she'd find her head pillowed on his chest, his arm draped possessively around her shoulders, keeping her close. She had woken to the steady beat of his heart for over half her life. Now he was gone, and the loss left her feeling empty and strangely adrift. If she couldn't take three nights, how was she going to get her plan to work?

"Why didn't you call me last night when Christine came back?"

If he had sounded accusatory instead of worried, she might not have answered. "There was nothing you could do. I called you this morning."

He paused with a crystal goblet in his hand, then nodded. "I couldn't get her at work so I decided to come over. Is she coming back here?"

Denise bit her bottom lip and hugged her arms around her waist. "I don't know. She told me she wouldn't call today because she would be in meetings. She was miserable when she left his morning. It tears me up, seeing her in pain."

"Dee, don't," he said and started toward her.

She wanted him to take her in his arms, wanted to accept the comfort of his arms, and it might have happened if the doorbell hadn't rung. In an instant, Edward's handsome face hardened.

"That better not be that realtor guy."

Denise quickly pulled herself together. That had been a little too close. "He has no reason to come back." Passing him, she tossed over her shoulder, "When you finish the glasses, the pots and pans under the cabinet need your attention as well."

He grunted.

Smiling, Denise continued to the front, then she opened the door and her smile vanished. Anthony, his head downcast, his hands shoved into the pockets of his slacks, stood on the doorstep. Guilt stabbed her. She hadn't meant to hurt her children.

"Baby." She gathered him into her arms before she remembered that he had stopped wanting her to hug him in the fifth grade. He'd been too big for that. As his arms closed tightly around her, she was glad he'd forgotten as well.

"Come into the kitchen. There's pecan and chocolate pie," she said, pulling him inside, hoping his favorite desserts would cheer him up.

"I'm not hungry," he said, finally lifting his head.

Her worry increased on seeing the despair and uncertainty in his eyes. "Anthony, please don't worry about your father and me."

"I can't help it. If you and Dad can't make it, who can?" Anthony asked, closing the door behind him.

Denise's gaze sharpened on her son, the carefree playboy. *My baby.* "Are you getting serious about Sherri?"

The horrified expression on his face was so comical she almost laughed. "No. I like Sherri, but jeez, Mama, I'm only twenty-one. I'm young yet."

She refrained from reminding him that Christine was a year old when her father was twenty-one. Edward had shouldered the heavy responsibility without grumbling a single time. He'd gotten up in the middle of the night during her pregnancy on several occasions to go across town and get her strawberry pie from the twenty-four-hour diner. He would come back home and tease her about keeping both of his ladies happy. They'd somehow known it would be a girl. Now, looking at her son, Denise couldn't imagine him shouldering the responsibility of a family. She still did his laundry.

"It's probably just as well." She tucked her arm through his. "Come on into the kitchen. Your father dropped by to see Christine."

They both halted in the doorway on seeing the cooking utensils on the floor surrounding Edward. "Hi, Daddy, what happened?"

"Hello, son. I was trying to straighten them out." Edward sat cross-legged amid the chaos. "Pull off your coat and give me a hand. Maybe your mother will take pity on you and feed you."

"I offered; he isn't hungry," she said.

Anthony slipped his hands out of his pockets. "On second thought, I guess I am a little hungry."

Denise shared a smile with her husband. *He'd always claimed Anthony had a hollow leg.* Then, becoming aware of the intimacy of their shared thought, she flushed and looked away. "I better get back to fixing dinner."

"Do you need anything from under here?" Edward asked, then frowned. "You need a pullout shelf under here."

Denise, who had been looking at Edward, saw him stiffen. She knew he had remembered that they were putting the house on the market. Suddenly she wanted to reach out to him, to hold and reassure him as he had done for her so many times in the past, but she couldn't. "The kitchen is fine the way it is." Turning away, she reached into the drawer for her carving knife. "Have you eaten?"

"No," came Edward's quiet answer.

"He didn't eat his lunch today," Anthony volunteered as he removed his jacket and dropped down beside his father. "I went by his office."

He hadn't eaten last night either, Denise thought. She knew she had said he was on his own, but it was *her* plan, and she was allowed to change the rules. "I'll fix enough for all of us. There's turkey and ham." Usually there wasn't enough left to make a sandwich after her family snacked all through the football games and his aunt and uncle took food home.

Just as she clicked on the electric knife, the doorbell rang.

"I'll get it." Anthony straightened and headed for the front door.

Denise stared after her fast-retreating son, then shook her head. "He's always been quick when it comes to getting out of housework."

"Yeah," Edward said, placing a broiler beneath the cabinet. "Guess I wasn't much help either. I didn't know where half this stuff went."

"It doesn't matter." She turned back to the turkey and clicked on the knife.

"I'm not signing the papers, Dee," he said quietly.

Denise whirled around, shutting off the knife as she did. Hope spiraled through her. She tried to look outraged instead of happy. He was going to fight for her and their marriage. "You have to. We agreed."

"I never thought you'd go through with it." He stood with

the same agile grace as his son and came to her. "I don't want to lose the house, or you."

Her spirits plummeted. Even now, he put the house first. He just wanted his orderly life back. "You promised, and I'm holding you to it."

"You better carve some more turkey, Mama."

Denise glanced around to see Christine, her eyes red and puffy, a suitcase in her hand. Denise reached her daughter seconds before Edward. "Christine, what is it?"

"C-can I stay here for a few days?" she asked between sobs.

Denise's heart sank. Her gaze went to Edward and saw his tight-lipped expression. He hurt for their daughter as much as she did. "Of course. I'll take your bag and go up with you."

Christine shook her head of long, straight hair. "No. I just want to be by myself for a bit."

"Pumpkin," Edward began, then sighed. "You're sure this is what you want to do?"

Christine brushed a tear away with the heel of her hand. "I wasn't given much choice in the matter."

Before Denise could ask her to explain, Christine turned and started from the room. Anthony stared after her.

"See that your sister gets to her room all right. I don't want her tripping on the stairs."

"Sure, Mama. This Christmas season is the pits," Anthony said, then followed his sister.

Denise's arms circled her waist. "What's happening? Christine's life is unraveling and there is nothing I can do about it. What I've done is just causing her more pain."

"Dee, don't." Edward pulled her gently into his arms.

She thought of resisting, but she badly needed the comfort. "I feel like this is somehow my fault."

Gently, he pushed her from him and stared down into her tortured face. "I hate like hell that you want to leave me and what I thought was a good marriage, but I won't let you take the blame for what's happening to Christine. You're a good mother, Denise." He brushed her hair back in an old, familiar gesture of affection he hadn't used in years. "That's why I could pull the long hours trying to get the business off the ground, because I knew you were here with the children and I didn't have to worry."

Her eyes widened in shock. "Y-you never complimented me before about the children."

He frowned. "I must have. All the things you do for us. It's impossible that I didn't tell you how I felt."

"She made it upstai—" Anthony's voice stopped abruptly.

Oddly embarrassed at being caught in her husband's arms, Denise pulled away. "Thank you, Anthony."

Busying herself with putting the turkey in the oven, she tried to ignore the warm feeling created by Edward's compliment, which made her feel almost as good as being in his arms again. Maybe, just maybe, her plan was working, even if it was killing her to go through with it.

TWELVE

Edward eased past his aunt and uncle's bedroom door in the hope that he could get to his room without letting them know he was home. The last thing he needed was another lecture from his uncle about his husbandly duties, or a scolding from his aunt about his bedtime. The floorboards squeaked and he held his breath. He felt like a kid sneaking in after curfew.

Finding Paul, or whatever his name was, in his house, smiling at his wife, had really done a number on his head. He was more upset about his presence than the idea that Denise was trying to sell the house right out from under all of them.

The jolly green giant had kicked in and he felt like doing the same to Mr. Perfect Teeth's teeth. "Probably caps," he grumbled.

He went into the bathroom, hoping that a nice hot bath would soothe his body and his mind. As he watched the steamy water fill the tub, he thought about the many nights and mornings that he and Denise had shared a bath together. Even after all these years, she still turned him on. The touch of her skin beneath his fingertips was enough to get his blood boiling.

From the moment he'd met Denise, he knew that she was the one for him. He wanted to do for her what his father had been unable to do for his mother. But it seemed that all his efforts and all his good intentions had been for nothing. Denise didn't want him in her life anymore and she didn't want anything he had to offer.

Well, he decided then and there, he was not going to be like his father. He was not going to walk away from everything he loved. Maybe it *was* some kind of spell that Denise was going through, like Uncle Eddie had said. But he was going to break the spell, and what he needed was some help.

He quickly finished what should have been a leisurely bath, donned the robe that hung on the hook behind the door, and darted off to his room. But he nearly leaped out of his skin when he opened the door to find his aunt and uncle sitting on the bed, waiting for him.

"'Bout time, boy," Uncle Eddie announced. "It's past me and Etta's bedtime."

"But what are—"

"I think it's about time we had a talk with you, son," Aunt Etta said.

"That's right. Now, have a sit down and listen."

"Uncle Eddie, if this is going to be another lecture about me coming in after nine—"

"You gonna listen, or run your mouth? That's why you're in the predicament you're in today," Etta admonished him. "Now, you do as your uncle told ya."

"Yes, ma'am," he muttered sheepishly. Slowly, Edward took a seat on the hard wooden chair with the bad leg. It rocked a few times, then settled.

Etta took her husband's hand. "Go head, Ed, talk to the boy."

"Seems to me, boy, that you've gotten yourself into a real fix with your wife."

Etta nodded in agreement.

"She done put you out of the house and wants a divorce." He shook his head. "Now, it's not that we don't want you here. It's nice having you back. But to be truthful . . . you're cramping our style . . . if you know what I mean." He winked, and Etta giggled.

"Now, you can stay if that's what you really have a mind to do," Etta said. "But a husband's place is at his wife's side. I know you just think we're two old eccentric codgers, but we haven't been together this long by luck."

"I may act the fool," Eddie admitted, "but so does she."

Etta popped him good-naturedly in the arm.

"Ow, woman!"

"Oh, hush. I ain't done nothin' yet."

"I got somethin' for ya in the next room."

"We'll just have to see now, won't we?" Etta said, her voice dropping to a seductive low that made Edward blush.

But what Edward saw beneath all the antics and talk of Wild Irish Rose and James Brown records was an unwavering love that radiated between them like lights on a Christmas tree. Maybe it didn't seem like they got along, but they did. They were a team—equals.

Then it hit him like a ton of bricks. That's what Denise had been talking about all along! Equality, being a full partner in the marriage. And he had been so wrapped up in being *the man* that he'd forgotten about being a husband.

Eddie leaned over and kissed his wife on the lips, not caring that they weren't alone, but just needing to show her that he cared, and Edward saw his aunt's eyes light up with joy the way Denise's eyes used to light up for him.

It was true that his aunt and uncle didn't have the great big, pretty house, two cars, and a six-figure income. But they had something more important—each other.

Eddie took Etta's hand and stood. "Hope you know you can't win her back by sitting on your hands, boy."

"That girl loves you, son," Etta said, brushing his cheek with the palm of her hand.

"You really think so?" Edward asked, needing reassurance.

"I see it in her eyes every time she looks at you. Just imagine, if you don't fix what's ailing in your marriage, you'll be living here with us!" She cackled at her own humor.

"Come on, woman. It's way past this boy's bedtime."

"And ours."

Eddie patted her bottom as they walked out, but not before Etta issued her closing comment.

"The same thing you did to get her is what you need to keep her." She closed the door gently behind them.

In bed that night, Edward thought about his odd counseling session with his aunt and uncle, even as he listened to "Sex Machine" and the bump and grind of their bed against his wall. If they could make their marriage work, so could he. What he needed was a plan. And that plan would begin tomorrow.

Morning couldn't get there fast enough. He'd have to get the help of his son and William, too, but it could be done. He put the pillow over his head to drown out the noise and smiled.

I t was a shame that he had to come up with an excuse to visit his own house, but he knew his wife. She would want to know why he wasn't at work. Well, he already had a story concocted.

Before he headed to his house, he made a pit stop at his son's apartment. He knew it was early, but he wanted to catch Anthony before he got on with his day. He just hoped he wouldn't walk in on anything other than his son.

He jogged up the short flight of stone steps that led to the townhouse where Anthony lived and rang the bell. Moments later his son appeared at the door, showered, dressed, and ready to face the world.

"Hey, Dad." He looked past his father to the lane behind him. "What's up? Is something wrong? You never just drop by."

"Can I come in? I need to talk to you, son."

"*Son.* Hmmm, this sounds serious. Sure, come on in. I have a few minutes."

"I'm not disturbing you, am I?" Edward asked, looking around at the apartment that could certainly use a woman's touch.

Every outfit that Anthony had worn for the past week and maybe longer could be found in various locations throughout the one-bedroom apartment. Empty containers of Chinese food and pizza boxes were lined up on the kitchen counter and on the living room table. If Denise ever saw this, she would have a natural fit. It was no wonder Anthony never invited them over.

"No, you're not disturbing me at all. Excuse the mess. I usually take my clothes over to the house for Mom to put in the laundry or drop off at the cleaners, but . . . with everything going on . . ." His voice drifted off and he looked expectantly at his father. "How are things with you two? You are going to work it out, aren't you, Dad?"

"That's why I'm here." He pushed aside a pile of clothes on the couch and sat. "I need your help and your advice."

"Me?" Anthony's dark eyes widened with surprise. To have his father come to him suddenly made him feel ten feet tall. For the most part, the family always looked at him as the baby of the family, the one who needed looking after. No one ever asked his opinion or advice on anything of importance. So it became easy, second nature, to play the role of the needy one, the comic relief. But now his Dad needed him and he was ready to rise to the challenge.

He took a seat opposite his father. "Sure, Dad, whatever you need."

Edward leaned forward. "Okay . . . here's the plan . . ."

THIRTEEN

Denise was nursing a cup of coffee when the doorbell rang on Monday morning. She ignored it. Thoughts about Christine filled her mind. Her daughter hadn't said one word about what had happened since she had arrived Friday night with a suitcase. Thirty minutes ago she had left for work without even a hint of what had happened to send her running back home in tears.

Denise might have pushed if her daughter hadn't looked so miserable, hadn't spent most of her time in her room. Both had stayed home from church Sunday. Denise couldn't honestly say if she stayed for Christine's sake—in case she needed her—or if she was trying to protect them both. There was bound to be talk once the parishioners saw Christine's red eyes and woebegone expression. Even more eyebrows would be raised on seeing that Denise and Edward weren't sitting together. He rarely worked on Sunday and they generally attended church services together.

Taking a sip of her coffee, Denise wondered if he had gone by himself. She hadn't wanted to ask when he had come by briefly yesterday afternoon. He had tried to talk to Christine and had been met with the same polite refusal she had given Denise.

The doorbell sounded again. With a heavy sigh, Denise placed the heavy yellow stoneware mug on the tiled counter and stood. Whoever it was, wasn't going away.

Opening the door, she was surprised, then worried, to see Edward standing there with a frown on his face. "Has something else happened?"

"No," he quickly said, reaching out to gently touch her arm in reassurance.

It ran through Denise's mind that he had touched her more in the last few days than in months. "Then why were you frowning?"

He sent her a self-conscious grin. "I thought you had gone to the grocery store or something and you weren't here."

"I do the grocery shopping on Mondays, but not until later," she told him, thinking how far their marriage had disintegrated that he didn't know that simple fact about her household schedule for the past fifteen years.

Edward sighed and shoved his hands into the pockets of his jeans. "I should know that, shouldn't I?"

"You're busy," she said. Despite everything, he loved his children and worked hard. He just didn't need her.

He studied her closely for a few moments, then said, "Can I come in?"

"Of course," she said. Flustered, she stepped back. "I'm sorry, I wasn't thinking. Would you like a cup of coffee?"

"If it's not too much trouble?"

For some odd reason, Denise felt tears sting her eyes. They

were so formal and distant. Resolutely, she continued to the kitchen. She just had to believe that things would work out.

"You're doing all right, Dee?" he asked.

His nickname for her caused more tears to sting her eyes. "Of course."

"Don't worry about the children. They'll be all right," he said, following her into the bright kitchen.

She took the out he gave her. "Christine won't tell me why she came back home." Taking down another mug, she filled it with coffee and automatically added two tablespoons of sugar and a dollop of condensed milk. She turned and paused in surprise. Edward was sitting on the barstool at the end of the counter, where she'd been sitting. Once she would have welcomed him there, but now she wasn't so sure.

Setting his cup in front of him, she picked up her own cup and remained standing. "Reese didn't call as he did at Thanksgiving. They were supposed to visit his parents this past weekend."

Edward's large, long-fingered hands circled the mug of steaming coffee. For just a moment she stared at his hands, the palms of which were ringed with calluses. But he had always touched her with aching tenderness and endless love.

"That doesn't sound too good," Edward said.

"I know," she admitted, coming out of her daze to lean a slim hip against the edge of the counter. "She kept glancing at the phone while picking at her breakfast this morning. I think she might regret her decision, but she's too full of pride and stubbornness to admit she might have overreacted."

"Pride makes for a cold bedmate."

The deep timbre of his voice, the sudden intensity of his eyes, had her hand tightening on the cup, her heat thumping in her chest. Only Edward had the power to awaken passion in her. Had he missed her as much as she had missed him? She brought the unwanted and now-cold coffee to her mouth. It was too late for second thoughts. "Christine is hurting."

He nodded. "Families should be happy and together, especially during the Christmas holidays."

Denise refused to rise to the bait and continued sipping her coffee.

"You think I should talk to Reese?" he asked in the lengthening silence.

Denise blinked. "You're asking me?"

Lines of confusion radiated across his strong forehead. "Yeah. You and he always seemed to get along, and he's a lot like Anthony."

Edward's observation was on the money, but the last time they had discussed a family matter was when they were building the house twenty years ago. Did he really want her opinion or was he saying what he thought she wanted to hear? Denise studied his open expression and decided to give him the benefit of the doubt. "I think we both should let them work this out on their own. Christine is worried about this woman, but if she isn't careful, she'll push Reese right into that nurse's arms."

"You're going to talk to her?" he asked.

"What about you?" she asked, deciding to test his sincerity. He was always the one the children ran to. They deferred to him in all things.

He shook his dark head. "I couldn't get a peep out of her yesterday. She came to you both times."

"She came to a place where she had always been loved and protected."

"Exactly," Edward said. "And you have always been here to give her whatever she needed."

No, it was you, Denise thought, but it went no further. She was here now for her daughter and she'd walk through hell to help her. "I'll do whatever it takes."

"Then I won't worry." Standing, he drained the coffee cup and set it down.

Denise saw the way he looked at her with complete confidence and felt almost light-headed. "I'll keep in touch to let you know how she's doing."

"You need anything?" He continued to stare down at her.

Looks like I'm getting what I need. "No. I'm fine."

He nodded, his reluctance to leave obvious. "Thanks for the coffee. I better get going. I'm already late to the office."

Denise glanced at her watch as she followed him to the door. It was 9:15 A.M. "You never go in this late. Is everything all right?"

He sighed in irritation. "Fine. I forgot to put my jeans in the dryer last night and had to go buy a pair."

Denise looked at the new jeans that encased his long, muscular legs and tight butt, and gave her own sigh of regret that she'd be sleeping alone tonight. "I hope you bought an extra pair in case it happens again."

His eyes narrowed as if he hadn't expected that reply. "Yeah." Then, as if he couldn't hold it back any longer, he said, "I miss you, Dee. I love you."

"Or do you love your orderly life? Are you willing to let me run mine?"

"Is this about you sewing for people?" he asked, his look accusing.

Hands on her slim hips, she stared right back. "It's about you seeing and treating me as your wife and partner, not house-keeper, cook, and bedmate."

"You enjoy our lovemaking as much as I do," he said, catch-ing her arms and pulling her against his hard body. "If you want to go upstairs, I can give you a demonstration."

Wrenching her arm free, she jabbed her finger into his wide chest. "Did you hear yourself? You completely glazed over the first two things I said and jumped to sex. And who said it al-ways had to be in the bedroom?"

His eyes bugged. "Dee!"

Seeing him off guard, she pulled away, walked to the front door, and opened it. "As I said, I'll keep you informed on how things go with Christine."

"Dee?"

She stared at the white silk draperies in the bay window in the living room. "Edward, you have to leave or I'll be late for an appointment."

"I'm going, but I'll be back," he said stubbornly.

Denise watched him slowly walk down the sidewalk toward the SUV parked at the curb. Against her will, she noticed again the width of his broad shoulders beneath the suede coat, the en-ticing way the blue denim cupped his butt, his long, muscular legs. A sigh fluttered over her lips. She felt a quickening deep inside her body. It had been almost a week since they had been intimate.

Edward climbed inside the vehicle and drove away. Denise closed the door, trying to get her mind on anything but Ed-ward's body joining with hers. He was right; he had always known just how to please her.

But so was she. They'd christened every room in the house during that first year.

Her gaze strayed to the carpeted area in front of the bay window. She could almost see them there after the children had gone to bed. They had been in the house less than a month. Edward had had an expensive bottle of wine, a couple of candles, and chocolate-covered strawberries. They'd been insatiable. He could love her body; he just had to respect her mind as well. And before she was through with him, he would.

FOURTEEN

When Edward was sure he was out of Denise's line of sight, he pulled to the curb and thought about what she'd said. How could she think he took making love to her for granted or used it as an excuse to gloss over their problems? Making love to his wife made everything right with the world. It replenished him, and he thought it showed her the depths of his feelings for her. It was obvious that although his intentions were good, the true meaning was lost somehow. Well, if she truly needed to be shown that she was number one in his life, he planned to do whatever it took—even if it meant keeping his raging libido in check. As for their daughter, he honestly believed that what Christine needed now was her mother's touch, as much as he wanted to butt in and protect his baby girl. Maybe that, too, would assure Denise that her presence, her opinion, and her help were still needed with their children. He'd been an idiot not to have realized it eons ago. He took out his cell phone and dialed Anthony at his office.

"How did it go?" Anthony asked the moment he saw his father's cell number on the caller ID. He swiveled his seat so that his back was to the opening of his cubicle, giving him a semblance of privacy.

"So far, so good," Edward said, leaving out the intimate details, of course. "Did you get your stuff together?"

"All done. I'll call Mom around lunchtime. I'll dart over to my place when I get off work, then on to the homestead."

"Great. I'll be at the office if you need me."

"Can you get phone calls after nine?" Anthony asked, then cracked up laughing.

"Very funny," Edward growled. "This won't last too much longer, I can guarantee that. Your mom has given me plenty to think about, but I want her to do some thinking too."

"Dad, I know I didn't say this earlier, but . . . you putting your faith in me and confiding in me really means a lot."

There was a poignant silence between father and son.

"Knowing that I can turn to you means a lot as well, son," Edward finally said.

There was a rally of throat clearing.

"Well, I guess I better get back to work," Anthony said. "I'll call you on your cell if anything goes wrong."

"I don't see how it could. If there's one thing I know about your mom, she won't let anything happen to her kids."

"That's true. She's like those lionesses in *National Geographic*. She may lurk in the background, but she's always ready to protect her cubs."

Edward smiled. Yes, Denise was all that, and more. It was the "and more" that he'd been too blind to see all these years. Being away from her helped him to realize what a fool he'd been. But his eyes were wide open now. He was going to prove to her that she was the center of his life, that they would be happier with each other than without, and he would battle his old ideals and demons if it meant keeping his wife and family intact. However, in the meantime, he had a trick or two up his sleeve.

"Well, Dad, I'll check in later," Anthony said, cutting into Edward's thoughts. He laughed. "You know what this reminds me of?"

"What's that, son?"

"Plotting with my boys to get the attention of some chick."

Edward's eyebrows rose. "Some chick?"

Anthony flinched. "Uh, young lady."

Edward chuckled. "I'd better get to work. We'll talk later."

"Roger that."

Edward shook his head and ended the call with the touch of a button. Anthony was really getting into this. Funny, but as traumatic as this whole situation was, it brought him closer to his son. He'd always had a special relationship with Christine, "Daddy's little girl," but he'd never developed that real closeness with Anthony. He'd gravitated toward his mother, who gave him everything he wanted, just as Denise did for him. As a result, they'd both taken all she did for them for granted. That was all about to change. But . . . in the meantime, he would have to use the old rules and old habits to his advantage, at least for now.

"Well, darling, I hope you know what you started," he said aloud with a wicked smile before pulling off and heading to work. "Now for step two."

It was hard for Edward to concentrate on the tasks at hand in his office. Lena had a million pieces of paper for him to read and sign off on. But his mind was on getting his wife back. It was a little more than three weeks before Christmas would arrive and he had no intention of spending it under the roof of his aunt and uncle!

Edward checked the clock that hung above his door. It was almost noon. William was scheduled to return from his meeting downtown any minute. He'd left word with Lena to send him in as soon as he arrived.

He flipped open his sketch pad and looked at the design that he'd been working on since last night. It was perfect. What made it great was that the entire layout would be prefabricated. A few nails, anchors, and fancy footwork, and it would be done. With William's help he figured the whole job should take about two to three days, tops. The trick was it would have to be completed without anyone knowing what they were doing. He added a few more touches to the design just as there was a knock on his door.

"Come in."

"Hey, man. Lena said you wanted to see me. What's up? Everything okay with the job site?"

"Yeah, yeah. Come on in and close the door." He waited for William to take a seat. "Listen, remember the day of the ground-breaking?"

William nodded, his expression pinching in concern. "Did something happen?"

"No." Edward cleared his throat and looked uncomfortable for a moment. Opening himself up was never something that he'd been good at; confessing his feelings or troubles to anyone, especially to another man, went against everything that made him who he was. But he also realized that if he was to accomplish what he set out to do, he was going to have to change. He took a deep breath.

"The day of the ground-breaking, you asked me if everything was all right at home. Well . . . everything is not all right at home. And hasn't been for a long time . . . at least, according to Denise. She decided to teach me a lesson."

"A lesson?"

"She asked for a divorce."

"Aw, Ed, I'm really sorry. You and Denise . . . I can't believe it."

"Neither can I. And I don't believe that she wants it any more than I do. But for the time being I'm staying at my aunt and uncle's house."

"Eddie and Etta?" he asked with alarm, knowing how loony those two were and how they drove Edward crazy.

"Yeah, and trust me, it hasn't been fun." He shook his head. "Those two might be nutty as fruitcakes, as Anthony would say, but I learned something since I've been there. Watching them, for all their antics, they are a team, something that Denise and I haven't been for a long time. I had this notion that I could do it all, be 'the man.' That's not what makes a marriage work. It takes two. This has been a marriage of one for a long time. Denise had been trying to tell me, but I wasn't listening. I just figured as long as I took care of everything, paid all the bills, and kept my nose clean, that was all that was necessary. And that's how it's been for a long time. I don't intend to let it stay that way. I want her to know that I'm finally listening." He paused for a moment. "I need your help."

William leaned forward, bracing his arms on his thighs. "Hey, man, anything I can do to help."

Edward smiled, and a slow sensation of relief filled him. He thought it would be hard unburdening himself, but maybe that's what he needed to do all along, just as his wife had done. There was so much that he needed to tell her, and he didn't believe that when he did, it would make him any less the man he should be.

"I was hoping you'd say that. Well . . . here's the deal . . ."

Edward laid out his plan in detail, as well as all the supplies and equipment that he would need. Once finished, he leaned back and waited for William's reaction.

"Wow." He grinned. "If she doesn't take you back with arms wide open after this, I'll take her place," he joked.

Edward laughed. "I don't think so, my man. I spent one night with you and that was enough to last a lifetime. I don't see how your wife can stand it."

William feigned hurt. "But I make up for it in very creative ways." He winked.

The two men slapped five.

"I hear ya," Edward said. "So, do you think we can pull this off in time?"

"Without a doubt."

"I want you to start gathering up the supplies. Keep a strict inventory. I'll cover it from my personal account."

"How are we going to manage to pull this off without anyone finding out?"

"I'll handle that. Keep your cell phone on you and not in the car. Every time there's an opening, I'm going to need you to be ready. Anthony has everything else covered."

"Tony?" William grinned.

"He's really stepped up to the plate. I guess I underestimated him too."

"Hey, sometimes all folks need is a good reason and they rise to the occasion."

Edward nodded slowly in agreement. "Exactly. And I have a damned good one."

FIFTEEN

How much do you love Reese?" Denise asked that night at dinner and watched as Christine, seated next to her, tensed, her fingers clenching on her fork.

Christine had come home from work an hour ago, as uncommunicative and miserable as when she had left. She'd cut her smothered pork chop into tiny pieces and had been pushing the meat around on her plate for the past five minutes.

When no answer came, Denise decided drastic measures were required. "Are you just going to let that woman have him?"

That brought Christine's head up. Her brown eyes glittered with as much pain as anger. "He doesn't believe me. The more I say, the more he defends her. He keeps insisting they're only friends since he was in med school."

"Reese, unfortunately like most men, can be naïve and gullible at times. They hear us talking, but not a word we say," Denise said, recalling her own experience with Edward.

"Exactly." Christine plunked her fork on the plate. "He kept defending her, telling me how immature I was. Then . . . then . . ." Her hands clenched.

Denise waited. Christine's temper was awesome when it erupted.

"That she-devil called not five minutes later and told me the bald-faced lie that she had no interest in my husband, and spouted that same lie about being just friends, the same put-down that I wasn't being mature. How could he have discussed me with that woman!"

"Men can be fools!" Denise said without a moment's hesitation. Edward was a prime example.

Christine blinked, then burst into tears. "But I still love him."

"I love your daddy too," Denise said. Rising, she went to her daughter and pulled her into her arms. "This may be hard to hear, but if you want him, crying is not going to help you get him back."

"I could pull her weave out."

"As satisfying as that sounds, it won't make Reese realize that she's after him or get you two back together." Denise rubbed Christine's back and appealed to her fighting spirit. "You didn't answer my question. Are you just going to give up on him or are you going to show that woman she can't mess with your man?"

Sniffing, Christine lifted her head. "You seem to have Daddy's attention, but I don't know what to do about Reese."

"Sometimes I wonder about your daddy," Denise said, then shook her head and continued. "But let's talk about you. I have an idea. I watched enough talk shows to learn a few things about the inconsistency of men. First, Reese, just like your daddy, needs a dose of reality to appreciate what he has in you. Your daddy was so jealous of your realtor friend he almost had a stroke. I'll just bet Reese would act the same way at the first hint of another man taking an interest in you. That nurse may be looking at him, but he needs to realize that other men might be looking at you."

Christine scrubbed her face, then looked thoughtful. "He did act jealous when I asked him how he would feel if he caught me kissing a doctor on his rotation."

"Perfect." Denise gestured for her daughter to continue her meal. "We'll strategize while we eat."

Christine picked up her fork, then glanced at her mother for reassurance. "You think it will work?"

Denise covered her daughter's free hand. It had been a long time since Christine had come to her for advice or assurance. She wasn't going to let her down. "Reese loves you, but unfortunately, men often become complacent with what they are assured of."

"Is that what happened with you and Daddy?"

Denise sat back in her chair. "Yes. Your father was busy building his business and I was busy with you, Anthony, and this house. We didn't take the time for each other."

"Daddy is miserable without you."

Denise smiled sadly. "I feel the same way, but if I want us to have the kind of marriage we once had, I have to play this out. Good marriages don't just happen. Love is a start, but you have to build on it and keep building. A coal will burn longer if you stoke it once in a while, otherwise it dies."

Christine grinned. "Is that what we're going to do?"

Denise grinned back. "You bet." She took a bite of her pork chop. "I seem to remember you and Reese were going to a Christmas dance Saturday night."

The happiness left Christine's face. "I had intended to buy a new dress, but I don't see the point now."

"The point is you're going to take your husband back," Denise told her. "I'll make you a gown that will make him salivate."

Christine blinked, then giggled. "Mama!"

Denise took a bite of her smothered pork chop and was pleased to see Christine do the same. "That woman doesn't have anything you don't, and in the creation I'm going to design and make for you, Reese will be able to see that very well."

"Oh, my goodness." Christine had to put her hand over her mouth full of food. "I've never seen you like this."

"No one threatens my family. No one."

"Do you think we could start with the design tonight?" Christine's eyes gleamed as she buttered her roll.

"As soon as I finish in the kitchen," Denise answered, relieved and thankful her daughter no longer wore that unhappy, defeated expression.

"I'll help. We can get through faster, and we can talk more strategy," Christine said with a pleased smile. "I should have talked to you when I was dating."

"I'm here now," Denise said quietly.

Christine paused in reaching for her tea glass. She looked at her mother. "I'm glad that you are."

"Me too," Denise said, feeling a lightness of spirit she hadn't felt in a long time.

F eeling good about her daughter, Denise phoned Edward after she retired for the night. As they talked, she realized that she had made a mistake by calling him while she was in bed.

The deep timbre of his voice brushed across her skin like a velvet caress. The empty side of the bed where he slept seemed to mock her.

She fought to keep her mind off her husband and on their daughter. "She's in fight mode now."

He chuckled. "Look out, Reese."

Unconsciously, Denise smiled into the phone. There had never been any stopping Christine when she wanted something. Her father was the same way. Christine was willful at times; Edward was simply determined.

"Is she going back home?"

"No, she's staying here for a while." That was part of the plan. Christine had to show Reese that she didn't need him. Men wanted what they couldn't have, but Denise didn't think it prudent to bring that up.

Edward sighed. "As much as I hate hearing that, part of me is glad. I don't like you staying there alone."

She didn't like it either. She glanced again at the empty side of the bed, then at the picture window. This year, unlike every year since they'd moved into the house, there wasn't a live Christmas tree filled with twinkling white lights in front of it. But if things went as planned, there might be a tree yet. Then they could snuggle in bed, enjoying the lights and each other. It couldn't be too soon.

She missed the warmth of his body when she crawled between the cold sheets, the comfort of his arms, the steady beat of his heart beneath her cheek. She closed her eyes as longing swept through her.

"Dee, I think we should put up the lights. I saw Mr. Long the other day and he asked why they weren't up."

She sprang upright. Mr. Long was a kind old man, but his wife was the worst gossip in the city—scratch city, make that the state. "What did you tell him?"

"That I'd been busy with work."

She made an instant decision. "You come by tomorrow. I'll have them out of the attic."

"You leave those heavy boxes alone," he ordered. "I'll get them."

"Edward, I'm not helpless."

"I never said you were."

Since that was far from the truth, she didn't dignify it with a response. "I just called so you wouldn't worry. Good night."

There was a long silence, and then, "I haven't had a good day or night since you asked for a divorce. I want you back in my life and us in our bed together," he told her tightly. "I'm going to keep reminding you of what we had until you remember."

"That's just it, Edward; I remember too much." Quietly, she hung up the phone.

SIXTEEN

Lying on his back, Edward hung up the phone and stared at the ceiling. He tucked his hands beneath his head. Yes, he remembered too. Those early years of their marriage had been a challenge. They were both young, full of energy, and madly in love with each other.

He'd never forget the night Denise told him that she was pregnant with Christine. It was a moment of pure joy and sheer terror.

They were in bed in their small, one-bedroom apartment on the outskirts of Atlanta. It was a hot August night with hardly a breeze to be had. The white sheer curtains that Denise had made for their bedroom windows barely fluttered. He only wore a pair of briefs and Denise had on a short, hot pink nightgown that showed off her fabulous legs and did wonderful things for her chestnut complexion. She curled up next to him and stroked his chest, the scent of her freshly bathed and oiled body almost edible.

"Ed," she whispered.

"Hmmm?" He kissed the top of her head, brushing aside her short curls.

"I was thinking that maybe we should start looking for a bigger place."

"A bigger place?" He turned on his side to face her. "We really can't afford a bigger place now, Dee. Not with me still in school. This one is fine for the two of us. Just hang on, babe. I promise one day you'll have the biggest, fanciest house in the neighborhood."

"But . . . what if it was more than two of us?"

He sat up and looked down into her eyes, which seemed to sparkle in the moonlight. "What . . . are you saying?"

"Well . . . in about seven months there will be three of us."

"Dee . . ." His heart raced, and it seemed that the room temperature had gone up at least another ten degrees. "Are you saying . . . ?"

She nodded. "I'm pregnant."

The world seemed to come to a standstill. For a moment, he couldn't think, couldn't breathe. How was he going to take care of a wife and child as a full-time student working two part-time jobs?

"Ed . . ."

He blinked and her face came back into focus.

"I know we said we'd wait. I know this means a big change in plans, but I can get a real job and help out with the bills and . . ."

He sat straighter. "Forget it. I promised you when we got married that I would take care of you. I mean that. If I have to work three jobs, that's what I'll do. I didn't want you working before and I certainly won't have my pregnant wife working now."

"But I want to help, Ed. This is my responsibility too."

"It's not up for debate, Denise. It's a man's responsibility to take care of his family and that's what I intend to do." He saw the disappointment in her eyes, but on this he had to be firm. He still had flashes of his mother coming home from work too tired to even look at him. He could still hear the arguments his parents had about bills, the lack of food, heat, and decent clothes. He refused to do that to his wife and especially to his child. *My child.* He was going to be a father! And whatever it took, he was going to be the best father he possibly could be.

"It's settled, Dee," he said. "I'm going to quit school and get a full-time gig. I'm sure Uncle Eddie can get me on one of the construction teams. It pays good money and I have some experience."

"You can't drop out of school! Ed, please . . ."

"What choice do I have, Dee? I'm not going to have you and my child want for anything. There's always time to go back . . . someday."

Denise lowered her head and he soon felt her tears on his bare chest. He gathered her close and stroked her back. "It's going to be okay, baby. I'll see to that. Don't you worry about a thing."

Have I been a thick-headed fool that long? he mused as the memories receded. Even back then she'd been asking—no, telling him—she wanted to be a part of the marriage. But in his macho mind, he wouldn't hear of it. What a fool!

So he'd dropped out of school and signed on with his uncle. Eventually, he did go back to school at night to master his trade in design and construction. And the more the money started rolling in, the easier it became for him to have the final say-so in everything, from where they lived, the kind of cars they drove, the schools the children attended. Everything. Little by little, like water beating on a rock, he wore away the fabric of his marriage.

"Oh, Dee," he said aloud. "I'm so sorry, baby. I'm gonna make it all up to you, I swear I will."

"Lights out in there, Edward! I know I didn't hear you talking on the phone this time of night," Aunt Etta yelled from the other side of his door before shuffling down the hall.

He groaned. Making it up to Denise couldn't happen fast enough.

Morning arrived and Edward was ready to take the day by storm. After a brief meeting with the construction staff, he took a few moments to talk with William.

"I've located just about everything we need. As long as your dimensions are correct, we should have enough material, with some to spare."

"Great. Well, I'm going to do a drive-by and see what's happening on the home front."

William chuckled. "No wonder you're looking so spiffy today. Not your usual work outfit."

Edward took a look at himself in the mirror. He'd purchased a new pair of black slacks and a lightweight burgundy turtleneck that showed off his abs. "If you're going to go a-courting, you have to go in style."

"I hear ya. Well, good luck. Think you might need me tonight?"

"Stay by the phone just in case. But I think I can handle some of it myself. And I have Anthony on call."

"Aye aye, Captain," he said, saluting.

Edward chuckled as William lock-stepped out of the office. Then he pressed the intercom for Lena.

"Yes, Mr. Morrison?"

"I'm going over to the construction site and I won't be back for the rest of the day. If anything comes up, give me a call on my cell."

"Sure thing, Mr. Morrison."

Edward made a quick pit stop to check on the progress of the site, then headed downtown to the mall. He'd seen the perfect gift for Denise and he wanted to get it and stash it away. He stood in line for a good half hour to have the present gift-wrapped and when he saw the exquisite finished product, he knew it was time well spent. After a few more stops to pick up some supplies, he darted to his temporary home to drop off Denise's gift and ran smack into Aunt Etta.

"Whatcha got there, son?" she asked, cornering him in the kitchen.

"It's my gift for Denise."

"Hope it's something romantic and not a vacuum cleaner." She laughed at her own joke.

"It's not a vacuum cleaner, Aunt Etta." He tried to get to his room.

Etta put her hand on his shoulder. "Sit down a minute, son."

He took a seat at the butcher block table.

"I want to tell you something you probably don't know anything about. It's about your dad."

"My father? What about him?" His brow creased in a frown.

"I know you got it in your head that your dad walked out on you and your mom. That he wasn't man enough to stick it out through the hard times." She lowered her head, then looked into his eyes. "It took a lot of courage to do what he did, Edward. Back in those days, if there was a man in the house, social services wouldn't help you. Your dad knew that and so did your mother. They decided *together* what was best. It broke both of their hearts. And your father stayed away because he couldn't bear to see you and your mother and not be a part of your lives."

Edward's eyes filled as a knot formed in his throat.

"The things your father taught you about being a man, taking responsibility, sometimes it means letting go of the reins, son. Understand what I'm saying to ya?" She reached out and touched his cheek as a tear ran over her thumb.

"Why didn't anyone ever tell me?" he asked, his voice choked with emotion.

"We should have. Maybe you wouldn't have made some of the decisions that you did in your own life. Me and your uncle tried to do the best we could by you, son."

"I know. And I appreciate it. I really do."

"And you may think that your uncle is an old fool and that I just run all over him. Humph . . . as wild as he is, I don't know what I would do without him. He makes me feel like I'm the most beautiful, most important thing in his life. And I try to do the same, even if I have to knock him upside the head every now and then." She chuckled lightly, which brought a half smile to Edward's face. "You do the same for Denise, you hear me, son?"

"Yes, ma'am."

"She's giving you a hard time now and rightly so. This is your knot upside the head. Hope she knocks some sense into you before it's too late."

"I think she has, Aunt Etta. I think she has."

SEVENTEEN

The sights and sounds of Christmas were everywhere. "White Christmas" played over the loudspeaker in the fabric store. The clerks all wore Santa hats. Holly looped around the checkout counter. People who a month ago would cut you off to get to the cutting table first were now full of the holiday spirit and insisted you go ahead of them. Denise had never felt less like joining in the festivities as she stood in line to have the fabric for Christine's dress cut.

Pushing the aching emptiness aside, she moved up in line. What was her next step in getting Edward to accept her independence and put the zip back in her marriage? She could guide him, but he had to get it on his own.

"You're making a party dress?"

Denise turned around to a smiling, middle-aged woman behind her. In her basket was a bolt of sheer red fabric, as well as fringes and tassels. "Yes, my daughter and her husband are going to a Christmas party this weekend. Is that what you're making?"

The well-dressed woman blushed, then glanced around and whispered, "My belly dancing costume."

Denise knew her mouth had fallen open and snapped it shut. The woman laughed. "That's the same reaction my girlfriend had, but I read it's good exercise." She looked down at her round middle. "I certainly need it. Plus, it's part of my husband's Christmas present."

Denise watched the twinkle in the other woman's eye and laughed. "I can tell he's going to be very pleased."

"Yes, he will, but then, so will I," she said with a wide grin.

"Next," called the harried clerk at the cutting table.

Placing the black jersey knit on the table, Denise told her how much she wanted, then impulsively turned back to the woman. "Would you happen to know if they have any more openings for the class?"

"I think so. Classes start Monday." The other woman dug in her small purse and pulled out a card. "Hope it works out."

"Thanks." Denise accepted the card, picked up the material, and headed for the checkout counter. *All right, Edward, time to get down.*

A fraid the class might fill, Denise had called immediately after reaching her car. When she was informed there was one opening left, she drove to the dance studio and signed up. She had practically skipped back to her car. Edward would have a conniption. She grinned all the way back to the fabric store. After purchasing the things she needed, she had driven to Christine's office to show her. They'd laughed and giggled like schoolgirls.

Her good mood continued as she put on a pot of beef stew

for dinner, then went to the attic to work on Christine's dress. They had settled on a design the night before. Her daughter had been almost as excited as when they'd worked on the sketches for her wedding gown.

Denise finished cutting out the dress, then frowned. The provocative creation only faintly resembled her original idea. While her own costume would be sheer, no one but the other women in the class and her instructor would see her. Christine's situation was different. Denise had wanted the long jersey dress to be backless with a high neck. Christine wanted it backless *and* cut artfully in front to show a bit of cleavage and stop just above her tiny waist. Denise hadn't been so sure about the idea.

"If I'm going to make his eyes pop, I might as well make them roll on the floor."

"Your father would have a fit," Denise had said while they were sitting on Christine's old bed, working on the sketch.

Her daughter had looked her in the eyes and said, "Daddy isn't doing this. We are."

Denise hadn't tried to dissuade her again. They were a team, and she wasn't going to let Christine down. The party was tomorrow night and by the time Christine came home from work, she'd have finished hemming the gown and Christine could have her final fitting. Denise could start on her own costume tomorrow. Classes started Monday.

The day passed quickly as Denise worked on the dress and kept an eye on the stew. Finished except for the hem, she slipped the gown over the mannequin. She had to admit it suited Christine's passionate personality.

"Now for the decorations." Dismissing Edward's instructions, she started dragging out the boxes. There were lawn decorations of Santa and his reindeer racing into the sky after dropping off a load of brightly lit gifts beneath a twelve-foot Christmas tree that Edward had specially made. Then there were the hundreds of feet of twinkling white lights that would follow the pitch of the roof. As she reached for another box, she realized that her family wasn't the only one who enjoyed Christmas and all its magic and joy. So did she.

With the upheaval in her life, she needed to believe miracles still happened.

"I thought I'd find you up here."

Startled, Denise whirled at the sound of Edward's voice, almost falling backward. He easily caught her, pulling her up in front of him. His easy strength had always pleased and fascinated her. "What are you doing here? It's only a little after four."

"Saving you from a wrenched back," he told her. "You've gotten stubborn on me."

"Independent," she corrected.

He shook his head in exasperation, but a slow smile curved his mouth, unerringly drawing her gaze. She became aware of how close he was to her, aware of how much she missed him, and aware how much she hated sleeping alone.

His fingers tightened. "You still care."

"I never said I didn't," she admitted a bit breathlessly.

Passion flared in his dark eyes. He leaned down until his warm breath caressed her lips. "We're going to talk before the day is over. If two of my men weren't waiting outside, we'd do it now and a lot of other things I've been thinking about."

Denise felt her body tighten, but she had to make one thing clear. "Things *can't* be the way they were."

His mouth flattened into a hard line. "We had a good marriage."

"It was good for you," she said with asperity.

A shadow crossed his face. Misery stared back at her. "I thought you were happy."

If he hadn't looked so lost, so hurt, she would have brained him. "A happy woman doesn't ask for a divorce."

Calloused hands flexed on her arms. "You were happy once. I know it. What if I could make you happy again?"

Hope spiraled through her. "You can try."

"I'll do more than try. I'm coming after you." Whirling, he left, every bit the self-assured man she had fallen in love with and married.

"Oh, my," Denise breathed. She could hardly wait.

Denise's day became even better later that evening on seeing the wide grin on Anthony's face when he greeted her at the front door.

"Hi, Mama. Reporting for duty. Did you remember to bake tea cakes?" he asked, picking up a box of decorations.

She laughed and pulled a palm-sized, golden brown cookie from behind her back. Another tradition. "Fresh out of the oven."

Leaning over, he took a sizable bite from the cookie, then chewed with relish. "More."

"Wait your turn." Edward, who'd been standing to the side with a box of decorations in his hands, leaned over and bit into the cookie, the tip of his tongue touching Denise's hand.

She gasped. Her eyes widened as tremors radiated through her body.

Edward's eyes narrowed as he slowly chewed. "Some things get better with time."

Denise's heart thudded. "C-Christine should be here shortly, and we can eat."

"Great. I'm starved." Anthony propped the box on his hip and reached for the remainder of the cookie with his free hand. "My turn, Dad." Munching, he went outside.

Denise's throat felt dry as she stared at Edward, and he at her. "He's waiting."

"How about dinner Saturday night?" Edward asked. "Any place you choose."

"I have plans."

"Doing what?"

Denise raised her eyebrow at his brusque tone. She wasn't about to tell him she planned on being at home in case things didn't go as planned for Christine. "That's not your concern."

Setting the box down, he stepped closer until he towered over her. "There was a time when I could change your mind."

Heat shimmered through her. Edward had coaxed and teased her out of her shyness during their courtship and marriage, teaching her to take her pleasure from him and give it in return. "You can't persuade me with sex," she told him softly.

"We never had sex. We had love, and it's still there." He leaned closer until she saw her own wide-eyed reflection in his deep brown eyes. "I see your pulse hammering in your throat, Dee. You want me as much as I want you."

"Intimacy was never our problem."

"You got that right." His hand touched her cheek before she

could evade it, then he just as quickly turned, picked up the box, and sauntered out of the house after his son.

D enise, this is great stew," Edward said, polishing off his second bowl. "Why aren't you eating?"

Because you keep looking at me like you used to when the children were younger and we couldn't wait to put them to bed so we could make love, she thought in rising irritation as she sat across from him. Who would have thought Edward could be devious?

"There's something about your cooking I always enjoyed. Maybe it's just knowing you cooked it." He laughed. "You remember the spaghetti you cooked for me when we were dating?"

She scrunched up her face as the memory came to her. Edward hadn't had the money to take her out, so she'd invited him to dinner instead. Her grandmother had been at Wednesday night prayer service and Denise had been on her own.

She'd overcooked the spaghetti, burned the meat sauce and the garlic bread. Edward had eaten it anyway and ended up with indigestion. She'd been so embarrassed and felt so bad she had refused to see him when he came over a couple of days later.

"Hard to imagine Mama not being able to cook," Anthony said, polishing off another tea cake. "If there are any left, I'm taking the rest home."

"I beg to differ." Christine shot an annoyed glance at her brother.

Unrepentant, Anthony grinned. "There's probably one or two left."

"If there isn't, you'll pay." Christine's eyes narrowed.

"You and what army?"

"I can still take you."

"Don't make me laugh."

"That's enough or I'll take all the remaining tea cakes for my-self." Edward grinned at the stunned look on the children's faces. "If you two are finished, we can help your mother wash the dishes and clean up the kitchen."

Denise leisurely sipped her iced tea. Edward was definitely making progress.

Edward picked up his plate and hers. "You sit there and re-lax, Dee. The kids and I have it."

"Thank you." She could get used to being waited on.

"I was going back out to finish the lights," Anthony said.

"I want to try on my dress," was Christine's excuse.

At the sink, Edward turned. "Then the sooner we finish, the quicker you two can do what you want. Afterward, I thought we'd go down to the tree lot and get a Christmas tree."

Denise opened her mouth to disagree, but the children bounded up, their faces shining. Another family tradition. This year it was Christine's turn to put the angel on top.

Denise sipped her tea and watched the unusual sight of her husband washing dishes. Time would tell if this change was per-manent or if he was simply going through the motions. She knew one thing. This round went to him.

No daughter of mine is wearing a dress like that," Edward railed, his hands on his lean hips as he stared at Christine in her party dress.

"I certainly wouldn't let Sherri go out in a dress like that." Anthony folded his arms across his chest. "Looks like that dress J.Lo wore at the Oscars."

In the middle of the family room, Christine's chin lifted a fraction. A sure sign that she was ready to fight. "I love you, Daddy, but I'm wearing this dress. It's just what I wanted."

"Denise."

"Mama."

All eyes converged on her. In Edward's face she saw disapproval and demand for her to follow his lead, just as she always had. In Christine's was a plea for help to fight for her husband. Unconsciously, Denise's chin lifted in an exact imitation of her daughter. "It's daring and provocative, but not risqué or vulgar. I think she looks stunning."

Christine squealed and ran across the room to grab her mother. "Thank you. Thank you. This will certainly make Reese take notice."

Edward's eyes narrowed with disapproval. "Is this how you're helping her?"

Denise felt Christine tense beside her. They'd never argued in front of the children, or anywhere else for that matter, because Denise always gave in. "Reese needs a wake-up call before it's too late."

"Wake up to what?" Edward asked.

"To realize that he has a beautiful, desirable wife and he had better pay attention to her before someone else does."

Edward's expression hardened. He stalked over to her. "Is that what this is about?"

"I'm going up to change." Christine headed for the stairs, dragging Anthony with her.

Denise didn't shrink from her husband's anger. She knew if she did, she might as well give up and give in. "I was talking about Reese and Christine. Not us."

"You don't think I pay attention to you, do you?" he asked, apparently not convinced.

Lying didn't enter her mind. "No, you don't."

Edward opened his mouth, then closed it and took a deep breath in an apparent attempt to calm down. "I do."

"If you can answer one simple question, I'll apologize."

"And call off the divorce procedures?" Edward quickly asked.

Denise hesitated. "Yes, but if I'm right, you sign the papers to sell the house."

The pleased smile on his face disappeared. "That isn't fair."

Denise shrugged carelessly, although she knew the outcome. Edward needed another wake-up call. "You said you pay attention to me. What's the risk? I'll answer the same question about you or any other question you ask."

Edward stared at her and rubbed the back of his neck as if trying to figure out if she planned to trick him. "Oh, all right. What's the question?"

"What was I wearing and what color was it the last time we saw each other?"

His eyes narrowed. Clearly, he hadn't expected the question. His gaze flickered over her red cardigan and jeans. "That's an easy question for you. I always wear jeans."

"But you had on a chambray shirt," she said calmly. "What did I have on? Forget about the color."

He moistened his lips "A sweater and pants."

Her smile was sad. "A white blouse and black skirt."

"Dee."

She stepped back from his reaching hands. "I'll get the papers. Afterward we can go get the tree." Quietly, she walked from the room.

If this new development didn't keep him on his toes and hustling to win her back, seeing her in her belly dancing costume certainly would.

EIGHTEEN

Edward watched in disbelief as Denise climbed the stairs and entered what was once *their* bedroom, shutting the door solidly behind her. He'd really blown it this time. Was he that out of tune to his wife? Did he really not see her and only took her presence for granted? No wonder she wanted out. He took a last look up the steps before heading out. "All of that is going to change, babe. I guarantee it. You're turning into a new woman and you're going to have a new man."

He opened the front door and stepped outside. He needed some air. The minute he crossed the threshold his cell phone rang. Checking the number, he saw that it was William. Damn, he'd forgotten all about calling him.

"Yeah, man. What's up?" Edward asked, closing the door behind him.

"How'd it go?" William asked. "I was waiting for your call. Will you be able to get her out of the house for a couple of hours tonight, or what?"

Edward frowned, faced now with the new ultimatum from

Denise. "I don't know, man, but I'll dial you back if the coast is clear and it's not too late."

"You don't sound good. Did something else happen?"

Edward walked over to his SUV and got in. He was pensive for a moment before finally confiding in his friend. He started in the middle.

"I don't know, man. I guess I have been living in my own world for so long that I really haven't been paying attention to anything or anyone. I've been under the notion that as long as the bills were paid, there was food in the fridge, and everyone was healthy, that it was all good."

"But that's what a man is expected to do," William said, using the remote to change the channels on his television. "I think you're being too hard on yourself."

"Yeah, but at the same time a man can't be so ignorant that he can't see or hear what's truly happening in his own house."

"What happened? When you left this afternoon, you were so positive and upbeat." He settled on an Atlanta Hawks basketball game. "Did you two have a fight or something?"

Edward shook his head and chuckled derisively. "I wish it was that simple."

"Then what happened?" William picked up a bottle of beer and took a long swig.

"Denise asked me a simple question. What was she wearing and what color it was the last time we saw each other."

"Oh, naw, man, don't tell me you went for that one? It's the oldest trick in the book." He laughed and shook his head. "That's the equivalent of 'Do I look too fat in this outfit?'" He put down the beer and took a handful of chips, chewing as he spoke. "They will get you every time with that one. Or 'Do you like this dress better than this one on me?' No matter what answer you give, it will be the wrong one."

Edward had to laugh. "Yeah, I see what you mean. So, do you think when Denise said that if I gave the wrong answer I would agree to sign the papers to sell the house that she was just pulling my leg?" he asked, his tone serious.

"Whoa. That's what she did?"

Edward nodded.

"Hmmm. To be truthful, Ed, I really think that Denise just wants you to pay her attention. I mean, really pay her attention. In all the years I've known you two she never seemed to want out, never seemed not to truly love you and the kids. I mean, have to admit, I'm no whiz when it comes to figuring out the complex minds of women, but on this one I would have to say she's trying to put the screws to you, my brother."

"Well, she's doing a damned good job of it. The thing is, the more I'm around her the less I seem to know her. She's a completely different woman. In all of our twenty-seven years of marriage, Dee has always been quiet, unimpulsive, loving, and dependable. Now when I drop by, there's no telling what or *who* I'm going to find."

"That's the joy of married life," he said with a chuckle. "What did Forrest Gump say in the movie? 'Life is like a box of chocolates, you never know what you're going to get.' Hey, that's what marriage is, a box of chocolates."

"They also say diamonds are a girl's best friend, but chocolate can go a long way too."

"Huh?"

"I'll call you later. I have to make a quick run."

"Okay, I'll be waiting. Leslie is at her mother's house for the weekend, so I have plenty of time."

*W*ho knew what Denise would think when she came back down-stairs and found me gone? Edward mused as he zipped down the street into the center of town. It was a little after six, but with the holidays right around the corner, the shops stayed open as late as possible, trying to entice shoppers.

He cruised around for a few minutes until he found a parking space not far from the Chocolate Factory. When he stepped inside, he was blown away to find the shop overflowing with men! He shook his head, wondering how many of them were in the same precarious situation as he.

After a good twenty minutes of waiting, it was finally Edward's turn in line.

"May I help you, sir?" the cheery salesclerk, dressed in a Ms. Claus outfit, asked. "Something for Christmas for your wife?" she asked, spotting his gold wedding band.

"Something pre-Christmas, actually," Edward murmured, fumbling for the right words.

The salesclerk looked at him curiously. "A make-up gift?" she whispered.

"Hmmm, more like a courting gift."

"I see." She smiled in understanding. "Do you have a price range in mind?"

"Price is no object," he said, tapping the wallet filled with credit cards in his back pocket.

"Well, let me show you what we have."

More than a half hour later, loaded down with a bright

red shopping bag tied with pink ribbon, Edward headed back home.

When Denise returned downstairs with the papers of sale in hand, Edward was nowhere to be found. She peeked out the window and saw that his SUV was gone as well. She started to go back upstairs to ask her children if their father said anything before disappearing, but changed her mind. The last thing she needed was for them to think things were even worse than they already were.

She dropped the curtain back in place. Had she pushed her hand too hard? Her goal had not been to run him away, but to bring him back into her arms—totally. Edward had never been a man who could easily be manipulated. He was single-minded and determined. His home and family were important to him and she'd threatened that.

Denise took a seat on the couch, her heart heavy and her thoughts in disarray. But on the other hand, Edward was not a man to give up easily either, she reasoned. He'd made it clear earlier in the day that his intention was to win her back. For a moment her hopes were renewed, but just as quickly, reality hit. Edward was gone. Gone. Gone after she'd told him he'd blown it for the last time. She told him he would sign the papers to sell the house, the last step in severing their relationship.

She covered her face with her hands to hold back a sob just as the doorbell rang. Blinking back tears, she pulled herself together and went to the door, figuring it was her nosy neighbor wondering when they were going to finish putting up their lights. She pulled the door open to find the last person she expected to see.

"Paul! I mean, Mr. Carter. What are you doing here?" She looked past him, praying that Edward really wasn't in the vicinity.

"Good evening, Mrs. Morrison. Sorry to just drop by unannounced. But I've tried to reach Christine and can't get ahold of her. I wanted to give her a small Christmas gift."

Denise's brows rose in surprise. "Oh, I see. Well . . . Christine is upstairs." She took another peek around him. "I can get her for you, if you want to wait a minute."

"That would be great, if it's not a problem."

She stepped back and let him pass. "Have a seat in the living room and I'll get her."

"Thanks."

He walked inside and Denise darted upstairs. She found Christine and Anthony sitting on the floor of his room listening to music.

"Uh, Christine, can I see you for a minute?"

Christine pulled herself up from the floor. "Sure, Mom."

The instant Christine was at the door, Denise snatched her by the arm and pulled her into the hall.

"You'll never guess who's downstairs," she said in an urgent whisper, her eyes wide with alarm.

"Who?" Christine hissed back.

"Paul Carter."

"What!"

"Yes, and he said he came to see *you*. He even brought a gift."

"What!"

"Are you having trouble hearing me? I'm telling you that man is downstairs bearing gifts for you! What in heaven's name did you tell him?"

Christine frowned. "I . . . I didn't tell him anything, other than I needed his help with my mom and dad and if he would mind just playing along. I didn't go into detail, if that's what you mean."

Denise rolled her eyes to the heavens. "Well, he must have read your signals wrong. Why else would he just turn up? He said he'd been trying to reach you."

Christine squeezed up her face. "Maybe I did kind of lay it on thick," she sheepishly admitted.

"Well, you better get down there and remove a few layers. We have enough to contend with at the moment."

"Where's Daddy?" she asked, heading downstairs.

"I have no idea. When I went back down, he was gone. And the last person I want him to see, if he decides to come back, is Paul Carter. He nearly had a seizure the first time." She giggled, remembering the thunder and lightning expression on Edward's face. "Go on, go on," Denise urged.

"All right, all right. But what am I going to say?"

"Just graciously accept the gift, tell him 'No, you shouldn't have,' and send him on his merry way." Denise bit down on her fingernail, imagining all the possible scenarios if Edward walked through the door. "Hurry up," she insisted.

"I'm going. Just wait right here."

Christine headed downstairs while Denise practically hung over the banister trying to overhear the conversation.

"What's going on?" Anthony asked, coming up behind her.

Denise almost leaped over the railing. "Boy! Don't you know

it's not polite to sneak up on people?" she squeaked, turning to her son.

"Jeez, I just asked a question. You don't have to bite my head off." He peered over the railing. "Who's Christine talking to anyway? I thought I heard the bell."

"Uh . . . just a friend who stopped by to say hello."

"Really? Who?" He started for the stairs.

Denise grabbed his arm just as the bell rang again. She let out a gasp.

"Mom! What's wrong with you?"

"Nothing. Go to your room."

"What?"

"I mean, why don't you go on back in your room and I'll get the door?" She forced a smile.

The bell rang again.

Before Denise could get to the door, Christine answered it.

"Reese! What are you doing here?"

"I wanted to see you." He slung his hands in his pants pockets. "Can I come in?"

"Uh . . ."

"Reese, what a surprise," Denise said, stepping up beside Christine. She slid her arm around her daughter's waist.

They both stood in the doorway like sentinels just as Edward's SUV pulled up in the driveway.

Denise groaned.

Christine turned to her mother, her eyes wide with alarm, asking the silent question, *What do we do now?*

"Reese, this is a surprise," Edward said, mounting the steps to the front door. "Are you coming or going?"

"I thought I'd stop by and see Chris, but . . ."

"But what?" He looked at the frozen expressions of his wife and daughter.

"Hey, Dad, Reese," Anthony said, joining the posse at the door.

"Can we come in or are you going to make us stand here?" Edward asked, brushing by Denise and Christine with Reese on his heels.

Both men came to a complete halt when they saw Paul sitting on the love seat in the living room, with Denise, Christine, and Anthony nearly falling over one another when the parade came to a stop.

Paul stood, his ever-ready smile in place. "Mr. Morrison." He stuck out his hand, which Edward reluctantly shook. "Happy holidays. Good to see you again."

Edward grunted something unintelligible.

He turned toward Anthony. "Paul Carter," he said by way of introduction.

"Anthony Morrison, Christine's brother," he said with a smile, oblivious to the tension in the room.

"Yes, Christine mentioned she had a brother." He shook Anthony's hand, then turned to Reese.

"Reese Evans, Christine's husband," he said, enunciating every word.

"Christine has told me all about you. Glad to finally meet you."

"Funny, Christine never mentioned you."

"Oh," he said and chuckled lightly. "Christine and I are old college friends. I stopped by to drop off a thank-you gift to the Morrisons."

"Thank-you gift?" Edward asked.

Denise and Christine shared a look of terror.

"Yes, I was working on selling the house for them. I generally pick up a token of thanks for all my potential clients during the holidays," he said, as smooth as a good shot of brandy. "Well, this is obviously a family night and I won't intrude any further." He started for the door. "Enjoy your holidays, folks."

Christine and Denise followed him to the door. He turned to face them.

"Thank you," they whispered in unison.

"No problem. I hope everything works out . . . for both of you." He handed the brightly wrapped gift to Denise. "Might as well make it look good," he said. He looked at Christine and smiled. "Ask your mom to share those with you." He winked and walked away.

Sighing deeply, Denise and Christine turned in unison and faced the questioning faces of the men in their lives.

"Well," Denise said, full of forced cheer, "a night of surprises." She smiled brightly. "We have our first gift." She marched over to the mantel and set the square box next to their wedding picture.

Christine straightened her shoulders and tilted up her chin. "You wanted to talk to me, Reese," she stated more than asked, and plopped down on the couch, folding her arms beneath her breasts.

Reese cleared his throat, looking uncomfortable for a minute. "Yes, about the party tomorrow night."

"I'll get working on the lights," Anthony said, finally getting his cue.

Edward stepped up to Denise at the mantel and cupped her upper arm. "I think you and I need to talk too," he said in a low rumble, hustling her out of the room and out the front door before she could utter a word of protest.

Once outside, he opened the door of his SUV. "Get in."

Denise huffed but got inside. "Are we going somewhere?" she asked.

"That's what I want to know. Are we, Dee?"

"It's entirely up to you, Edward," she said, holding her ground.

"If it were entirely up to me, we wouldn't be having this conversation in the first place."

"I see."

"Do you?" he said, his voice dropping to a throbbing, low tone. She turned to look at him and her heart knocked hard in her chest. He was so close, close enough to . . .

He reached into the backseat and pulled up the red shopping bag. "I got something for you."

"Edward, you didn't have to buy me something," she murmured, taking the bag and holding it to her chest.

"I know I didn't. I wanted to." His smile was gentle. "I want things to be the way they were, Dee. Well, maybe not exactly, but . . ." He took a breath. "I'm not signing any papers. I just want you to know that. You're going to have to make me truly believe that you don't love me, that I can't make it up to you, and that you don't want to live with me anymore. Until you do that, I'm going to make it hard as hell for you to walk away from me." He turned the key in the ignition. "Now, let's go get that tree."

He pulled off into the twilight, and Denise wondered how much longer she could hold out.

Several hours later, the tree was up, the house was lit, and the ragtag family stood around admiring their handiwork.

Anthony yawned. "Well, folks, I think I'll be heading

home." He stood and stretched, said his good-byes, and headed out.

"Me too," Reese said shortly, after looking longingly at his wife.

Christine swallowed hard. "I guess I'll see you tomorrow . . . for the party. That is, if you still want to go."

"I'll be here," he said quietly. He picked up his jacket from the back of the couch and slipped it on. "Can you walk me to the door, Chris?"

Christine got up from the floor and followed him out.

"Chris, I don't like this. I miss you. I'm sorry about everything. I want you to come home." He took her hand in his.

"I still need some time to think, Reese," she said. "I have to learn to trust you all over again."

"You will. I promise." He leaned forward and kissed her cheek. "See you tomorrow."

"Good night, Reese."

She watched him get into his car and couldn't wait until tomorrow night when he saw her in her dress. The days and nights of being without him would be well worth it when she saw the look in his eyes. She closed the door, smiled, and practically skipped upstairs, waving good night to her family on the way.

"Guess that just leaves me and you," Edward said with a sparkle in his eyes as he eased closer to Denise on the couch. "The kids are gone, the house is quiet . . ." He leaned over and kissed her gently on the ear.

A shiver like an electric shock raced through her. "Ed . . ."

"What?" he whispered, his warm breath running along her neck. He traced the shell of her ear with his fingertip.

She closed her eyes, relishing the sensation of his touch,

and then suddenly, as if cold water had been tossed on her, he jumped up.

"Gee, look at the time," he said, checking his watch and then shrugging into his jacket. He looked down at her and smiled that boyish smile of his. "Gotta be going." He put on his baseball cap and tugged it down over his brow.

It took all the control she could muster not to scream.

She let out a breath and returned his smile. "Yes, it is getting late," she said from between clenched teeth.

"Maybe I'll see you tomorrow. If not, I'll call." He walked to the door. "Rest well," he said, and shut the door behind him.

Denise jumped up and stomped her foot in frustration. *So that's how he's going to play it*, she thought, her hormones raging. *Fine*.

She glanced across the room and saw the red shopping bag. Snatching it up, she took it to her room. Sitting on the big king-size bed, she debated opening it before Christmas.

"He did say it was a pre-Christmas gift," she muttered, reaching for the box.

When she finally got past all the ribbon and wrapping and got the box open, she sat back and nearly cried.

Inside were two twelve-inch chocolate figures of a man and woman surrounded by an assortment of chocolate delights. But what stole her heart was the note tucked in the box.

Marriage is like savoring a box of chocolates . . . some moments will be sweet, others sticky, some will bring tears to your eyes, and others will make you see heaven. Each one is like a day with you, Denise, filled with surprises. Whatever it might hold, I want to discover it all with you.

Love, Ed

"Oh, Edward," she said, nearly weeping as she reached for one of the delicacies and popped it into her mouth.

She curled up on the bed with the box tucked beneath her arm. "Maybe you are getting it after all," she whispered, a smile blooming on her lips. "But just for assurance's sake, I still have a trick or two up my sleeve."

NINETEEN

Reese perched on the edge of the living room sofa on Saturday night, his head bowed, his folded hands between his long legs. Denise watched the silent young man and waited for her daughter to come downstairs. She felt sorry for him, but he did need a wake-up call. "I'm glad you and Christine are going to the party together."

Slowly, he raised his head. Misery stared back at her. "I didn't want her driving back by herself late at night, especially with all the heavy holiday traffic." He pushed his glasses back on the bridge of his nose. "I love Christine. I want you to know that. I'm not sure what's happening, but I just wanted you to know."

Denise sent him a warm, encouraging smile. "I'm sure you do, Reese, but Christine is the one you have to convince."

"Ready."

Reese jerked around at the sound of Christine's voice. His mouth gaped. Slowly he came to his feet. "Christine." There was awe in his voice as he stared at her standing in the doorway.

Denise glanced at Christine. She was stunning in the provocative gown.

"I'm ready to go," Christine said, then crossed to her mother and bent to kiss her on the cheek. "Thank you."

Denise briefly clasped her hand. "Have fun."

Christine's eyes twinkled. "I intend to." Straightening, she turned her back to Reese and held out the wrap for him to help her.

Reese's sharp intake of breath cut through the room. The backless gown barely skimmed the smooth brown curve of her back. "Christine!"

She glanced beguilingly over her shoulder. "Yes, Reese?"

He gulped. "Your—your dress."

"Beautiful, isn't it?" she replied. "Mama made it for me."

Reese's wide eyes swung to Denise. She smiled sweetly. He couldn't very well say anything bad about a gown her mother made, and certainly not while Denise was in the same room.

"If you've changed your mind, Reese, I can go by myself. Since it's being given by the hospital, several of my friends will be there," Christine told him.

Denise smothered a laugh as Reese, moving faster than she'd ever seen, raced across the room and took the wrap from her hand. "No. You're going with me." He draped it around her smooth bare shoulders, his hands lingering possessively.

"Thank you. We'd better get going."

He nodded absently. "All right."

"Good night, Mama."

"Good night," Denise said, coming to her feet and giving Christine a discreet thumbs-up. "Have fun."

"I certainly plan to. I can't wait to dance."

Reese's arm tightened. "Maybe you should just dance with me."

Christine batted her lush, long eyelashes. "But you don't like to dance."

"Tonight is an exception."

"We'll see," she said, stopping in front of the door and waiting for Reese to open it.

Denise's lips twitched. Christine was in a reckless mood.

Frowning, Reese opened the door. "We'll talk in the car."

"Talk about what?" asked a deep male voice.

"Daddy!" Christine greeted, going up on tiptoes to give him a hug.

Reese swallowed. "Good evening, Mr. Morrison."

Edward peered down from his six-inch advantage at his son-in-law. "Good to see you again, Reese."

The young man visibly relaxed. "Thank you, sir."

Edward stepped aside. "Don't let me keep you."

"Good night, Mr. Morrison. Mrs. Morrison." Taking Christine's arm, he guided her down to his late-model Lexus.

Denise waved as they drove off, then came inside. Edward followed. "I'm glad you got here in time to see Christine off. She did look beautiful in her gown."

"I saw that, but that's not why I'm here."

"Oh?" Denise tried to read his expression and couldn't.

"The first reason is to apologize for the way I went off about her dress. I called her today and told her. It was a knee-jerk reaction. I've always trusted you to make the right decisions for the children, and you have."

Denise felt like pumping her fist. *Go, Edward!* "The second reason?"

"Guess?"

Butterflies took flight in her stomach at the intense way he was looking at her. Was he there to take up where they had left off last night? Would she let him?

"We're going to spend some time together where I can pay attention to the woman I love." He grabbed her hand and pulled her back outside. "Let's go for a walk and look at the Christmas decorations."

She stared at him. "It's fifty degrees out here."

Shrugging off his suede jacket, he wrapped it around her shoulders, then grinned devilishly down at her. "Come on, I'll keep you warm just like I used to."

As always Edward tempted her, but she had too much to do to catch a cold. "I have things to do."

Ignoring her protests, he closed the front door. "They can wait. You have on a thick sweater and wool pants. I'm wearing a flannel shirt and jeans. So stop stalling."

"My body doesn't generate heat like a furnace the way yours does." She couldn't believe this. He wasn't the impulsive type. "I didn't get my key and I have nothing on my head."

"I have my key." He frowned at her as if he'd like to shake her, then plopped his baseball cap on her head. "Now, will you stop complaining?"

Denise opened her mouth to say she wasn't complaining, then snapped it shut. "Are they showing reruns of your favorite TV programs? On Saturday nights, you wouldn't budge from that hideous chair from seven until you went to bed . . . unless it was to get food or a soft drink."

"Jeez." He slung his arm around her shoulder and started down the curved walkway. "This is what I get for listening to Uncle Eddie and Aunt Etta."

"Whoa." Denise stopped and stared incredulously at Edward.

"You're taking advice from your uncle and aunt?" she asked, laughing.

"They certainly know something I don't. They're at each other every night," he said with an equal amount of envy and admiration.

Denise choked. Edward's large hand pounding her back made it worse. "Stop." She coughed, then caught her breath enough to look at him. "You're serious?"

Grim-faced, he nodded. "They want me in bed every night by nine."

They looked at each other and started laughing so hard they had to hold each other up. The laughter ceased when Denise realized Edward's arms were around her waist, pressing her body firmly to his, his face inches from hers. She couldn't move, and when his mouth settled on hers, she ceased to think.

Hunger shot through her. She reached for him, her need as desperate as the arms locked around her. She missed the taste, the texture, the overpowering desire he ignited in her.

The sudden blast of a car horn tore them apart. Passing down the street in his twenty-year-old Cadillac was Mr. Long and his wife, who had her nose pressed to the car window.

"Spoilsports. We were enjoying the show."

Denise and Edward jerked around to see Jeff and Monique Patterson, the couple next door, standing midway on their walk and grinning from ear to ear. They'd moved in a few years ago and were expecting their first baby in January.

"W-we were going to look at the lights," Denise said.

"Yeah, right," Jeff said, hugging his wife as she elbowed him in the side.

"I think it's sweet," Monique said, leaning her heavy body against her husband's. "I hope we're as affectionate in the years to come."

Denise felt like a fraud. "You doing all right, Monique?"

She smiled. "The baby is practicing kicking field goals again." She was bundled up with a heavy wool coat that couldn't possibly reach around her protruding stomach, a scarf, and boots. "I thought walking might help."

"Why don't you join us?" Edward said, sliding his arm around Denise's shoulder. "I can give Jeff some pointers on changing diapers and making formula, and I don't think there's ever been a better mother than Denise."

Denise stared up at her husband, a pleasant warmth stealing into her heart. He was definitely doing and saying the right things tonight. She just might get her Christmas miracle.

They set off at an easy pace, with the Pattersons in front. Edward still had his arm around Denise's shoulder. She certainly wasn't going to complain. She had missed having him close to her.

Occasionally they'd stop to admire the glittering Christmas lights in a rainbow of colors or in stark white on almost every house. Those that weren't decorated soon would be. Many homes had the new icicle lights, but a few still had the old rope lights. As they ambled down the street, people waved and asked the Pattersons about the impending birth of their baby. They had good neighbors. Their decision to raise their children here had been a sound one.

Seeing a Nativity scene on the lawn at the end of the block, Monique stopped and placed her hands on top of her stomach. "It's beautiful. I can't wait to hold our baby in my arms."

Denise came up beside her and felt Edward's arms go around her waist. She was powerless to keep from leaning back against him. "You fall totally, hopelessly in love the moment you set eyes on your baby. I couldn't stop crying."

"I wasn't too dry-eyed myself," Edward admitted quietly, his chin resting on top of Denise's head. "Yet I'd never been more scared in my life."

"Of what?" Jeff asked. "The worst part was over."

Edward's arms tightened. "It was just the beginning. I now had two people depending on me. I never wanted Denise or Christine or Anthony, who came later, to want for anything."

"We didn't," Denise admitted truthfully; Edward had held down two jobs to care for them. "We couldn't have asked for better."

"My father wasn't there for me when I got older," Edward said, his voice quiet in the night. "I swore I'd always be there for my family."

"That's just how I feel," Jeff said. "A man's got to take care of his family."

Out of the corner of her eye, Denise saw the almost imperceptible shake of Monique's head. So Jeff was another man who thought women's brains turned to mush when they married.

"But don't smother your wife and children or try to live their lives for them," Denise said to Jeff before she thought. "Love them, but give them room to grow, to make their own mistakes."

For a moment Jeff looked taken aback, then he grinned sheepishly. "You've been talking to Monique."

"No. I've been living with Edward for twenty-seven years." The younger couple laughed. Denise joined in. Only Edward was silent.

Edward remained quiet as they started back. After saying good night to the Pattersons, she invited him in for coffee, but he made no attempt to drink it. "Would you like a tea cake?"

He looked up from sitting at the island in the kitchen. "It wasn't my intention to smother you."

Without thought, she crossed the room and placed her hand on top of his. "You're a wonderful man even if you make me want to strangle you at times."

His other hand settled on hers. "What about the other times?"

"I felt as if I was the luckiest woman in the world," she admitted honestly, then stepped back when he reached for her. "But sometimes isn't enough."

"All or nothing, is that it?" he asked, a hint of challenge in his voice.

"Yes."

He finally picked up his coffee cup. "Is Christine coming back tonight?"

Denise wasn't sure how to take the change of subject. "I don't know."

He stared at her over the rim. "What was Reese's reaction to the dress?"

Relaxing, Denise smiled and picked up her own coffee. "He wasn't able to take his eyes off her."

"So, he's going through sensitivity training too."

Denise straightened, remembering why she never played card

games with Edward. He'd lull you, and then . . . wham! "He's learning to appreciate her."

"Hmmm." Setting the cup aside, Edward came off the stool and didn't stop until his body was pressed against hers. She felt the hard delineation of his muscled body from her suddenly aching nipples to her quivering thighs.

"Edward," she said breathlessly. "W-what are you doing?"

His arms bracketed her, preventing her from moving. "I've been thinking about what you said about not making love in bed all the time."

"E-Edward."

His tongue grazed her lower lip, causing her to shiver. "I think you're right. I seem to remember one memorable occasion right where we're standing, while the kids were at the movies." He nuzzled her neck. "You came apart in my arms."

"*Edward.*"

"I'm here, Dee," he crooned. "I'll always be here."

Denise felt herself slipping under his spell. It had been so long, and he felt so good.

The ring of his cell phone shattered the spell. Edward muttered an expletive.

Denise didn't know if she was thankful or annoyed. She did know she wasn't sure if her legs could support her if she tried to move.

Edward snatched the cell phone from his belt loop. "Yeah!"

"Don't you take that tone with me, boy," Denise heard Uncle Eddie yell. "It's past nine. If you're not home in fifteen minutes, you'll be sleeping outside." The line went dead.

Edward's head fell forward. "There's not a jury in the world that would convict me."

Denise's lips twitched. "They love you."

"And I was about to get some good loving," he growled.

"That's what *you* think." Denise shoved him aside and headed for the front door. "Good night. I have things to do."

"Denise."

She turned and found herself in his arms. Her hands pressed against his broad chest. "You'll have to sleep outside," she warned.

It will be worth it." His mouth pressed possessively against hers, taking, giving, sending heat and desire racing through her. Her body yielded. She felt herself being lowered to the area rug beneath her. His mouth left hers to roam greedily over her face. Lights flickered. It took Denise a moment to realize they were lights from the Christmas tree.

They'd made love beneath the Christmas tree too. But if they made love now, before things were completely settled between them, it would only complicate matters. He was doing and saying the right things, but she wasn't entirely convinced he'd continue if she called off the divorce. Could a man change twenty-seven years of behavior in a matter of weeks? She was betting he could if the love were strong enough. But in the meantime . . .

"Edward, stop."

His mouth hovered above hers. "You don't want me to."

"Yes, I do."

His eyes shut briefly, then he stood gracefully. "I want you back in my life and I'm not going to rest until you are."

Denise watched him leave, then came up on her knees in

front of the twelve-foot pine decorated with twenty-seven years of memories and love. Directly in front of her was a handmade ornament she'd sewn of white satin and red thread that said *First Christmas*. Her finger traced the words. They'd been poor, but so in love. She wanted that love for them again.

Leaning back on her heels, she looked at the beautiful Black angel on top of the tree, with her wings outspread and arms open. "Please, let it be the real deal."

TWENTY

Edward was up with the sun, having barely slept through the night as sexy visions of his wife kept him on a simmer. It had taken all his home training to keep from ravishing her, but, as he'd slowly come to realize, a good marriage needed more than just good loving. With it being Sunday morning, short of a natural disaster, Denise went to church—with or without him—where she spent the better part of the morning, followed by a late brunch with Christine. He grinned as the steamy water streamed over his body. Thank goodness for habits. But this would be a Sunday without him.

Drying quickly and donning a pair of jeans and a work shirt, he called Anthony and then William and told them both to meet him at the house in an hour. He'd already called Denise to ensure that she was gone. He had less than two weeks to pull this off, and it was one deadline he had no intention of missing.

By the time Edward arrived at the house, Anthony's Acura and William's Jeep were parked out front. They stepped out of their vehicles when Edward approached.

"Hey, guys. Thanks for coming."

"No problem," William said, shaking Edward's hand. "Let's do this."

Edward clapped Anthony on the back. "Thanks, son."

"Sure. But we should get busy. Mom usually gets home around three."

Edward checked his watch. "That gives us five hours."

"We can get plenty done in that time. Let me start unloading." He headed for his Escalade.

"I'll help," Anthony offered.

"Naw. I'm cool," he said, waving Anthony off. "You two can get started inside."

"Good idea. Come on, son."

"I'm glad you're doing this, Dad," Anthony said as they strolled down the driveway.

"Really? Why?" He looked at his son expectantly.

Anthony shrugged. "I think it will mean a lot to Mom."

"I hope so."

"Dad?"

"Hmmm?"

"Are you and Mom really getting divorced? I mean, the other night with the real estate guy . . . she seems serious. But then sometimes I see her looking at you when she doesn't think anyone is watching and . . . well, I don't know . . ." He looked at his father, hoping for answers.

"In my heart I have to believe it's not what she really wants."

"Then why?" he asked, truly perplexed.

Edward halted at the end of the driveway and turned to Anthony. "Your mother wants me to wake up and smell the coffee. She wants to put the fear of God in me."

"Has she?"

"You better believe it." He chuckled halfheartedly. "To be honest, son, when your mother told me she wanted a divorce and wanted to sell the house, I've never been so scared in my entire life. It terrified me to think that I could lose everything I loved in one fell swoop." He shook his head. "I can't imagine my life without your mother."

"Have you told her that?"

Edward blinked and focused on his son. He put his hand on Anthony's shoulder. "It's not that simple. It has to be more than words."

"Like what?" He frowned in confusion.

"I'm still trying to figure that out. But in the meantime, this is a start. And I'll keep trying until I get it right."

"Hey guys, your Uncle Eddie just pulled up," William said, hauling supplies on a dolly.

"Uncle Eddie!" they cried in unison.

"And your aunt."

"Oh, no," Edward groaned.

"What are we going to do, Dad? You know Aunt Etta couldn't keep a secret even for a fifth of Jack Daniel's, and Uncle Eddie is worse."

Edward ran his hand across his face. "I'll take them in the house. You two get as much done as you can. I'll chat them up for a few and get them out of here as soon as possible."

"Okay."

Edward darted to the front of the house just as Etta and Eddie alighted from their 1968 Cadillac Seville. The car was enormous, and a gas guzzler. It sounded like all the screws were loose when it came down the street, but Eddie refused to get rid of it. "Just 'cause something is old and noisy doesn't mean you get rid of it," Eddie would say in defense of his car whenever someone suggested that he get a new one. "Etta's old and noisy. What if I traded her in for a new one?" To which Etta would promptly pop him in the head with whatever was available. "Ouch, woman!" And then it would be on. Oh, Lawd, he couldn't take those two today.

"Uncle Eddie, Aunt Etta," he greeted them, full of good cheer, catching them at the front door. "What are you two doing here?"

"We were coming home from early church service," Etta began, "which is someplace you needed to be this morning." Her eyes squeezed into two slits. "Need to get down on your knees and pray for forgiveness."

"Forgiveness for what?" he asked, and knew he shouldn't have given her an opening the moment the words were out of his mouth.

"Well, you musta done something to get yourself in this here predicament," she said, adding a "humph" for emphasis.

"You're probably right, Aunt Etta, but that still doesn't explain why you both are here."

"Passed by and saw the cars parked out front, boy," Eddie said, jumping right in. "Thought you folks were having some sort of shindig and didn't invite us."

"Exactly!" Etta said, slipping her arm under Eddie's and jutting out her chin.

"Trust me, there's no party going on."

"So whose Jeep is that?" Eddie demanded.

"And isn't that little Tony's car? What's he doing here? I've never known that boy to get up on Sunday mornings before noon."

"Anthony, uh, spent the night. And, uh, he called me this morning and asked me to join him for breakfast. You know, a father and son thing," he added, hating that he had to lie to them. He smiled, looking from one skeptical face to the other, hoping that they bought his story.

"Breakfast," Eddie said, his eyes suddenly sparkling. "I could sure use some." He turned to Etta. "How come you never fix me any breakfast?"

"Never!" Etta squealed. "You old fool, I fix you breakfast every morning, just the way you like it." She sucked her teeth in annoyance. "You can't remember a darn thing." She sucked her teeth again and rolled her eyes for good measure.

Eddie scratched his head. "You know, you're right. You sure do." His brows rose when he turned to his nephew. "But I could sure go for a cup of coffee."

"That's right," Etta chimed in. "Where are your manners? Got us standing out in the street like two vagabonds. Your own blood relations. I brought you up better than this." Her eyes welled up as if she was going to cry.

"Now, look what you done, boy. Gone and got your aunt all worked up. All we asked from you was a cup of coffee, but that seems to be too much. And after all we done for ya."

"Oughta be 'shamed, treating your kinfolk like this," Etta said, her voice cracking with emotion.

Dumbfounded, Edward momentarily stood there and wished that the ground would open and swallow him whole. He couldn't believe how the situation had deteriorated to this level in a matter of seconds.

"There's no reason to get upset," he said in his best cajoling voice. "Let's all go inside and I'll make some fresh coffee. I'm sure Denise has some sweet rolls to go with it. How's that sound?"

"Sounds like you finally located your good sense," Etta said, and pulled Eddie up the three steps to the front door.

Edward darted around them, stuck his key in the lock, and opened the door.

They stepped in with authority and took a good look around.

"Denise sure keeps a nice place," Etta said, taking off her good church hat with its drooping two-foot baby-blue feather that had seen better days. If Edward remembered correctly, it looked like the same hat she used to wear to church when he was a kid. It had to be the same hat, he concluded as he watched her place it reverently on the chair. There was no way there could be two of them.

"Make yourselves comfortable. I'll put on the coffee."

"See you finally got the tree up," Eddie commented, opening the buttons on his royal blue sharkskin suit.

"Yes, finally," Edward said.

Etta sniffed. "Christmas just won't be the same this year with you kicked out of the house."

Edward flinched.

"Told you what you need to do, boy, to keep that woman happy," Eddie advised. He patted Etta's thigh. "I know how to keep my woman happy, don't I, baby?" He gave her a wink.

Etta giggled and popped his hand playfully. "You old fool." She leaned over and kissed him on the lips.

Edward smiled at the old couple and hoped that one day when he and Denise were their ages, they'd still be able to share those precious loving moments, and still enjoy each other even with their quirks and shortcomings. Etta and Eddie may not have had much, but they had each other. That's what was most important. And Edward was willing to give up all that he'd acquired to keep Denise in his life.

He walked into the kitchen and prepared the coffee, then snuck out the back door to check on Anthony and William.

"Everything cool out here?" Edward asked.

"We got it, Dad. How are you making out with the folks?" He wiped sweat from his brow with the back of his hand.

"I think I have them under control. But you're going to have to make an appearance at some point. I told them you spent the night."

"Aw, Dad, can't you make up an excuse?" His handsome face twisted into a grimace. "Aunt Etta is going to quiz me to death about my entire life since birth, and Uncle Eddie will want to give me another dance lesson."

William and Edward roared with laughter, feeling the young man's pain.

"Son, if I'm going down, everyone is going down with me," he said, fighting back laughter. "They're really quite harmless."

Anthony cut a look at his father from the corners of his eyes and shook his head in defeat.

"In the meantime, I'd better get back inside before they get suspicious."

Edward returned to the kitchen, poured two cups of coffee, added cream and sugar, took two sweet rolls from the bread box, and placed everything on a tray.

"Here you go," Edward said, returning to the living room. He set the tray on the coffee table.

Etta picked up her cup and took a testing sip. "Not bad."

"What time is your wife getting home?" Eddie asked.

"About three."

"You plan on being here when she gets in?"

"I, uh, hadn't really thought about it."

"Didn't she put you out?" Etta stated more than asked.

"We just have a difference of opinion at the moment."

"You got more than a difference of opinion. You got two different addresses! You young folks have some strange ways of working things out. Pass me my purse, Eddie."

Eddie handed Etta her purse and she promptly took out her silver flask and splashed a capful in her coffee.

"For my nerves," she muttered, then looked at her nephew. "If you're gonna set around in the woman's house, the least you could do is fix dinner so she won't have to be bothered when she gets in."

"Fix dinner?" Edward looked almost frightened. "Dee doesn't like anyone messing around in her kitchen."

"Son, you are about as silly as they come. Of course that's what she says because you've never allowed her to have nothing else around here that she was in control of, except the kitchen!"

"But I . . ."

"Do you want your wife back or not?"

"Yes, ma'am."

"Then act like it." She pushed herself up from the couch. "Come on, son." She took him by the arm and pulled him into the kitchen. "You just show me where she keeps her ingredients and we'll have dinner cooked up in no time. Watch and learn."

To his amazement, Aunt Etta helped him whip together a wonderful meal in an hour flat. She'd chopped up a bunch of collard greens, tossed in some seasoning, and had them simmering on the stove while Edward diced potatoes, carrots, onions, and celery. Wild rice boiled merrily and after a thorough wash and seasoning, the chicken was roasting in the oven. All the while she made sure Edward paid attention to everything she did. Maybe he should have paid more attention to those cooking shows, he mused as he checked on the pot of greens.

"You need to do this more often," she said, her voice taking on a soft tone. "Women appreciate things like this." She washed her hands at the sink and wiped them on a yellow-and-white kitchen towel, then turned to her nephew. "That's all any of us want, son, is to be appreciated. If you want a good marriage, it has to be equal. Both of you have to share the load. No roles, no special duties, just equal. Know what I'm sayin'?"

"Yes, ma'am, I think I do."

She patted his cheek. "Good. That's a start. Now get this kitchen cleaned up and me and your uncle are going to be heading home." She started out.

"Aunt Etta . . ."

She turned to him and he leaned down and kissed her cheek. "Thank you."

"Thank me when you get your wife back. Make her want you as much as you claim to want her. Give her some time. She'll come around." With that, she walked out.

Edward thought about his aunt's words of wisdom as he washed utensils and wiped off countertops. Although her choice words of advice only came in spurts, when they did, they were well worth listening to.

When Edward returned to the living room, Anthony was sandwiched between Eddie and Etta, taking their usual grilling.

"Dad!" he cried out with much too much enthusiasm, jumping up at the sight of a reprieve. "I was just telling Aunt Etta and Uncle Eddie that I *really* needed to be getting home."

"Sure, son."

"We should be leaving too," Eddie said, rising from his seat. He darted over and helped up his wife.

Etta retrieved her precious hat, setting it at a jaunty angle on her head. "Don't forget what I told you," she said, wagging a finger at Edward while blowing the feather out of her face.

"And make sure you're home by nine," Eddie warned, then turned to Anthony. "You too. Young folks need their rest."

"Yes, sir," Anthony said.

"That chicken should be done in about an hour," Etta said at the door. "Then turn the oven to warm and it will be just right."

"Thanks, Aunt Etta."

Anthony and Edward waved good-bye as the old couple drove away, the car rattling and clanging down the street.

"Whew," Anthony breathed.

"We better get finished up out back before your mother gets home."

"We've done about as much as we can for today," Anthony said as they headed out back.

William was packing up his tools.

"Wow," Edward said in admiration, looking around. "I'm impressed."

"We still have a lot to do," William said, wiping his hands on his jeans. "But it's a good start. When do you think we can get back in here?"

"I can come by tomorrow and check out what's going on,"

Anthony offered. "I can always use my laundry as reason for dropping by."

"Good idea," Edward said. "Your mother would never be suspicious about that. Find out what her plans are going to be and then give me a call."

"Will do."

"Okay, fellas, let's cover our tracks and get out of here."

When Denise and Christine returned from brunch, the house was filled with the aroma of Sunday dinner.

"Did you leave the oven on?" Christine asked as they stepped in and closed the door behind them.

"No." Denise put her purse on the foyer table and headed for the kitchen. When she pushed through the kitchen door, she stopped cold. Pots were on the stove, and when she pulled the oven open, a perfectly browned chicken was in the roasting pan, surrounded by baby potatoes, carrots, and onions.

She stood in the center of her kitchen, totally perplexed, until she noticed the note on the fridge.

Dee,

Just wanted you to know I was thinking of you. I realize you need some time. And I'm willing to give that to you. Enjoy your dinner.

Love always,
Ed

She held the note to her chest and smiled.

TWENTY-ONE

Denise was in a rotten mood. In the days since leaving that wonderful Sunday dinner, Edward ignored her. In the beautiful note he'd left with the food he'd said she needed time and he was going to give it to her, but for how long? When was he going to resume trying to win her back?

Her teeth tore viciously into a slice of toast. The rat. She wished she knew what was going on in his head. One thing she was certain of, was that he was purposefully wearing those skin-tight jeans to get her all hot and bothered when he dropped by to check on Christine. He knew she liked him in jeans, just as he knew things with Christine and Reese were going great. Reese was stepping up to the plate, courting Christine, sending flowers, taking her out when he was off duty.

From the conversation with Christine that morning, Denise had learned Reese had finally seen through Loretta. Apparently, she'd hit on him last night at the hospital. After setting her straight, he'd called Christine to apologize. He was coming over to dinner tonight. If Denise wasn't mistaken, Christine would be going with him when he left.

Denise's eyes narrowed as she looked at her little bag on the table. Inside was her belly dancing costume. The gold fabric was so sheer it could be pulled through her wedding ring. When she danced for Edward, the undergarments would be of the same fabric. Maybe she could work it out so that the next time he came over she'd be practicing with her costume on. She grinned. He'd swallow his tongue.

Her mood brightening, Denise finished the toast and took her breakfast dishes to the sink. She didn't want to be late for her dance class. Tomorrow, December twenty-third, was the last day. She'd need every minute, she thought as she tried to undulate as her instructor had shown her for the past weeks. Her upper torso went up and down, her stomach didn't budge. But she was determined. She was going to do a little tempting herself.

Grabbing the bag and her purse, she headed for the front door. With all of Christine and Reese's things in the garage, it was impossible to walk through to the back where her car was parked. Locking the door, she started around the side of the house.

"Mama, wait."

She turned to see Anthony get out of his Acura Legend. He'd always loved her old car and she had given it to him when he was a junior in high school. The gray sports car's paint gleamed. Anthony might not have kept a neat room, but he'd always kept the car in top condition. "Good morning, Anthony."

"Hi, Mama." Popping the trunk, he hauled out a duffle bag stretched to the seams. "I'm going in late this morning and thought I'd bring my laundry over."

Her gaze roamed over his sweat suit. "Going to the gym?"

He grinned. "I got a racquetball match. I'm going to cream Dale."

She placed her hand on his shoulder when he stopped in front of her. He planned on playing while she worked. Her fault. "Anthony, you know I love you, don't you?"

His eyebrows knitted. "Yes, ma'am."

"Then do your own laundry from now on." She removed her hand. "I have an appointment."

"You're serious?" His brown eyes widened. "You're not going to do my laundry?"

She sighed. It had definitely been a mistake to do all the housework so her family would have more leisure time. "No, I'm not. You have to learn how to do things for yourself."

"But I don't know how," he told her.

"I'll be home tonight. Come back and I'll show you, but I won't do it for you." She checked her watch. "Sorry, but I really have to leave."

For a moment Anthony stood there perplexed, then snapped out of it when his mother started walking away. "Where are you going that's so important?"

He sounded so much like his father her eyebrow lifted in annoyance. "I beg your pardon."

Anthony shifted uneasily. "I mean, are you all right, Mama?"

She touched his cheek reassuringly. "Don't worry about me. I'm just going to class."

"Class?"

"Belly dancing."

His mouth fell open.

She held up the small bag. "My costume. Goodbye, honey, see you tonight if you want my help." She almost skipped to the car. She didn't have a doubt where Anthony would go. My, she'd like to be a fly on the wall when he told his father.

Belly dancing!" Edward yelled, shooting up from his desk.

Anthony shook his head as if he still couldn't believe it. "Daddy, she had this . . . this little bag that she said her costume was in. Daddy, you've got to do something. She's acting strange. I went over there to get the dirt just like we discussed, using my laundry as an excuse to talk to her. I still can't believe she refused this time."

"Her not doing your laundry might be a good idea."

"But Mama has always done it," he said. "Even when I was in college."

Edward stopped, stared at his son, then continued pacing, his hands shoved into his front pockets. "I think your mother has decided we need to learn to do things for ourselves. I think she's right."

Anthony's shoulders slumped. "But it's hard when you've always had it done for you. Nobody takes better care of us than Mama."

Edward's head came up, his hands snatching out of his pockets. "What did you say?"

"Just that it's hard to accept since Mama has always taken such good care of us."

"And we've always taken without any thought of giving." Edward shook his head. Aunt Etta was right again. "How could we—I—have been so selfish?"

"We do things for Mama," Anthony defended.

"Name one," Edward said, his hands on his hips.

Anthony opened his mouth, then closed it. "Jeez."

"Exactly." Edward began to pace again. "It's a wonder she didn't throw us all out sooner."

"Christine is still there."

"Because she has a husband who is, rather was, as thick-headed as we were." Edward stopped and braced a hip on the corner of his desk. "I just hope and pray my plan works. I've got to get my wife back and get her to call off this wild idea of a divorce. I know she still loves me just as much as I love her."

Anthony grinned. "You asking me for pointers, Daddy?"

Edward almost smiled. "Get out of here and go to work. I'll let you know if I can't handle things."

"Good luck, but if I were you, I'd put a stop to that belly dancing." Anthony opened the door. "That costume had to be triple X–rated."

As the door closed, Edward visualized Denise in something flimsy, with a half veil across her face, her brown eyes promising untold passion, her supple body moving sensuously to the music, her slender arms moving beguilingly. But he wasn't in the picture.

He snatched his coat from the rack. He couldn't get out of his office fast enough. The only man looking at his wife was going to be him.

Yummy. Now that's what I call tall, dark, and delicious."

"If he were a few years younger I'd like to practice my moves on him."

The two women from Denise's dance class laughed uproariously as they stared at Edward, arms folded, long legs crossed as he leaned against the hood of his SUV with a lazy grace. Denise had to admit he looked good dressed in a denim shirt and blue jeans. The temperature, in the low fifties, didn't seem to bother him.

She might have smacked her lips if he weren't watching her so intently. She couldn't help but remember all the times in her senior year when, after school was dismissed, she'd come outside and find him waiting in his beat-up car. Edward had always taken care of his own, he just had to learn that his own could take care of themselves.

"Wonder who he's waiting on?" Helen, a divorcée and the more outspoken of the two women, asked.

Denise felt compelled to say, "Me."

Two pairs of slightly envious eyes converged on her.

"You go, girl," they chorused.

Denise didn't know whether to say thanks or tuck her head in embarrassment.

"With a hunk like that, I can see why your outfit is off the chain," said Carrie, a young college student at Grambling. Her stomach was so tight you could probably bounce a dime off it. "We're still on for tonight?"

Denise nodded, her gaze still on Edward. "I'll see you tonight around seven."

Waving, the women took off in different directions to their cars. Denise was left alone to face the silent man watching her. She stopped about a foot from him, glad she had refreshed her makeup after leaving class and that the cranberry-colored turtleneck she wore complemented her amber complexion. Now that she had Edward's attention, she planned on keeping it. "Good morning, Edward."

"Morning, Denise." He didn't move, just continued to watch her.

"Anthony?" she asked, knowing the answer. Her son had certainly been predictable.

He nodded.

"Christine?" she asked.

He nodded again.

Her delight at seeing him began creeping toward annoyance. "My, you're talkative this morning."

"I was listening like you always wanted and thinking how beautiful you are and how blessed and lucky I am to have you for my wife."

Denise felt her throat clog with emotion. Sneaky. Very sneaky and very effective.

Straightening, he pulled her between his legs. "So, when are you going to give me a demonstration?" His voice was low and inviting.

She'd expected him to blow his top, not practically seduce her in the parking lot. She felt herself melting against him, her body fitting itself to his with a will of its own. It had been so long.

His dark eyes glittered down at her, as if reading her thoughts. "We can be home in twenty minutes."

Mentioning home snapped her out of her sensual haze. Time to get back on track. He'd been doing so well before the note. "The realtor is becoming anxious. You can't keep putting off signing the papers. He said he may have a buyer," she fibbed.

He glowered down at her. "He's wasting his time. That's our house and it's going to remain ours."

"That's debatable," she said, stepping back and slipping her gloved hands into her coat pockets.

"You didn't used to be this stubborn," he said, clearly annoyed.

Denise grinned. "Thank you. Now, if you'll excuse me, I have errands to run." She started down the sidewalk.

He fell into step beside her. "You're going grocery shopping?"

"Yes." She stepped off the sidewalk of the strip shopping center and headed for her car.

He caught her arm. "I could go with you."

Edward had gone grocery shopping with her exactly once: the week they were married. "You'd be bored in five minutes."

His hand slid down her arm to catch her hand. "Not with you, I wouldn't."

She simply stared at him.

He sighed. "Maybe so. Just answer me one question. No evasion, no double questions. I'm ninety-nine-point-nine percent sure I know the answer already, but I need to hear you say it."

"If I can." Realizing it was going to be a very important one, Denise hugged her purse and bag to her chest.

"Do you still love me?"

She stared up at him. Suddenly she felt afraid of what she had started. What if he got tired and walked away? Two hours ago, she'd been miserable because he was ignoring her. But if she said yes, would she lose her advantage?

"Dee," he said, and the word seemed torn from him.

She reached for the door handle but couldn't make herself open the door. "If . . . if I didn't love you, this wouldn't feel like my soul is being ripped from my body."

"Dee." He pulled her around, holding her tightly, desperately. "I . . . I . . ."

She held him just as tightly as he held her. The curious stares of people passing, the biting wind, meant nothing, only this man and this love of a lifetime.

"I may have made you want to pull out my hair, but I've never let you down, have I?" Edward asked.

"No."

He stepped away and stared intently down at her. "I'm going to get you back."

"You better," she threatened, brushing at the moisture pooling at the corner of her eyes.

He looked as if he didn't know whether to laugh or cry. "This new you will take some getting used to."

"Stop complaining, Edward, and go to work," she said, pushing against his chest and opening her door. "I have things to do."

He caught the door before it closed. "Mind if I come over tonight? If you're busy, I can show Anthony how to wash."

The new Edward might take some getting used to as well. "Is this a way of inviting yourself to dinner as well?"

"Am I that obvious?" he said, flashing a smile.

Starting the motor, she activated the window. "Rocking Around the Christmas Tree" played on the radio. "It's gumbo tonight."

He grinned roguishly. "I love gumbo, especially yours."

She grinned back. *Maybe we'll have a chance to rock around the Christmas tree together yet.* "See you tonight, Edward."

"I'll be there," he said, brushing his hand gently against her cheek. "If you don't mind, could you pay the monthly bills? You know where everything is kept."

Her throat was too full to do anything but nod. From the

first day of their marriage, Edward had always kept the check-book.

"Great." He stepped back. "Drive carefully."

"Good-bye," she finally managed, then drove off, grinning from ear to ear.

TWENTY-TWO

With Denise out of the way for a few hours, Edward darted over to the house to get as much work done as he could before she returned. When he pulled up out front, he was surprised when Anthony greeted him at the door.

"Hey, Dad. Did you find Mom?"

"I found her, all right," he said, mounting the three steps to the house and imagining his wife in some skimpy outfit.

"And?"

"Let's just say we have a truce—for the moment." He could never admit to his son that he couldn't wait for Denise to show him everything she'd learned.

Anthony frowned. "If you say so."

"What are you doing here anyway?"

"Trying to figure out this laundry thing," he said, looking like a stray puppy.

Edward shook his head and walked inside. He'd been gone from his house for nearly a month, but it felt like an eternity. He missed the comforts of his home, but more importantly, he missed his wife and what he thought they had together. But he promised himself that when he came back—and he would—

he'd be a better man, a wiser man, and the husband that Denise deserved. Each day away from the people and things he held dear offered him a new lesson.

"Well, don't just stand around, let's get busy," Edward said. "No telling what time your mother will be back."

"But what about my laundry?"

"We'll figure it out later." He headed to the back of the house with Anthony trailing behind.

"Dad?" He handed his father a plank.

"Yeah?" Edward expertly measured the surface, then lined up the board.

"I know this might be kind of personal, but are you cool with this belly dancing thing? Don't you think Mom has gone a little too far? I just can't imagine Mom . . . well . . . you know. She's my mother."

Edward worked hard at beating back his laughter, listening to the forlorn tone of his son. The fact of the matter was, kids could never see their parents as sexual beings, just two people who got together long enough to have them.

"What I've come to understand in these past few weeks is that your mom is her own woman. She's entitled to spread her wings and do the things that make her happy, not always working on someone else's happiness and needs—namely ours."

"But . . ."

"It's not as if she's running around town in that outfit or per-forming for an audience in a club."

"What if she did? 'Cause to be truthful, I don't put anything past her lately."

For a hot second, Edward envisioned Denise on a stage in

some dimly lit dive, dancing for a room full of howling men. His blood pressure rose.

"I'm sure your mother wouldn't do something like that," he said, as much to convince his son as himself. "I know your mother." At least he thought he did at one time. But did he now?

Sultry music rang in his head as Denise stepped onto the stage of *The Jerry Springer Show* to reveal to the world her hidden life as a belly dancer for hire. He would sit there appalled as Denise slinked her way across the stage, undulating to the beat of the audience's applause.

Suddenly, it took all of his willpower to restrain himself from scouring the town, looking for her and demanding that she give up all of her ridiculous plans and schemes and come back home where she belonged.

"Dad?" Anthony tapped him on the shoulder. "Are you okay?"

Edward blinked and focused on his son. "Yes, fine. Come on, we have work to do. And don't worry. All of this is going to work out. We're going to be one big happy family again, celebrating the best Christmas ever." He wanted to believe that. He had to believe that.

The moment Edward was out of sight, Denise pulled the car to the curb. She pulled out her cell phone and called Christine.

"Operation Wake-Up Call is working like a charm," she said to her daughter.

"Dad didn't blow a gasket?" she asked, totally surprised.

"Nope. He was quite charming," she said wistfully. "And he actually turned over the bill-paying to me. I still can't believe it." She grinned and shook her head in amazement. "Bills and finances were always your father's domain. I think he truly sees that there can be two heads in a household."

"Wow! Maybe I need to take up belly dancing," Christine said, laughing.

Denise chuckled, but didn't encourage the idea. "How about just inviting Reese to dinner tonight, for starters?"

"That's an idea. I'll give him a call. Do you need anything?"

"No. I'm on my way to the market now. I think I'll ask two of my classmates as well. And maybe even Aunt Etta and Uncle Eddie."

"Now that sounds like a party," Christine said, delight lifting her voice.

"It sure does. See you around seven."

"I'll be there."

Denise hurried over to the market to pick up everything she needed for dinner. She wanted it to be special. With Christmas only days away, the holiday season was finally seeping into her pores.

As she walked up and down the aisles, she couldn't help but smile when she thought about the moment she'd stepped out of class to find Edward waiting for her. At first, from the stern look on his face, she was certain that he was going to insist that she give up her dancing, the same way he'd wanted her to give up her sewing. But he'd surprised her—totally. Not only was he pleasant about the whole thing, he actually wanted a private demonstration.

She giggled, causing a woman coming up the aisle to look at her suspiciously and hurry by, clutching her infant close to her chest.

Ducking her head in mild embarrassment, Denise continued her shopping while thinking about the show she was going to put on for Edward when she got him alone. She was more than determined to be really good at it. She wanted his eyes to roll in the back of his head when he watched her put the moves on him. Just the thought of what would come after her performance sent a surge of heat racing through her body. The moment of truth couldn't come fast enough.

TWENTY-THREE

The house was filled with people, just the way Denise liked it. Impulsively, she'd invited Monique and Jeff over to dinner. Christine and Reese were keeping them company and keeping an eye on the seafood gumbo while she finished measuring Carrie and Helen.

"That should do it," Denise said as Carrie pulled her black knit sweater back down. It stopped an inch above her belly button. "I'll have them ready by tomorrow for the last day of class."

"So soon?" Helen asked, excitement in her voice.

"I sew fast," Denise said, not wanting to admit they were her only clients. But she planned to change that. "Shall we go back downstairs? I'd like both of you to stay and have dinner with us."

"I was hoping you'd ask," Carrie said, and made a face. "The food at the college cafeteria is the pits."

Helen laughed. "How well I remember."

Denise opened the attic door to lead the women to the kitchen. "I never went to college, but my family has stories about the food that will curl your toes."

"Don't get me started," Carrie said.

The women started down the stairs just as Anthony started up. He took one look at Carrie and she at him, and both stopped and stared. Denise sighed and said a silent good-bye to Sherri. "Helen Boyd, Carrie Sims, my son, Anthony."

Anthony remembered his manners, but his interest in Carrie was clear. His gaze kept skipping back to her as he talked to Denise. "If you have time, I'm ready for my first lesson."

"You're going to learn belly dancing?" Carrie asked, with a teasing smile.

"Something much more mundane. Washing my clothes," he answered, smiling back at her.

"Your father is going to help you," Denise said. "In the meantime, why don't you take Carrie to the kitchen? She's staying for dinner."

"Great!" Anthony lightly grasped Carrie's arm and went back down the stairs.

"Can you ever remember being that young and that carefree?" Helen asked.

"As a matter of fact, I can," Denise said as they continued down the stairs. At the landing, the doorbell sounded. "Excuse me." The beating of her heart increased with every step. Her hand actually shook as she turned the deadbolt and opened the door. Her gaze flickered from Edward to the two elderly people who pushed past him.

"Get out of the way, boy. My bones are getting cold," Aunt Etta admonished.

"You think the boy would want to get to courting," Uncle Eddie said. "Must have been dropped on his head as a baby, but I don't 'member."

"You don't remember yesterday," his wife said.

"Yes, I do, but I 'member last night better." Grinning, he helped her off with her coat and opened the hall closet door.

Denise stood there with her mouth open until a lean, brown finger lifted her chin. "I can't believe it," she whispered.

Edward sighed. "At least you don't have to listen to them talk about it and you're not getting any."

Denise's cheeks flamed and she shushed Edward.

"Tell the truth and shame the devil," he said with a mischievous grin.

Aunt Etta's head perked up. "Don't talk about the devil in my presence, boy. You'd think we didn't raise you right."

Uncle Eddie shook his graying head. "Must have been dropped and they didn't tell us. Got no sense of decency to come dragging home after everybody trying to sleep. Won't happen again. I'm driving tonight."

Denise put her hand over her mouth until she could control the laughter threatening to bubble out. "We were about to sit down to dinner. You're right on time."

Aunt Etta opened her black patent leather pocketbook. "Got my special sauce."

"Come on, Etta. Let's leave them while you go fix the food." They started for the kitchen.

Denise took off after them, completely ignoring Edward's laughter.

She'd served her gumbo and, after everyone had eaten, they all moved to the family room. The Christmas tree glittered like spun gold. Looking at her family, Denise glanced at the angel on top of the tree again and felt Edward's hand on her shoulder.

"We'll make it," he whispered in her ear.

"Stop that, boy," Uncle Eddie said from the comfort of Edward's favorite chair. "Time and place for everything."

Denise heard a distinct growl from Edward. Her lips twitched. "Coffee or soft drinks anyone?" She glanced at Monique. "Or in your case, tea?"

"I'm fine and stuffed," she said, reaching out her hand for her husband's, which he immediately took.

"Thank you for inviting us," Jeff said from his seat on the floor by his wife. "I'm not the best cook and we both were getting tired of takeout."

"How well I remember," Denise said. "I'll bring over a dish tomorrow." The young couple quickly started to protest, but she talked over them. "I'll just make a little extra."

"Don't argue with her, Jeff and Monique." Edward placed his hand back on his wife's shoulder. "She takes care of those she cares about."

"That's the way it should be," Aunt Etta said from across the room. "What time is it getting to be?"

"Eight-ten," came the answer from Reese and Jeff. A muscle ticked in Edward's temple. Christine and Anthony looked at their father in sympathy.

Folding her hands back over her wide girth, Aunt Etta leaned back in the easy chair.

Carrie rose. "I better get going. My first class is at eight. Thank you for dinner, Denise. I can't wait to see the belly dancing costume you're making for me."

Edward gave Denise a look, but didn't say anything, for which she was thankful. She certainly didn't want a scene in front of her friends.

Helen came to her feet as well. "Denise has the sexiest outfit in class."

Uncle Eddie jerked upright. "Denise is taking a sex class? Edward, boy, you need to put your foot down!"

Christine quickly walked over to the agitated older man and put a comforting arm around his thin shoulders. "No, Uncle Eddie, Mama is not taking a sex class."

"She better not be, or I won't let that boy come courting anymore," he said.

There was a stunned silence for a moment, then a lot of clearing of throats and coughing. Edward groaned and covered his face with both hands.

"I'll show you to the door," Denise said, her mouth twitching.

Anthony hopped up from his seat beside her. "I'll go with you, Mama."

Denise had expected as much as she showed Helen and Carrie to the door, then watched Anthony walk Carrie to her car. Wanting to give them some privacy, she came back inside as soon as Helen drove off.

She was just in time to see Jeff help Monique to her feet. "I'm glad you could come over. I'll bring the dinner over tomorrow around five," she told them.

"Thank you," they both said and in seconds they were gone.

"I guess I better get going as well. Early day tomorrow." Reese looked pointedly at Christine. "I'm off tomorrow night. I made reservations at your favorite restaurant. Or we could have dinner at home? I could cook."

"Why don't we talk about it tonight . . . at home?" Christine said.

He whooped, then grabbed Christine, his voice trembling as

much as his body when he said, "I love you." He leaned her away and stared down into her face. "I was an idiot not to listen to you. It'll never happen again. I promise you that."

Christine kissed him gently on the lips. "Let's go home."

Grinning broadly, Reese ushered his wife toward the door. "We'll pick up Christine's things tomorrow."

"Good night," Denise and Edward said as the young couple hurried from the house.

"They're deserting this place like rats on a sinkin' ship," Uncle Eddie said as he came slowly to his feet. "We better go, too."

"I'm staying to help Anthony," Edward told him. "He can drop me off."

"He shouldn't be out late either." Aunt Etta stuck her pocketbook beneath her arm. "Get your coat and let's go."

Edward leaned back on the sofa and folded his arms across his chest. "I'm not going."

"Now see here, as long as you're under my roof, you'll abide by my rules." Uncle Eddie walked over to Edward and stared mutinously down at him.

"He can spend the night," Denise heard herself say. Edward loved his aunt and uncle, but they'd try the patience of a saint.

They all stared at her. "He's going to help Anthony do his laundry while I do some sewing. I'll see that he goes to bed when he's finished."

Her eccentric in-laws grinned at each other, and then Uncle Eddie slapped Edward on the shoulder with surprising strength and winked. "Don't forget what I told you."

Denise didn't want to think about what he might have told Edward or if she'd been had. She quickly got their coats. She didn't breathe easier until they drove away. Carrie pulled off behind them.

"You want Anthony and me to help you with the kitchen?" Edward asked.

She was no longer surprised by his offer to help, but she felt strangely nervous. "I wrote out the bills and plan to mail them in the morning."

"I never doubted," he said. "You're a remarkable woman, Denise."

"Well." She moistened her lips. "Anthony, your father is going to help you. I'm going up to my sewing room." Denise didn't think of her quick escape as cowardly, just a strategic retreat. But how was she going to deal with Edward under the same roof and not in the same bed?

TWENTY-FOUR

With everyone gone, it was finally just the two of them. But not the way Edward imagined. He flipped onto his side in the narrow single bed, careful not to find himself on the floor.

Less than ten feet away was his beautiful wife. The only thing that separated them was an inlaid wood door that he could easily plow his way through with a shove of his shoulder. He flipped onto his other side and stared at the wall. Suddenly an image of Denise clothed in nothing more than a sheer miniskirt and bra-like top appeared in front of him, with jingle bells dangling from every tempting location. The room became suddenly warm and he threw the light blanket off him.

"This is ridiculous." He got up and headed out into the hall. The house was silent. He could hear the crickets outside the hall window. He tiptoed down the hall and pressed his ear to the bedroom door. Silence. *What would she do if I came in and slipped in between the sheets?* he wondered—then the sudden flash of Denise wielding that nail file popped into his head. He exhaled a deep breath.

Ravishing his wife was not the answer, he realized. Sex was not their problem; it never had been. Denise admitted as much. It was more than that. It was him learning to respect and accept her as not simply an object for his desires or to fulfill his needs and the needs of their family, but as a whole woman. That's what she had been asking for all along. And maybe it took these past weeks, experiencing the thought of losing her, of being without her, to finally help him to understand that fully. She didn't need him to just make love to her, she needed him to be *in* love with her, to romance her and make her feel like the bride he married.

Smiling, he turned away and returned to the single bed alone.

Denise stared up at the ceiling, counting the sheep that skipped merrily across the off-white surface. She turned toward her closed bedroom door and wondered if Edward was just as restless as she. She kicked off the covers, got up, and made her way across the darkened room. Inching the door open, she peeked out into the hallway. A sliver of moonlight could be seen coming from behind Edward's partially opened door.

Easing down the hallway, she stopped short of the door, listening for any movement. Edward's deep snores greeted her. Her heart sank to her feet. Here she was driving herself crazy with wanting him and he slept as soundly as a babe. Fine! If he could sleep, so could she.

Marching back into her room, she practically threw herself into her bed. By the time she drifted off into a fitful sleep, the sun was cresting over the horizon. *The best-laid plans,* was her last tormented thought before her eyes finally closed.

By the time she awoke the following morning, it was nearly ten. She jumped up from bed and hurried down the hallway. Edward's room was empty, the bed neatly made. Sighing, she slowly returned to her room to straighten up. *All he needed was a place to sleep,* she thought miserably as she pulled the sheets from the bed and replaced them with fresh ones. That mundane task completed, she took her shower, dressed, and went downstairs with the intention of fixing a light breakfast before tackling the task of finishing the costumes for her classmates.

But when she entered the kitchen, she couldn't have been more surprised than if Santa had been sitting there to greet her.

On the table was a perfect place setting for two, with a single rose in a slender crystal vase. Braced against the vase was a note:

Dee,

I thought you needed your rest, so I took the liberty of trying my hand at breakfast. I hope I didn't leave too much of a mess. Your food is in the warmer in the oven. I know the place setting is for two because I wanted you to think of me as sharing this morning with you, as I hope we will share many more together. It would give me great joy if you would be my date tonight for a Christmas Eve dinner. If your answer is yes, I'll pick you up at seven thirty. You know my number.

Love, Ed

Denise beamed with delight and did a great imitation of James Brown across her kitchen floor. Coming up short, she realized she had tons of things to do before her date. A date— with her husband!

Quickly eating her breakfast, which wasn't bad, she cleaned up the kitchen and darted upstairs to the attic to finish the costumes. Her class was at 3:00 P.M. today and if she hurried, she could stop at the hair salon for a touch-up and a rinse afterward. She wanted to look extra special tonight. Before she left the house, she called Ed's office—only to find he was out on a job.

"Can I transfer you to his voicemail, Mrs. Morrison?" Lena, his secretary, asked.

"That's okay, Lena, I'll call his cell phone. Thanks." She hung up, then dialed his cell.

"Morrison," he answered on the first ring.

"Seven thirty sounds fine," she said softly.

"I'll be there with bells on."

"I'll be waiting." Slowly, she hung up the phone, and her heart beat with the same anticipation it did when she would sit by the window waiting for him to pick her up in the early days of their courtship. Old folks often said you couldn't go back, but maybe she could prove them wrong. In the meantime, she had work to do.

Class flew by. Carrie and Helen were thrilled with their outfits and couldn't compliment her enough on the wonderful job she'd done, especially in such a short period of time. Thanking them profusely, she darted over to the hair salon and went into a mild panic when she was informed that the wait would be at least an hour before they could get to her. While she waited, she decided to get a manicure and a pedicure. *Why not?* she reasoned. Tonight was special. Finally, she was in the chair, and a bit more than an hour later, she looked into the mirror and was thrilled with what the stylist had done. A little cut, a little rinse, and she looked ten years younger. The woman insisted on arching her brows as well, which highlighted her almond-shaped eyes. With a little more than an hour to spare, she darted home and got ready for her date.

She was just applying the last touches of her makeup when the doorbell rang. Willing her heart to be still, she took a deep breath and slowly descended the stairs. But when she opened the door, her breath caught in her chest.

Edward Morrison looked like one of those mature male models from the catalogues. Always a handsome and fit man, he was even more dashing in his midnight blue suit, matching tie, and pale blue shirt. From the looks of him, he'd been to the barber for a perfect shave and shape-up, his dark hair, sprinkled with gray, cut close to his head.

"You look beautiful," he said, and leaned down to kiss her chastely on her cheek. "You always did look good in red."

She'd decided on her red velvet sheath with the cowl neckline, cinched waist, and body-hugging length. It hit her just above the knees and she knew that Edward always had a thing for her legs.

"You're looking quite gorgeous yourself," she said, smiling like an infatuated teen.

"Ready?"

She nodded briskly. "Let me just get my jacket." She took her matching jacket from the chair in the hall and picked up her purse.

"Let me help you with that."

He eased the jacket around her shoulders, and she shivered when she felt his warm breath against her neck and his fingers gently pressing into her flesh. For a hot minute, she thought about calling the whole night off and just taking him upstairs and having her way with him. But his voice in her ear jolted her out of her daydream.

"The car is out front."

When she stepped outside, she was momentarily confused. She turned to him. "Where's your car?"

"I decided that I would rent a car for us tonight so that I could concentrate on you and not on driving."

The chauffeur stepped out and opened the door for them.

"After you," Edward said, helping her into the car.

Denise thought she was in a dream, but if she was, she didn't want to wake up anytime soon.

Edward had selected an exquisite Italian restaurant just outside the city limits. And when Denise looked around everything came rushing back. It was the same restaurant he'd brought her to when he proposed. As the waiter showed them to their table, she promised herself that she wouldn't cry.

"Do you remember?" Edward asked once they were seated.

Against her will, her eyes filled and she dabbed at them with the linen napkin. "Yes," she whispered.

He reached across the table and took her hand, slipped off her wedding band and engagement ring, and placed each one in a box that he pulled from his jacket pocket. He placed both of them on the table between them.

"Twenty-seven years ago," he began, "I asked you to be my wife. We had visions of being together happily ever after. Somewhere along the way, we hit a detour. Or maybe I did. I started to believe that things, possessions, and control were what made a marriage work. It took the thought of losing you, Denise, to make me finally understand that marriage is so much more than that."

"Ed . . . I . . ."

"Wait, let me finish. Somewhere along the line, the romance disappeared, the courting, the fun, and the partnership. In the beginning, we struggled together. All we had was each other, a little one-bedroom apartment, and a black-and-white television." They both chuckled. "Now we have more than any couple could ask for, but we lost each other along the way. You gave me everything I needed to make me strong, but I didn't do the same for you. It may take me some time, but I want to work on fixing that. I want to hold onto these rings and present them to you when I'm the man you deserve to call husband. If you can be patient, I'll make it happen. If you know nothing else about me, you know I'm determined."

Denise didn't know what to say. On the one hand, she was thrilled that at least on the surface, Edward truly seemed set on making the marriage work and allowing her to be an important part of it. But on the other hand, she was terrified, terrified that this could very well be the end. He'd taken back the very symbol that bound them together. She had to think. But she couldn't. Instead she tried to focus on her meal, which began to taste like sawdust.

She wasn't sure how long the dinner lasted or what it was that they talked about. Her mind was sludge. Absently, she kept touching her bare fingers and another surge of dread would tramp through her.

At some point, the night finally came to an end as the driver pulled up in front of their house. Desperate, Denise gave it one last effort, the one thing that Edward had never been able to resist—her.

Standing in the doorway, she suddenly felt like an awkward teenager on a first date deciding if this would be the night. But a part of her deeply believed that if it wasn't, she might truly lose her husband for good.

"Uh, it's getting really late," she said, looking up into his eyes. "Why . . . don't you spend the night? I could make us some coffee . . . we could talk." She wanted to touch him, but dared not.

Edward gave her a half smile, then leaned down and kissed her lightly on the lips. "I don't think that would be such a great idea, especially on a first date. You wanted a new me and the first thing on my list is to respect you. So in light of that, I'm going to head over to my aunt and uncle's and try to get some sleep. I hope it's okay if I stop over tomorrow and open the gifts with the family."

She swallowed the lump in her throat. "Of . . . course."

He smiled gently. "Good night, Denise."

"Good night." She stood there for several unbelievably long moments as she watched the limo whisk him away.

Slowly she turned away and closed the door, letting the tears she'd held onto for hours flow down her cheeks.

TWENTY-FIVE

She was alone on Christmas Eve and it was her fault. Huddled on the four-poster she'd once shared with Edward, Denise fought a losing battle to keep tears from streaming down her cheeks. She ached so badly she didn't know if she could stand it. The house was silent instead of ringing with the joyous laughter of years past.

My fault.

Hugging a throw pillow to her stomach, she drew her knees up toward her chest. Her finger kept running over the empty space where her wedding rings had once been. Edward had worked an extra job to buy her the fourth-of-a-carat diamond. The symbol of their love had mattered more than the size of the stone, and he had taken her rings from her hand.

The only thing that gave her any hope was that Edward hadn't taken off his wedding band. He'd also explained his reasoning, but it was hard to accept with her alone in bed and aching for her husband.

In the past weeks since she'd asked for a divorce, he'd shown he understood her need for independence and to be an active part of the decision-making for them. He had become the partner she wanted, but he wasn't there with her.

Her Christmas miracle wasn't going to happen.

Denise woke with a splitting headache and eyes that felt as gritty as sandpaper. The throw pillow was still clasped tightly to her chest. As usual, she was on Edward's side of the bed.

It was Christmas Day. People everywhere were celebrating with family and friends. All she wanted to do was pull the covers back over her head and try to block out the impossible mess she'd made of her marriage.

Half a loaf is better than none. Too late. Much too late.

Opening her eyes, she sat up on the side of the bed. She couldn't wallow in misery all day. Christine and Anthony would come by. Maybe they'd take the food she'd cooked, thinking there would be a celebration.

Foolish woman. Making herself stand, she went to the shower.

Thirty minutes later, Denise slowly went down the stairs. She hadn't meant to, but her eyes went almost accusingly to the Christmas tree. Her brow knitted on seeing it lit. She distinctly remembered unplugging it last night. Still frowning, she walked over.

Her eyes widened as she saw a note dangling from the hand of the angel. *Merry Christmas. Look for a slender gold-wrapped box.*

Her heart thudding, she dropped to her knees, prepared to

throw all the carefully wrapped packages aside if need be. But there it was, on top. Her hands shaking, she tore the paper off, then gasped on seeing the gold nameplate: DENISE K. MORRISON, DESIGNER. She was so shaken she almost missed the note underneath that said, *Look in the bottom cabinet in the kitchen.*

Springing up, she raced to the kitchen to throw open door after door until she saw it—bolt after bolt of fabric. Dangling from the top was another note. *Pick up your next gift in the garage.*

Shooting upward, she whirled and was off again. Her hand was shaking so badly she could hardly open the door. Then, when she did, she burst into tears.

"Merry Christmas, Dee."

"Merry Christmas, Mama."

"Merry Christmas, Mrs. Morrison."

She could hardly take it all in. Her family and in-laws stood in the middle of a newly constructed sewing salon with state-of-the-art equipment.

"When . . . how—" she stammered.

Edward stepped forward and pulled her into his arms. "Whenever you were out of the house."

"You really do understand." She blinked back tears of happiness.

"Finally," he said. "I'm sorry for all those years I heard but never really listened. All I ever wanted was for you to be happy."

She gazed up at him with complete love and devotion. "I know that now. I guess I just needed to hear the words."

"I love you, Denise Morrison. You're the most wonderful, the most beautiful, the sexiest woman in the world to me, and I will do whatever it takes to remind you of that every day."

"So will we," the children chorused. "All except the sexy part."

"Sex is the best part," Uncle Eddie said with an emphatic nod of his graying head. "Told the boy that."

Everyone laughed. Denise leaned against Edward, then straightened. "Your chair! Your chair is out here!"

"While you are out here working, I thought I'd keep you company sometimes."

Her hands palmed his face. "You won't miss your television programs?"

His hands covered hers. "I'd miss you more."

Denise kissed him.

"I think the boy finally got it," Aunt Etta said. "About time. I'm hungry and I want to see what I got under that big tree."

"I ain't eating no tree," Uncle Eddie said, following her inside.

Laughing, the family followed. Soon the house rang with love and good cheer, and the rocking sounds of James Brown.

While the family was making merry in the living room and tearing through the brightly wrapped gifts, Denise pulled Edward aside.

He wrapped his arms around her waist and pulled her close. "Merry Christmas, baby."

"Merry Christmas. I have something special for you, too."

"Really?"

"Yes. Follow me." She took him by the hand and led him upstairs and into their bedroom. "You sit right there and don't move."

"Your wish is my command."

She darted out of the room and into the attic. Moments later, she returned and got the reaction she'd dreamed of. Edward's eyes really did roll back in his head.

Remembering the moves she'd learned in class, Denise rotated her belly and shimmied her hips, all to the beat that danced in her head.

Edward's mouth dropped open as the sensual moves set off the tiny bells on her skimpy costume, signaling her approach. This was better than he'd imagined and he couldn't wait until he could get to what was beneath.

"This is the dance for lovers," she whispered from behind her veil. She reached out for him and pulled him to his feet, then placed her hands on his waist. "Follow me," she instructed.

Laughing and giggling, Edward did an admirable job of matching her beat for beat until their bodies were pressed against each other, dancing to a rhythm all their own. Piece by piece, the sheer fabric fell away from Denise's body, followed by Edward's clothing, which all wound up in a pile at their feet.

"Can I take the lead now?" he whispered in her ear.

"I was hoping you'd say that."

Taking her in his arms, he placed her on the bed gently, like the precious jewel she was. Looking into her eyes, he knew that there was no better Christmas gift than the one she would give him. He leaned over the side of the bed and pulled the little black boxes from his pants pocket. Bracing his weight on his elbow, he opened the boxes. One at a time he lifted the rings from their cushioned cases.

"I truly believe that I'm the man you need and want in your life. And if you think that's true too, then I pray you will accept these rings as a token of my love and respect for you and consent to be my wife, my partner, from this day forward."

Tears of complete joy spilled from her eyes as she looked at the unbroken circles that he offered.

"Always and forever," she said through her sobs.

Edward took her hand in his and slipped the rings back onto their rightful place. And, taking as much time as his willpower allowed, he tried to show her with every touch, every dip of his body into hers, how special she was, how important, and how much he deeply loved her.

Her cries of joy were muffled by the sounds of music and laughter bubbling up from downstairs. As she held her husband close, she smiled, realizing that miracles still did happen. She and Edward would be rockin' around the Christmas tree for many years to come!

The Wish

FRANCIS RAY

CHAPTER 1

Nicholas Darling hefted a head of iceberg lettuce in the palm of his right hand, then plopped it unceremoniously into his shopping basket. Next came tomatoes, onions, cucumbers, baby carrots. By the time he left the produce aisle, the bottom of his cart was loaded with vegetables and looked as colorful as the Christmas decorations hanging in the grocery store.

"Jingle Bell Rock" blaring over the loudspeaker did nothing to smooth out his bunched brows. With a resigned sigh, he stared at the jumble and wished his younger brother, Ronald, had wanted to eat out instead of staying in. Small towns like Jubilee, Texas, might not have much to offer in the way of restaurants, but at least Nicholas wouldn't have to struggle with preparing a huge meal. Ronald ate like a bear right out of hibernation.

"Stop frowning, Nick," Ronald said, dropping several red and golden apples in a plastic bag into the cart. "How hard can this be?"

Nicholas lifted a dark brow and stared at his brother. Twenty-four years old, self-assured, and unflappable. "Then you can cook."

Ronald grinned and shoved his hands into the pockets of his jeans. "I'm your guest."

"An uninvited guest," Nicholas reminded him.

Ronald didn't appear the least disturbed by the comment. "You know you're glad to see me. Especially since you won't be home for Thanksgiving next week. Let's go check out the meat department." Whistling, he strolled off.

A reluctant smile tugged the corner of Nicholas's beautifully shaped mouth. Ronald had been sure of himself since he started talking. In this case, he was right. Nicholas *was* glad to see him. This would be the first Thanksgiving he wouldn't spend with his family. He'd been delighted when Ronald called and said his business meeting had wrapped up earlier than anticipated and he was driving from Austin, an hour away, to spend the night with him.

Nicholas hadn't seen his brother or their parents since he'd left Philadelphia four months ago to take a position as administrator of Memorial Hospital in Jubilee. His employer at his old job had given Nicholas a going-away party only after their considerable efforts failed to get Nicholas to stay.

Nicholas thrived on challenges, and Middleton General Hospital in Philadelphia ran beautifully after being under his direction for four years. He planned the same thing for Memorial Hospital here in Jubilee. In a year, the red ink would turn to black.

From twenty feet away, Ronald held up a package of red meat in one hand and one of fish in the other. Twisted strands of silver and gold garland hung from the counter behind him. "Which?"

Considering Nicholas's plan to eat the rest of his leftover lasagna tonight, both looked appealing. The problem was, he realized, he burned water. He was working his way through a family-sized frozen lasagna dinner because of it. Ronald cooked worse. Their mother had refused to let any of the men in her family near her spotless kitchen.

In Philadelphia, it had not been unusual for them to go by their parents' house to eat dinner. Both lived nearby. And if the brothers didn't have time to sit down, their mother would put it in microwavable dishes. What Nicholas wouldn't give for some of her cooking right now.

"Toss them both in and we'll decide later."

The meat plopped on top of the vegetables. "DJ loves to cook."

Nicholas sighed and refrained from glancing at his watch. Ronald didn't appear capable of going over ten minutes without mentioning his latest girlfriend. "Unfortunately, she isn't here."

Ronald's long-suffering sigh matched his brother's. "Don't remind me. If she hadn't been out of town on a business trip, I would have flown home tonight."

"It's nice to know how I rank," Nicholas said dryly, picking up a pound of sausage for breakfast, then a pound of bacon for good measure.

Unrepentant, Ronald grinned. "She adores me and has certain other appeals you can't match."

"So you keep repeating."

"Nick, she's gorgeous. I think I'm in love this time."

"Uh-huh," Nicholas replied, giving his brother's statement all the attention he thought it deserved. Ronald fell in and out of love regularly. For someone who worked with concrete data—Ronald was a systems analyst—he was as fanciful as they came. Nicholas was more pragmatic and less emotional.

Old-fashioned, lasting love like their parents had was rare these days. Nicholas didn't even plan on trying to look. Too many of his friends and associates were divorced or going through a divorce, and it was seldom amicable. As a kid he might have wished for a wife and family, but no more. He had better things to do with his time. Stopping the cart in the dairy aisle, draped this time with red and blue garlands, he placed a gallon of milk in the small basket near the handle.

"Mom and Dad like her."

"Uh-huh." Nothing unusual there. His parents liked all the young women Ronald brought over. They were fun-loving, energetic, and intelligent, just like Ronald. Nicholas picked up a can of country-style biscuits and sighed. He'd burned the last biscuits he'd tried to bake. He hadn't heard the timer in the shower. His hand flexed on the can. His mother's biscuits were light and fluffy. He could almost smell them, taste them.

"I'm going over to DJ's house tomorrow night for dinner. We're having veal."

The vision burst. Nicholas's breakfast had been toast and stale coffee. Lunch was a dry tuna sandwich from one of the vending machines in the hospital. He'd had back-to-back meetings or inspections and didn't have time to go to the cafeteria. Veal. His mouth watered. "Too bad she's not here to cook for us. I wish she was your wife."

"Don't worry, young man; you'll be married soon."

Nicholas jerked around at the soft-spoken Southern voice and saw an elderly Black woman smiling serenely up at him. Small and fragile, she barely came to the middle of his chest. "I beg your pardon?"

Reaching over, she patted his arm with her small, white-gloved hand as if to reassure him. "I said you'll be married soon. Your wish has been granted."

Having worked in hospitals for the past twelve years, since he was twenty-one, Nicholas remained calm. Unfortunately, the elderly often suffered from dementia or Alzheimer's. He looked around to see if there might be someone with her and only saw two other women nearby. Both looked vaguely familiar, probably people from the hospital. They were openly watching the interaction, but neither moved toward him and the woman. His attention switched back to the woman, who appeared to be patiently waiting for something.

She wore a yellow straw hat with a little bouquet of flowers on the brim. The dress she wore had flowers on it, too. Her arm was hooked through an empty blue plastic shopping basket. Unobtrusively, he tried to see if she was wearing a hearing aid, but he couldn't detect one. He shot a glance at the watchful women and said, "Thank you." There was no reason to embarrass the elderly woman by telling her she'd made a mistake.

"You're welcome. You'll be engaged by Christmas." Smiling at him again, she walked away, disappearing down the next aisle.

Laughing, Ronald slapped Nicholas on the back. "You don't even have to ask. I'll be happy to be your best man."

Nick lifted a heavy brow. "Very funny. Let's go to the bakery and get a chess pie for dessert."

Still chuckling, Ronald fell into step beside Nicholas. Neither noticed the excited chatter of Nicholas's coworkers as they hurried to check out.

Nicholas pushed open the double glass doors of Memorial Hospital at a quarter to nine the next morning. He felt as if he could conquer the world. After the overcooked steak and undercooked fish last night, he and Ronald had decided against trying to prepare another meal. Instead, they'd gotten up early and gone out to breakfast and stuffed themselves. Afterward, Ronald had left in his rental car for the airport in Austin. His last comment had been a teasing remark that he was going to start looking for a tuxedo because he wanted to look good as Nicholas's best man.

"Hello, Mr. Darling."

"Morning, Mr. Darling."

"Good morning," Nicholas returned to the two smiling nurses who had greeted him, then hastened his steps to catch the elevator.

"Morning, Mr. Darling," an attractive woman in a stylish red suit said as he got on. "You didn't have to rush. I would have held the door for you."

"Thank you," Nicholas said, stepping aside to make room for three other passengers, all women.

"I don't think we've had a chance to meet," another woman in a white uniform said, extending her hand. "My name is Gwen Stradford. I'm the charge nurse on the west wing of the med-surg floor from seven till three."

No sooner had the woman finished speaking than all the other women on the elevator introduced themselves. Puzzled, Nicholas shook their hands, almost glad when the door opened on the second floor and he could get out. Wishes for a good day followed him down the hall, but he also heard the distinct sounds of giggles. Shaking his head, he kept walking.

"Morning, Mr. Darling."

"Good morning," Nicholas replied to a tall woman in green

scrubs who looked at him as if he were the last piece of birthday cake and she intended to have it. His pace quickened. He didn't relax completely until he opened the outer door to his secretary's office.

"Good morning, Mr. Darling." Michelle Rhodes, his secretary, glanced up at him from digging in the file cabinet.

"Morning." Continuing to his connecting office, Nicholas covertly watched her pull out a file and flip through it. She hadn't acted any differently toward him. With each decisive step across the room, his uneasiness faded more and more.

In his office, he saw the stack of files he'd left on his desk when Ronald arrived unexpectedly Monday afternoon. After loosening his tie, Nicholas promptly forgot about the women and set to work.

By eleven, he'd made a decent dent in the records for the last quarter. Stretching, he tightened the tie he'd loosened earlier and then pulled on the navy blue double-breasted jacket to his suit. He was meeting with the head of radiology in five minutes. She wanted a new MRI machine. They cost upward of a million and a half dollars, but if it would help with early detection or diagnosis, he'd certainly see if there was a way for the hospital's overtaxed budget to obtain one.

He was barely in the hallway before it started again.

"Hello, Mr. Darling. Have you eaten lunch yet?"

"We're going out; do want us to get you anything?"

"It'll be our treat."

"They have fantastic stuffed baked potatoes."

Nicholas looked from one smiling woman to the other. They worked in the administrative offices on his floor. Until now they'd been cordial, but not overly so. Now they were acting as if he and they were old friends. Something wasn't right. "Hello. Thanks for the offer, but I'll pick up a bite later."

"If you change your mind, I'm two doors down from your office. I'm Carolyn Johnson."

"Alice Wilson."

"Sylvia Atkins."

"Gloria Quigley."

"Thank you," Nicholas said, and hurried away. He stopped and turned when he heard what sounded suspiciously like giggling again. Yet when he turned, the women were simply staring innocently at him. He rubbed the back of his neck and continued to the elevator. Perhaps he was working too hard.

Nicholas kept the thought until he stepped off the elevator on the ground floor, where radiology was located. Every step he made, women were saying hello, introducing themselves. It was so bad that he was late for his meeting with Dr. Bradford and two of her staff members. Nicholas relaxed on seeing they were men. Thirty minutes later, when he was the first to leave her office, he paused briefly, hand on the doorknob. Then, feeling foolish, he opened the door and strode down the hall.

He made it ten feet before it began again. Women were everywhere. He couldn't seem to get away from them. Any men he saw just shook their heads as if they felt sorry for him.

Opening the door to Michelle's office, he strode across the room to her desk and planted both hands on top. "What is going on? Why is there a woman smiling at me everywhere I go?"

Her hands left the computer keyboard and she swiveled in

her chair toward him, tucking her long, braided hair behind her ear. "Don't you know?"

"If I knew, I wouldn't be asking," he said tightly. He sighed and made an effort to relax. This wasn't her fault. Michelle was hardworking and ran his office efficiently. And, as his predecessor had informed Nicholas, she was privy to all the latest gossip in the hospital. Until now, he hadn't availed himself of that particular talent of hers. "Please, tell me."

She sighed dreamily. "You've been granted a wish."

"A wish." Nicholas straightened, a strange foreboding sweeping through him.

"Yes," she said. "Mrs. Augusta granted you your wish to be married. Isn't it wonderful?"

Nicholas's jaw dropped. "Mrs. Augusta . . . ? You mean that little old lady in the grocery store who was hard of hearing? She got it all wrong. I did not wish to be married."

"You didn't?" Michelle's large eyes rounded in uncertainty.

"I most definitely did not," Nicholas said, beginning to pace in front of her desk. "I was teasing Ronald, and that woman . . . Mrs. Augusta or whoever she is . . . well, she simply misunderstood what I said. You know how elderly people get things mixed up."

Michelle shook her head. "Despite being up in age, Mrs. Augusta is still as sharp as they come."

Nicholas spun and pinned his secretary with his fierce gaze. "If you mean an elderly Black lady wearing gloves and a hat in a grocery store at five in the afternoon, I think the way she dresses says otherwise."

"She always dresses that way. She's a real Southern lady," Michelle said, as if that explained everything.

"She's a kook." Nicholas started pacing again. "Spouting off about my wish being granted and that I'd be married soon. I should have walked away from her instead of thanking her."

"Oh, Mr. Darling."

Nicholas spun around and saw the distress in Michelle's face. "What?"

"You thanked her."

"I was being polite."

Michelle shook her head again. "In thanking her you accepted the gift of your wish being granted. I told you, Mrs. Augusta is a real lady. She wouldn't bestow a gift on someone who didn't want it."

Nicholas rolled his eyes. "Look, I don't know how you know her and why you believe any of this nonsense, but the simple truth is, I did not wish for a wife."

Michelle brightened. "That's what makes Mrs. Augusta so unique and magical. She has this uncanny ability to grant unspoken wishes. Did you ever wish for a wife?"

Nicholas opened his mouth to emphatically tell his secretary that he hadn't, then recalled his wish as a young boy, a wish he had thought about only moments before Mrs. Augusta had appeared. He scoffed at the absurdity of it all. "Maybe when I was a kid and believed in fairy tales and happily ever after," he admitted reluctantly, then quickly added, "but after watching so many marriages go bust, I've come to realize that lasting happiness seldom happens in marriages these days."

"Simon and I are very happy and we plan to remain that way," Michelle told him, her face glowing.

Not wanting to point out that a year was hardly enough time to test a marriage, Nicholas said, "I'm glad you and Simon are the exception." He took a calming breath. "I can't believe I'm getting worked up about this. By tomorrow, it will all be forgotten." He waited for his secretary to confirm his words, and when she didn't, he plopped down in the chair in front of her desk. "Drop the other shoe."

She twisted uneasily in her seat. "Mrs. Augusta's predictions and wishes have always come true. Since she's a Christian lady and the wishes are welcome, people usually want her to grant them a wish."

"No one can grant wishes," Nicholas scoffed.

"Five years ago, after church, Mary Kennedy wished that she wouldn't die an old maid. She wished that she'd find a good man to marry and have a big family to love. Mrs. Augusta heard and right there in front of everybody granted her wish. Before a year had passed, Mary was married and had a baby girl."

Nicholas waved a dismissive hand. "Sheer coincidence."

"Before Mary dated John, her husband, she'd been on one date. They now have five children and are as happy as can be. There have been several others whose wishes were granted, including the mayor's unspoken wish for his son to stop drinking and settle down with a loving, Christian woman."

Nicholas continued to look dubious.

"And if that's not enough, Mrs. Augusta saved the lives of hundreds of schoolchildren when she called the sheriff's department to tell them to evacuate the elementary school. There wasn't a cloud in the sky. The tornado hit less than two minutes after the last kid got out. The building was flattened. Me and my sister and three cousins were at school that day." Michelle folded her arms. "At the beginning of the school year, the principal, Yolanda Thompson, had wished that all the school children have a safe year. You'll never convince me Mrs. Augusta made a mistake."

Seeing the surety on Michelle's face, Nicholas realized what he was up against. Augusta had had one lucky guess, albeit a miraculous one, and the townspeople took her word as gospel. The rest of her "wishes" were all coincidental. "This time she's made a mistake."

"Mrs. Augusta never makes mistakes." Michelle turned to her computer. "If I were you, Mr. Darling, I'd accept the wish and start thinking about who you plan to invite to the wedding."

"This is ridiculous."

The door behind them opened and three women surged in. Nicholas barely kept from grinding his teeth. Just what he needed. More women!

"Mr. Darling, I just had to tell you the good news," said Delores McKinnie, the hospital's director of human resources. Her smile grew as she crossed the room. "You won't believe how many tickets we've sold." She glanced between the two women on either side of her. "Eula and Rachel just gave me the good news."

"We're on our way to post the tabulations of the most wished-for items on the bulletin board of the cafeteria," Eula said.

"We thought you'd like to be the first to know," Rachel added, staring at him with undisguised interest. "I bought twenty tickets myself."

Delores hugged the notebook to her chest. "It looks like this year will be the biggest in the ten-year history of the wish list. You're new to this, but half the money raised goes to one lucky winner to make their wish come true, and the other half goes to charity. Since news started circulating this morning, sales have tripled for the wish list for Christmas, and we have you to thank for it."

Nicholas went very still. She couldn't possibly mean what he thought she meant. She just couldn't.

"I wanted to tell you personally," Delores said, grinning. "You're at the top of the wish list."

CHAPTER 2

Andrea Strickland sat cross-legged in the window seat of the family room, her upper torso bent with an unconscious grace over the sketch pad in her lap, her slim hand making quick, decisive strokes as she brought the young prince to life once again. This was the last scene in the children's book she'd been hired to illustrate, and the most important. The handsome prince had just professed his unending love to the beautiful but poor young woman standing before him in a tattered dress.

The story had been told hundreds of times in varying ways, but it had never lost its appeal. What young girl, poor or rich, hadn't yearned at one time or another to marry a handsome prince? Andrea would settle for a simple man who was honest, kind, and intelligent.

Her mouth curved ruefully as she outlined the prince's muscular thigh. All right, she wouldn't mind if he had a body like an Adonis, a voice that made her shiver, and a face to make an angel weep with regret. His large hands would be slow, inventive, and clever.

"Andrea, stop daydreaming and answer the front door."

Andrea jumped. Her startled gaze flew to her diminutive

aunt in the doorway. Heat flushed Andrea's amber cheeks as if Aunt Augusta could read her thoughts. "Ma'am?"

"The door," Aunt Augusta repeated with unending patience and love. "The timer is about to go off for the tea cakes."

At that second, a bell sounded on the gas stove that was almost as old as Andrea. "The door," Aunt Augusta repeated with a smile. She left the room and went down the hall toward the kitchen in the back of the house.

Placing the sketch pad on the window seat, Andrea stood, then stretched her slim arms over her head to loosen the stiff muscles in her back and shoulders. When she worked, she often forgot time. She lowered her arms and headed for the front door, her thoughts returning to the man she'd envisioned.

Melissa Manning, the heroine of the romance novel Andrea was writing on speculation, would have such a man in Braxton Savage. Tall, dark, and brooding, Braxton, an ex–army ranger, was a cynic who didn't believe in love . . . until he met warmhearted Melissa, who was nobody's pushover. She'd proven that when she escaped from the two men sent to kill her. Melissa intrigued Braxton as much as she aggravated him. For the first time in his lonely life, he had found someone he could love, someone he couldn't walk away from.

Andrea readily admitted living vicariously through her heroine, since she didn't have a man of her own. She'd had fun with Melissa and Braxton's verbal sparring while the sexual tension crackled around them like a downed electrical wire. The chemistry between them was explosive, the loving hot and intense.

Aunt Augusta would probably be shocked if she knew what her niece had written. On second thought, perhaps not. Her aunt was definitely a woman of the twentieth century, even if her gift dated back centuries.

Augusta Venora Evans was a modern-day fairy godmother. She had no idea why she was the conduit to tell people their wish had been granted. She simply accepted her unusual gift, since the wish always led to happiness.

That ability alone should have alleviated Andrea's worry about being called home by Aunt Augusta a month ago. When she had called Andrea in New York, insisting she come home immediately, she'd come, afraid her aunt had had a premonition that something bad was going to happen to her.

Since Andrea's return, her aunt remained as spry as the day nine-year-old Andrea had come to live with her. Andrea's parents had died in an automobile accident eighteen years ago. Dr. Jones, Aunt Augusta's doctor, had assured Andrea her aunt was in excellent health for a seventy-three-year-old woman.

However, Aunt Augusta still became agitated if Andrea mentioned returning to New York. Thank goodness that as an illustrator for a children's book publisher, she could work anyplace. Although she'd been hoping not to spend another Christmas holiday dateless, Jubilee had slim pickin's when it came to eligible bachelors.

Her mouth twitched. If Aunt Augusta could grant Andrea a wish, she knew exactly what it would be: the man she'd envisioned earlier. What a wonderful Christmas present he would make. Her aunt wouldn't even have to put a bow on him. Laughing, Andrea reached to open the front door.

Nicholas, tired and irritated after another day of being ogled by women, was in a foul mood. After he'd rung the bell several times and there was no answer, he was strongly considering pounding on the door when it opened. "I'd—" His thoughts scattered as he stared at the woman in the doorway.

Small, delicate, vibrant—his breath caught at the sheer joy she radiated. The fading sound of her silken laughter shimmered down his spine. Thick black lashes shaded deep chocolate eyes in a stunning, almond-hued face. Her lush mouth was painted a rich raspberry color that he instinctively knew would taste sweeter than any fruit.

The laughter died on Andrea's lips as she stared at the man in the doorway. He was absolutely gorgeous, with a strong jaw, piercing black eyes, a beautifully shaped mouth. His shoulders were broad beneath the tailored wool sports coat, his chest wide, his legs long in gray charcoal slacks. He was six fabulous feet of toned, mouthwatering muscle.

At five foot two, she usually didn't like big men, but she irrationally felt this man would protect her with his life if need be. His skin was the color of honey poured through sunshine. The thought made her want to touch the tip of her tongue to his skin to see if he tasted as good.

"Andrea, where are your manners?" Augusta said from down the hallway. "Invite the gentleman in."

Andrea flushed, hoping the man hadn't been offended by her staring. But considering what a handsome specimen of manhood he was, he probably had been stared at before. "I'm sorry. Won't you come in?"

"Thank you," Nicholas said, stepping inside the foyer, trying not to stare at her, or notice that she had on shorts that revealed legs that demanded a second look, or that her long-sleeved knit shirt clung enticingly to her high breasts. He cleared his throat. "I'd like to see Mrs. Augusta Evans, please."

"Auntie?" Andrea frowned, hoping he wasn't a salesman who preyed on the unsuspecting elderly. "I'm her niece. What's this about?"

"I want her to take back her wish or do whatever she has to do so my life can get back to normal," he said, annoyance creeping into his deep voice.

"She granted you a wish?" Andrea asked.

"No one can grant a wish," he stated emphatically. "However, the women at the hospital seem to think she can."

Andrea glanced behind her to see her aunt come out of the living room. Her quickness never ceased to amaze Andrea. "He's here to see you, Auntie."

"Good afternoon, Mr. Darling," Augusta said as she came toward them. Hardwood gleamed beneath her feet. "This is my niece, Andrea Strickland. Andrea, Mr. Nicholas Darling."

Andrea nodded and thought how aptly named he was. "Mr. Darling."

"Andrea," he said, then switched his attention to her aunt. "You know my name?"

Aunt Augusta smiled. "Of course. You don't think I'd go around talking to strange men, do you?"

"I'm not sure," he said slowly. He wasn't committing or agreeing to anything Augusta Evans said.

"Auntie, Mr. Darling wants to talk about his wish," Andrea said, wondering what the wish had been.

"I expected as much." Augusta extended her small hand toward the first door on the left. "I already have refreshments set up in the living room."

Nicholas shook his dark head. "Thank you, but I just want you to take back your wish and then I'll be leaving."

"We can just as well talk while we eat." She affectionately patted his stiff arm. "I have iced tea cakes. I'm sure you're hungry."

His unhappy stomach rumbled in agreement. He hadn't had a good meal since breakfast with Ronald two days ago. Since then, Nicholas hadn't dared venture out of his office or go to a restaurant for fear of women throwing themselves in his path.

"We had fried chicken and macaroni salad for lunch, if you'd care for some," Andrea said. The poor man looked as if he were at his wit's end. "It won't take me but a minute to fix a plate."

Nicholas thought of telling her not to bother, then caught himself watching the alluring sway of her hips as she hurried down the hall.

"Mr. Darling."

Nicholas jumped and jerked his head around, half-afraid Mrs. Evans had picked up on his lustful thoughts. He didn't believe she had any special powers, but she had eyes. "Yes, ma'am."

"Why don't you follow Andrea to the kitchen? You'll be more comfortable eating at the table. I'll get the tea tray."

"I'll get it for you," he said.

She gifted him with another smile. "I knew you'd be a gentleman."

Nicholas said nothing, just followed her to the living room filled with antique furniture. He picked up the heavy silver tea set from the claw-foot coffee table and took it to the kitchen. He licked his lips as he stared down at the golden palm-sized cookies glistening with buttercream icing on a white doily.

Entering the bright yellow-and-white kitchen, he saw Andrea spooning macaroni salad onto a stoneware plate laden with crispy-looking fried chicken, black-eyed peas, rice, and two corn muffins.

She threw him a glance over her shoulder. "I nuked it already." She placed the plate on the scarred round oak kitchen table that seated four. "There's also iced tea, coffee, fruit juice, and soft drinks."

Nicholas placed the tray on the spotless Formica counter, his eyes on the plate of food. His mouth watered. "Coffee. Black."

"Please sit down and eat," Andrea instructed, and went to pour him a cup of coffee. She didn't like the stuff, but Aunt Augusta couldn't start the day without it. "Here you are."

"Andrea," Aunt Augusta said, "I need to make a phone call. Keep Mr. Darling company." When Nicholas looked as if he'd object, she said, "By the time you finish I'll be back." Then she was gone.

"Don't worry, Mr. Darling. I'm sure everything will work out."

Nicholas turned to Andrea and felt his body stir. "Call me Nicholas and have a seat." Hearing her say "Darling" conjured up a fantasy he wasn't ready to deal with.

She shook her head of short auburn curls and smiled impishly. "If I hurry, I can grab my sketch pad and be back before Auntie returns. You probably can't eat with me staring at you."

Nicholas picked up his fork. For some odd reason, he didn't object to her being near him, unlike the other women he'd had to deal with over the last two days. "I don't mind if you sit with me."

Her face dimpled into a pleased smile. "I'll be back in a minute."

Nicholas stared after her, then dug into the macaroni salad.

One bite and he closed his eyes and sighed. He hadn't had food this good in weeks.

By the time Andrea returned and slid into a seat beside him, he had finished off a chicken thigh. Giving him a shy smile, she propped a pad on her knees. Her brows bunched in concentration as she sketched. His food was forgotten as Nicholas watched the quick, graceful movements of her small, delicate hand and her beautiful profile as she worked.

Afraid she'd catch him staring and see the desire in his eyes, he looked down at his plate and began to eat again. He enjoyed the food, but he was very much aware of the woman sitting near him.

Finished, he pushed his plate aside. "That was the best meal I've had in a long time. Thank you."

"Would you like your tea cakes with ice cream?" Andrea asked.

"I think I've stuffed myself enough." Nicholas picked up his coffee cup.

"Then I'll put some in a tin for you to take home." Placing the sketch pad on the table, she went to the cabinet, then bent to open the bottom door.

Her shorts lovingly cupped her rounded hips, and Nicholas looked away, disgusted with himself. He'd never been this lustful over a woman in his life. Needing a distraction, he drew her sketch pad toward him. "Do you mind?"

Straightening, she glanced around and shook her head. "Help yourself."

As he flipped though page after page of pencil drawings, he was captured by the fine detail of the sketches. "These are wonderful."

"Thank you," she said, pleased as she finished putting cookies in the round red canister lined with wax paper. "Let's hope
the author of the book and her editor think so."

"You're a book illustrator?" he asked with genuine interest.

"Yes." Placing the canister beside him, she retook her seat.
"After I graduated from art school, I headed to New York. I got
lucky when I was sketching on the train and an author of children's books sat beside me. He introduced me to his editor and,
as they say, the rest is history."

"That's amazing," Nicholas said, not sure if he meant her suc-
cess, or the allure beckoning in her deep brown eyes.

She nodded. "People in Jubilee thought Auntie was crazy to
let me go to New York on my own without a job. She told me
to follow my dream. She never doubted."

Something about Andrea's statement caused uneasiness to
run through Nicholas. "How long were you in New York before
you found a job?"

She wrinkled her nose and laughed. "Three days. I know I'm
blessed, and I never take my good fortune for granted."

"Did you wish for a job?" he asked, unable to keep the skep-
ticism out of his voice.

If she heard it, she didn't appear offended. "No, but it wouldn't
have mattered."

"Why is that?"

She smiled sadly. "Auntie has never been able to grant anyone in the family a wish."

He was outraged. What kind of sense did it make to grant a
wish to him that he didn't want and keep one from a person as
vibrant and beautiful as Andrea?

"Sorry to have kept you waiting, Mr. Darling," Augusta said as she entered the room. She waved Nicholas back into his seat and took the cane-backed chair beside him. "How can I help you?"

"By taking back your wish. I don't want it," he promptly told her.

She folded her hands in her lap. "Are you sure?"

"Positive." Nicholas placed his arms on the table and leaned toward her. "I was joking with my brother. Marriage is the furthest thing from my mind."

"Your wish was to get married?" Andrea asked softly.

"I wished my brother was married," he stated emphatically.

"But you accepted the gift," Augusta reminded him.

Nicholas straightened, then shoved his hand over his head in frustration. "I only did that because people were watching and I didn't want to embarrass you by telling you you had made a mistake."

"That was very kind of you, Nicholas," Andrea said. "Thank you."

He looked over at her and became ensnared in Andrea's dark gaze and soothing voice for a long moment before wrenching free. "I have to be honest and admit that knowing the consequences as I do now, I'm not sure if I would have acted the same way."

"What consequences?" Andrea asked.

"Women," he answered tightly. "Everywhere I go, they're there. Introducing themselves. Asking me out. Offering lunch. It has got to stop. I can't run a hospital like this. Take the wish back."

"Once accepted, it cannot be given back." Augusta patted his arm, then rose. "A wish has never brought anything but happiness. You'll see."

"Mrs. Augusta, I beg you to help me," Nicholas said, pleading for the first time in his life. He didn't care.

"By Christmas, you'll be happily engaged. Andrea will see you to the door. Please come back anytime."

With stunned disbelief, Nicholas watched Augusta Evans leave the room. He'd been so sure when he obtained the address from his secretary that he would be able to get Augusta to publicly announce that she'd been wrong. He oversaw the operation of millions of dollars. When he talked, people listened. But Augusta Evans had fed him, patted him on the arm, then politely dismissed him. His visit had been futile. Standing, Nicholas pushed back his chair, then walked to the front door.

"This cannot be happening to me," he mumbled, his hands clamped around the top railing of the porch.

"If there was any way to help you, I would."

He spun toward Andrea. Hope glittered in his eyes. "If you mean that, then get your aunt to take back the wish."

"I'd never interfere with Aunt Augusta."

"Then wish my wish away." Nicholas knew his words were ridiculous, but he was desperate.

Slowly, Andrea shook her head. "As I've told you, Auntie's abilities have never extended to the family. No family member has ever been involved with anyone who was granted a wish or benefited in any way from a granted wish. My wish doesn't count." At the doubting expression on his face, she continued, her voice barely above a whisper. "I remember my first wish when I was nine."

Thinking she was going to say she had wished for a doll, Nicholas was ready to dismiss it as being frivolous.

"I wished my parents were alive." Her words were like a sharp punch to his gut. "That there had been some horrible mistake and that they hadn't been killed in an automobile accident."

"Andrea, I'm sorry," he said, wanting to take away the pain and shadows that had appeared in her eyes. His situation was nothing in comparison to that of a young child who had lost both parents at once. "I'm so sorry."

"My mother was Auntie's only sister, her only sibling. Auntie held me and we both cried." Andrea swallowed. "I've never wished for anything again. Not that I don't believe in Auntie's power and am not happy for others she's granted wishes to, but I see how it hurts her when she can't help her family."

Nicholas stared at Andrea and hadn't a shred of doubt that she was telling the truth. He'd seldom seen that kind of selfless love and devotion. Without thought, he brushed his fingers across her cheek in wordless comfort. He watched her eyes widen in surprise, felt the warmth and silky softness of her skin, and experienced the need to keep on touching.

His hand tightened into a fist. "I should be going. Thanks again for the meal."

Andrea remained on the porch as Nicholas backed his big black Mercedes out of the driveway. Almost immediately, a late-model sedan pulled up in its place and two middle-aged women piled out. They kept looking over their shoulders at the disappearing Mercedes as they hurried along the flagstone walk, then up the three wooden steps.

"Good evening, Mrs. Freeman, Mrs. Kimbrew," Andrea

greeted both women, members of the church she and her aunt attended.

They returned the greeting, but it was obvious their minds were on the man in the Mercedes. "Wasn't that Nicholas Darling?"

"Yes," Andrea answered. Both women had single daughters. It didn't take much to guess why they had dropped by.

"Wonderful," Mrs. Freeman said. "Perhaps now Mrs. Augusta can tell us who the lucky woman is."

"I hope it's my Annie."

Cheryl Freeman shot her best friend, Evelyn Kimbrew, a proprietary look. "My Jackie would be better for him."

"Why don't we ask Mrs. Augusta?" Mrs. Kimbrew sniped.

Without waiting for Andrea to invite them in, they surged inside, each trying to get through the door first. Instead of following them, Andrea propped her shoulder against the square white post on the porch, her hand lifting to her cheek. She could almost feel the warmth and tenderness of Nicholas's powerful hand.

Strong, sensitive, and caring, he was the kind of man women dreamed of finding, of loving. But that woman could never be her. She'd told Nicholas the truth. For some unknown reason, her aunt's gift didn't extend to family members. Andrea would never find out how it felt to be held against his hard body, if his mouth was hot and greedy, if his hands were slow and thorough. Blushing at her uncharacteristic thoughts, she went inside and closed the door.

CHAPTER 3

Nicholas's bad day on Tuesday was turning into a bad week. It was Friday afternoon and the number of women who somehow managed to ambush him increased hourly. It had gotten to the point where he was afraid to leave his house.

Women seemed to materialize out of thin air. He'd try to avoid one and end up facing three more. He hadn't known women traveled in groups or giggled so much. And he could have happily gone to his grave ignorant of those two facts. His orderly, well-organized life had been turned upside down by a mite of a woman.

Nicholas pulled into the driveway of Augusta Evans's house and parked. He wasn't sure why he'd come. He didn't hold out any hope that she would change her mind. Besides being stubborn, she believed she had right on her side. Sighing, he draped his arm over the steering wheel and studied the house in front of him.

Neat and inviting, the pale yellow house had a second floor with gabled dormers. The trim around the arched windows, the railing, and the four posts on the long porch were white. The shutters and roof were slate blue. White wicker furniture with colorful cushions was tucked in a corner of the porch. At the end of the meandering flagstone walkway stood a mailbox, an exact replica of the house.

Despite it being the middle of November, blooming flowers were everywhere. They trailed from baskets on the porch and sprouted from the well-tended beds. The house had an air of grace and serenity that reminded him of Andrea. It sat on a huge lot at the end of a two-lane gravel road. The nearest house was half a mile away.

On the green lawn was a five-foot burlap scarecrow. Straw protruded from the stuffed sleeves of the denim shirt and the legs of the overalls. Beneath one extended arm, pumpkins overflowed from a wheelbarrow. Several clay pots of yellow and rust-colored chrysanthemums sat nearby. In his mind's eye, he could almost picture Andrea laughing with delight as she created the scene.

It was quiet and peaceful here, with only the wind sailing through the branches of the maple trees, causing the leaves to shimmer like quicksilver. Colorful beds of snapdragons and pansies circled the trees. Monkey grass marched up the sides of the driveway of the detached garage off to the left. In one of the double bays, he could see the back of an older-model blue Pontiac.

When he had visited yesterday, there had been a much older model Pontiac there as well. The missing car most likely belonged to Augusta.

Picking up the empty red canister on the seat beside him, he got out, went up the steps, and rang the doorbell. When there was no answer, he knocked, then knocked again. Reasoning told him they could be out together, but that didn't stop him from stepping off the porch and going around the side of the house. In the back he saw more trees, and underneath one, a yellow legal pad in her lap, was Andrea.

He was unaware of the tension leaving his body. Today, in deference to the twenty-five-degree drop in temperature, she wore faded jeans, a bulky red sweater, and sneakers. A bright purple wool scarf lay beside her. Wind playfully tossed her hair. She looked serene and breathtakingly beautiful.

He was almost to her when she glanced up. Surprise widened her eyes; she scrambled to her feet.

"Nicholas."

"Andrea." Now that he had found her, he had no idea what he wanted to say. He finally admitted to himself he'd been searching for her. Why, he wasn't sure. He handed her the tin. "I ate every crumb." Bending, he picked up the discarded scarf and looped it around her neck. "It's chilly today."

She stared into his warm eyes, inhaled his spicy cologne, and wanted to go in search of the elusive fragrance, just as Melissa had done with Braxton in her novel. She moistened her dry lips. "I guess I was busy and didn't notice."

He frowned. "You're so delicate. You have to be careful that you don't get sick."

She grinned. She had a black belt in karate. Another thing she and Melissa shared. "I'm tougher than I look. Country girls have to be."

"I suppose." Finally releasing the scarf, he glanced around the well-tended yard. "My mother would love it here. Dad's due to retire from the accounting firm he works for in a few years, and when he does, she wants to move out of Philadelphia to a little town where the pace is slower, but close enough to visit me and my brother and her future grandchildren," he finished with a derisive twist of his mouth.

"Is that where you're from?" she asked. He'd have beautiful children.

"No. I was born in Flint, Michigan, and lived all over the country while Dad climbed the corporate ladder. He transferred to Philadelphia from Akron when I was a freshman in high school." He chuckled. "Mom told him point-blank once we were settled that if he moved again before he retired, he'd go without us."

"Four generations of Radfords have lived here. My great-great-grandfather was the town's blacksmith and built the original house," Andrea said with pride. "Each generation has worked to improve the place without changing its personality." She laughed. "I still have the claw-foot tub in my bathroom my grandmother ordered from the Sears and Roebuck catalog."

Nicholas's black eyes narrowed; then his gaze traveled leisurely over her body. "I'd like to see that."

Andrea's body went hot. She wasn't sure if he meant the tub or her in it. Self-consciously, she drew the tin and the tablet closer. "I'm sure you wouldn't be interested."

"You'd be surprised in what interests me lately," he said cryptically, then nodded toward the tablet. "Another drawing?"

"No. I'm working on an entirely different project." She wasn't ready to tell him about her book. Most people laughed themselves silly when she mentioned wanting to write a romance novel.

His finger traced the top of the tablet, coming precariously close to the rounded curve of her breast. "Can I take a peek?"

Her heart thudded. There it was again. The double meaning. "No," she said, her voice a wobbly squeak.

"Perhaps some other time." His hand fell, but his eyes watched her with the intensity of a large cat studying his next meal.

Andrea gulped. "You just get off work?"

The seductive laziness vanished. In its place was the same frustration she'd seen when he'd visited yesterday. "Yes."

"Things haven't been going well, have they?"

"It doesn't seem to matter that it's illogical for women to think they can win the wish pot and get me like I'm some toy in a box of Cracker Jacks." He snorted. "I'm running five to one ahead of everything else on the wish list. I can't go anyplace without women looking at me as if I'm the cherry on top of a sundae."

Andrea caught herself before she licked her lips hungrily. Then she shook herself; Nicholas had felt safe coming here. "Auntie's gone to visit a friend, and I was just about to go in and make biscuits for supper. Would you like to join us?"

"I don't want to be any trouble," he told her.

Andrea smiled at the grudging wistfulness in his deep voice. "You won't be. I love to cook and so does Auntie. Come on in." She crossed the backyard and went into the house.

Inside the kitchen, she placed the pad on the counter and washed her hands. "Have a seat or, if you want, you can go to the living room and watch TV." She dried her hands on paper towels and turned on the oven. "It's a black-and-white, I'm afraid. Neither of us watches much television."

Folding his arms, Nicholas leaned against the counter next to her. "How do you spend your spare time?"

"We both like to read. At night, Auntie knits and I do the

less meticulous sketch work." Taking a bowl from beneath the counter, she mixed the ingredients for the bread.

"What do you read?" he asked, watching her quick, easy motions.

She cut him a sharp glance, transferred the dough to a lightly floured surface, then picked up a rolling pin. "Fiction."

"What kind of fiction?" he asked when she didn't elaborate.

Picking up the round pan of biscuits, she put them in the oven and faced him. "Romance."

Nicholas came out of his slouched position. He almost took a running step toward the door until he remembered the little girl who hadn't made a wish since she was nine, and why. Girls dreamed and wished for their Prince Charming just like the young woman he'd seen in Andrea's sketches. What must it be like for her to see other women's wishes come true, but not her own?

"If I could give you my wish, I would. I'd wish that you'd find a man to love you as much as you'd love him. As much as you deserved to be loved." The words just slipped out. No one could have been more surprised than Nicholas. After the fiasco with his last wish, he thought he'd completely removed that word from his vocabulary.

He swept a hand over his face. Maybe he should give more thought to ordering the MRI machine. He could be the first to have his brain scanned.

Andrea's face softened. "Thank you."

"For what? I don't believe in your aunt's power."

"I know. That's why I thanked you, because you wished from your heart."

The way she was looking at him did strange things to his

body. Mercy, she was gorgeous. Delicate and beautifully proportioned. He'd have to be careful of her when they made love for the first time.

His mouth dropped open.

"Nicholas, what's the matter?"

Clamping his mouth shut, he swallowed. He scoured his face again. He was definitely losing it. The one woman in town who wasn't coming on to him, and he wanted her more than he'd ever thought possible to want a woman. "I-I just remembered I have an appointment. I'd better go."

"Wait!" she called as he started toward the door. "I'll fix you a plate."

He was already shaking his head. "That's not necessary."

Andrea wasn't listening. She quickly put smothered steak and rice into a microwavable container. "Here."

Nicholas's unsteady hands clamped around the container. She was treating him like his mother did, and he wanted to pull her into his arms and make love to her until he had just enough energy to breathe . . . maybe not even then.

He swallowed again. "Thank you."

"You're welcome. Once you finish with your appointment, you can stop back by for biscuits."

Nodding, Nicholas tore his gaze away from her mouth and hurried to the door. If he came back, it wouldn't be for biscuits.

Tuesday evening, the women in the Beauty Boutique cheered and applauded Augusta as she entered the salon with Andrea. A week had passed since Augusta had granted Nicholas

Darling his wish. Women whistled, stomped their feet, and waved their hands. Augusta took it all in stride, nodding to the women as she made her way to a padded green chair in the small reception area.

Andrea glanced around at the cheering women and felt sorry all over again for Nicholas. Perhaps if he wasn't handsome enough to make a woman lick her lips, he wouldn't have half the single women in town after him.

"Mrs. Augusta, you sure have livened things up," Glenda Hobbs, the owner of the shop, said. She removed the cape from around the neck of a customer she'd just given a finger wave and gave it a brisk snap with her wrist. "I'm ready for you."

"Thank you, Glenda." Augusta took her seat in the stylist's chair, her black patent leather purse dangling from the crook of her arm. She placed her purse in her lap as Glenda whipped the cape around her neck with a flourish.

"Yeah, Mrs. Augusta," Hazel, the beautician at the next station, said. "I saw him yesterday at the post office. He's one fine-looking man."

"I wouldn't mind finding him under my tree Christmas morning wearing a big red bow," Rebecca, getting her waist-length braids redone, commented with a wide grin.

"Why waste the bow, since you'd rip it off?" joked Glenda. "I know I would."

The women howled with laughter. Glenda, robust, with dyed blond hair, had been married three times and made it no secret she was looking for number four.

Andrea smiled, remembering her similar thought about a man for Christmas, and wondered if she'd be bold enough to rip the bow off. If the man was Nicholas, it would be gone in seconds. The smile faded. Nicholas was not for her. Why did she keep forgetting?

"Come on, Mrs. Augusta. Let's go to the shampoo bowl," Glenda said as she helped Augusta to the floor. "I don't suppose you know who the woman is?"

Hair dryers clicked off; scissors and curlers halted. Breaths were held. Ears strained to listen. Eyes locked on Augusta.

Augusta kept them waiting until her head was over the shampoo bowl. "She's one of our own."

An excited buzz raced through the shop.

"I think the hospital should open the wish list to the whole town," Glenda suggested, squirting shampoo into her hand. "Give some of the rest of us a chance to win that pot. I can think of ten ways to use that money right off the bat to get his attention and him."

This time the excitement rose higher as women listed ways they'd use the money to entice and lure Nicholas. *Poor Nicholas*, Andrea thought. It would be all over the town by tonight. Gossip from the beauty shop traveled faster than the speed of light. "Auntie, I have an errand to run. I'll be back in an hour."

Eyes closed as Glenda worked up a lather in her thick gray hair, Augusta answered, "I'll be fine. Take your time."

Andrea headed for the door. By the time she reached her car, she had her keys out. Six minutes later, she was parked at Memorial Hospital. Another three and she stood in front of Michelle's desk. They'd gone to elementary and high school together. "Hi, Michelle. Is Nicholas in?"

"Hi, Andrea," Michelle greeted her, then frowned and glanced toward the closed door behind her. "He's in, but he asked that he not be disturbed. I guess you know why."

Andrea's fingers tightened on her bag. *And it's about to get worse.* "This is important. Please ask him if I can have a few minutes of his time."

"Well, since you're Mrs. Augusta's niece, he probably won't mind." Leaning over, Michelle pressed the intercom. "Nicholas, Andrea Strickland is here to see you. She says it's important."

"Send her in."

Swallowing nervously, Andrea opened the door. Nicholas was already striding across his office toward her. The sight of him caused her heart to pound, her pulse to leap. She'd almost forgotten how handsome he was.

He frowned. "What is it? What happened?"

Andrea moistened her dry lips. "I don't know how to tell you this except to just say it. Auntie just told the women in the beauty shop that the wish woman is one of the town's own. In a couple of hours it will be all over town. While it will stop the women from surrounding towns who may have heard about the wish by working in the hospital or through gossip, those from Jubilee will be even more enthusiastic about the wish."

For a long moment he simply stared at her. "Do you know how difficult these last days have been for me?"

Andrea heard the underlying frustration in his voice and reached out to touch his arm. A little jolt raced from the tips of her fingers back up her arm. She quickly withdrew her hand, but not before she felt the muscled hardness beneath the fine woolen suit coat. "It's difficult now, but it will work out."

"In the meantime, what am I supposed to do?" he asked, gesturing toward his desk. "I can't get a thing done. The hospital board hired me to get Memorial out of the red, to make it profitable and efficient. I can't do that now with these women showing up every place I go."

She'd already guessed he was conscientious. He took his responsibility to the hospital seriously. He didn't like not being able to do the job he'd been hired for . . . or being on display. Everywhere she'd gone for the past few days, his name had been mentioned. Successful, intelligent, and handsome—what woman wouldn't want him? "I'm sorry, Nicholas."

Nicholas saw the distress in her eyes, and his irritation evaporated. She had such a capacity for empathy. Her eyes were clear of guile and deceit. She'd want him for himself, not because of some wish. The thought brought him up short. He stepped back. "Is there a problem?"

His pager vibrated, saving him. Pulling it from his belt, he threw it a sharp glance, scowled, then deleted the number. "I've changed numbers twice and they continue to find me."

A knock sounded on the door, then Michelle stuck her head inside, a worried frown on her face. "I think you'd better take this call. It's Kay Smith, a reporter from the local newspaper."

"What does she want?" Nicholas asked.

Michelle glanced from Andrea to Nicholas. "She's heard about the wish and she wants to do a story."

He scowled. "Tell her I'm not in."

"I'll tell her, but it won't stop Kay." The door closed.

Nicholas shoved both hands over his hair. "This has got to stop."

"It will. Unfortunately, the women have tied the wish pot and your wish together. But once . . . once you find her, the other women will realize they don't have a chance and they'll leave you alone," Andrea said, experiencing a pang of remorse that it wouldn't be her.

"What?" His hands lowered.

Happy that she could finally help, Andrea continued. "Everyone knows it's just a matter of time before you find the woman you wished for. Once you find her, the other women will bow out."

"You mean a woman got me into this mess and a woman can get me out?" he asked.

She shifted uncomfortably. "I wouldn't have put it that way, but essentially what you said is true."

A wide grin split his face. "If that's all it takes, I've already found her."

Misery swept through her. "Who is she?"

"You."

CHAPTER 4

W hat!"

"You said you'd help me. This is your chance," Nicholas rushed to say. "If people believe you're the woman I wished for, they'll leave me alone and I can get back to running the hospital."

Andrea looked at the excitement on his face and wanted to kick him on the shin for making her foolishly hope he felt anything for her, and at the same time wanting to join him in his happiness. "This wasn't exactly what I had in mind, Nicholas."

He stepped closer. "Please. You have to help me. You're the only woman I can turn to."

Andrea gazed into his dark eyes and gorgeous face and felt herself weakening. "I don't like the idea of fooling people."

"Please," he repeated, an engaging smile on his face. "You're my only hope."

She shook her head. Nicholas wasn't for her. "Family members have always been excluded from Auntie's wishes."

His hands gently circled her upper arms. "The townspeople don't know that, do they?"

"I-I don't think so." It should be against the law for a man to touch a woman and fry every circuit in her brain. Why wasn't she telling him no?

"Then this will work." He grinned like a little boy on Christmas morning who'd had every wish granted.

"What about the woman you wished for?" she asked weakly.

He tsked. "If there is such a woman and we're fated to be together, it won't matter what you and I do. This wish woman and I will see each other and no power on earth will be able to keep us apart."

Andrea's spirit sank. Nicholas was joking, but that's exactly how it would be. "I believe in my aunt's gift."

"Then prove it," he challenged. "Go out with me."

"Out?"

"If, as you say, this wish woman and I are destined to be together, you and I going out won't matter, and it would get all these women out of my face," he said, obviously warming to his plan. "You aren't seeing anyone, are you?"

"It would certainly put a cramp in your plan, wouldn't it?" she evaded. It wasn't fair that he could turn her into mush when he'd never be hers.

His dark eyes narrowed, the look in them hard. "Are you?"

She allowed herself all of two seconds to think that was possessiveness she saw in Nicholas's eyes and not simply irritation because a man in her life would interfere with his plans. "No. I'm not seeing anyone."

His fingers flexed. "Good." Releasing her, he stepped back and slipped his hands into the pockets of his dress slacks. "What are you doing tonight?"

"I thought I'd work on my special project," she said slowly.

How ironic; she had reached the part in her book where Melissa had to rescue Braxton.

"Could you spare a couple of hours? The president of the hospital board is having a small get-together at his house. I'd like to take you."

"You certainly aren't wasting any time putting your plan into action, are you?" she asked, the hurt she'd tried to keep from feeling surfacing.

His hands whipped out of his pockets. "I don't use people, Andrea."

"But you're not above using a situation to your advantage."

"No, I'm not. But if this is going to make us enemies, let's forget it." He strode behind his desk and picked up a folder.

His cavalier dismissal infuriated her. "I suppose now you'll find another woman to take my place." She tried to be blasé, but her hands shook.

Slowly his head lifted until their gazes locked. "I don't think that's possible."

The deep timbre of his voice caused her insides to shiver. Her problem, not his. She had promised to help. It wasn't his fault that he was the first man who'd interested her in a very long time. "What shall I wear and when should I expect you?"

He arched a dark brow. "Just like that?"

She shrugged carelessly. "I did say I'd help."

"And we'll still be friends?"

"And we'll still be friends," she repeated. Friendship was better than nothing, and she'd get over whatever this was in fifty or sixty years.

Pulling out the leather chair, he finally took his seat. "Dressy, and I'll pick you up at seven thirty."

"I'll be ready. See you then." Hefting the strap of her bag over her shoulder, she went to the door.

"Andrea?"

She glanced around. "Yes?"

"There's something you should be aware of."

"What?" *Please don't tell me you have a woman in Philadelphia.*

"If I did believe in wishes, you would be the woman I would have wished for."

Andrea felt the heat and desire in his gaze, felt the softening of her own body in response, felt her regret. "She's out there, Nicholas."

"There is no wish woman," he said stubbornly.

Arguing would settle nothing. Time would prove him wrong. "I'll see you tonight." Opening the door, she said good-bye to Michelle and went to her car.

Andrea had no intention of keeping her date with Nicholas a secret from her aunt. They had always been honest with each other. The instant they returned home from the beauty shop Andrea told her aunt that she was going out with Nicholas and why.

Augusta's fragile hands palmed her niece's cheeks. "What will be will be."

"He doesn't think so," Andrea said.

"He will. In the meantime, we'd better find you a dress to wear." Augusta took her niece's arm and steered her into her bedroom. "It's not ladylike to keep a gentleman waiting too long."

"It's not like it's a real date," Andrea said, sorrow creeping into her voice.

Augusta paused in front of the door to Andrea's closet. "It's always important to look your best." Reaching inside, she pulled out an indigo light wool sheath with long sleeves. "You always look lovely in this."

"You aren't going to let me mope and worry about this, are you?" Andrea said, taking the dress from her aunt.

"Each breath we take puts us that much closer to our reckoning day. Wasting life is stupid. You've never been stupid."

Practical and straightforward, Augusta Venora Evans never minced words. Andrea hugged her aunt, who was two inches shorter and fifteen pounds lighter. "I love you."

"Enjoy life. Don't take a backseat." Patting her niece's arm, Augusta left the room.

Holding the dress to her, Andrea gazed into the mirror. "Auntie's right. You aren't stupid. So why can't you stop thinking about Nicholas?" There was no answer, only the slow beating of her heart.

Nicholas had gone on his first date at the precocious age of eleven. His parents had taken him and his girlfriend to a Saturday movie matinee, then picked them up and taken her home. Nicholas remembered handling the entire affair like a pro. Tonight, as he walked onto Andrea's porch and rang the bell, he was caught between anticipation and annoyance.

He hadn't been able to get out of his mind what he'd said to her about her being the woman he would have wished for. While he'd spoken the truth, the reason behind why he'd said it bothered him.

He simply had been unable to let her leave his office thinking he was callous or that she didn't matter. This tendency to want to protect a woman from the slightest hurt was a new experience for him. Ever since he'd made that foolish wish, he'd lost control of his life. But after tonight, he'd have it under control again.

The door opened, and he realized he was wrong.

Andrea stood in the doorway, the light from the chandelier in the hallway framing her. She was exquisite. The dress skimmed over her to reveal the sensuous curves of her body. He wanted to grab her and gobble her up. He wanted to savor her inch by luscious inch.

"Good evening, Nicholas. Come in. I'll get my shawl."

"Good evening, Andrea," he managed, stepping inside, then following her into the living room. Augusta sat in an old-fashioned rocking chair, knitting a red scarf. A colorful basket of yarn sat by her feet. Gold-framed eyeglasses were perched on her nose. "Good evening, Mrs. Augusta."

"Good evening, Mr. Darling." Metal clicked as she continued to rock and knit.

"Please call me Nicholas," he said, wondering when his annoyance at her had left.

She sent him a smile. "I'd be honored."

Picking up her black cashmere shawl, Andrea leaned down and kissed Augusta's thin cheek. "We shouldn't be too late."

"I'll be fine," Augusta said. "Drive carefully, Nicholas."

"Yes, ma'am." Taking the shawl from Andrea's hands, he draped the soft material around her shoulders. "The temperature's dropped again."

"Thank you." She smiled up at him over her shoulder, her warm breath caressing his lips.

Every nerve in Nicholas's body went on full alert. He hoped Augusta was paying close attention to her knitting and not to him. He cleared his throat and placed a white card near the telephone on the end table. "The name and phone number of where we're going is on the back of my business card, if you should need to contact Andrea."

The needles and chair stopped. "Thank you, Nicholas. That's very thoughtful of you."

For some reason he felt like shuffling his feet. "I should have her back by eleven."

Augusta set the chair in motion once again. "I won't worry, since she's with you."

It occurred to Nicholas as he escorted Andrea to his car that Augusta trusted him with Andrea because she, like Andrea, was under the misguided belief that his wish woman was out there and that he was a gentleman. That was a gross miscalculation on both their parts. He went after what he wanted. Always had. Always would.

Try as he might to control it, he wanted Andrea, not some mythical woman. And the need grew stronger each time he saw her.

Cars were lined up on both sides of the street where Bob Hawkins and his wife, Beverly, lived. The stately neighborhood of two-story homes had long been the enclave of the wealthy and elite of the city. Bob Hawkins, as president of the largest of the three banks in Jubilee, was both. His appointment as president of Memorial Hospital's board only served to elevate his stature.

Nicholas helped Andrea out of his car, his mouth tight. "I've been in Texas four months and I know size is relative, but it's stretching it to call this a small gathering."

"Thanksgiving is only a couple of days away; maybe there's another party," Andrea said hopefully.

"Somehow, I doubt it."

When the maid let them inside the entryway, with its twenty-five-foot ceiling and double crystal chandelier, Andrea saw that Nicholas was right. The "small" get-together of the six other board members, their spouses, and a few others had expanded to over thirty people. Most of them were women.

Their eagle eyes centered on Nicholas the instant they entered the spacious den, then jerked to Andrea. Clearly, they were trying to determine if she might be an obstacle in their path to Nicholas.

Unconsciously, she stepped closer to Nicholas. Almost simultaneously, he moved closer to her.

The dual stimulus of his warmth and the hardness of his body aligned with hers drew her gaze to his face. His black eyes burned into her as much as his possessive hand on her waist. Time stood still. The other people in the room vanished. His eyes drifted to her lips. Her stomach muscles tightened. She had the overpowering impression that he wanted to kiss her. Her lips parted.

"Hello, Nicholas, Andrea," Beverly Hawkins greeted them, holding out her hand and breaking the spell that had held them. Diamonds and sapphires glittered. "There're going to be some very disappointed women when this gets out."

Bob Hawkins, likable and robust, sent his wife of thirty years a stern look. "I told you not to let all those women talk you into letting them come over. Perhaps now you'll listen when I tell you not to interfere."

"That will be the day," she said with a laugh, then hooked her arms through Nicholas's and Andrea's. "Let me introduce you to the other people you may not know. Andrea, be thankful you're Mrs. Augusta's niece or you'd have to watch your back. If Dianna wasn't engaged, I might be a little upset myself."

"Beverly!" Bob said through gritted teeth, then shook his balding head. "But I must admit that I'm glad it's over and you can concentrate on Memorial. We want Memorial financially sound."

"It will be, Bob. Count on it," Nicholas said, not a trace of doubt in his voice.

"Excellent. Business comes first." Nodding, Bob walked off.

Beverly harrumphed. "Good thing Dianna takes after me, or she'd be snuggled up to a calculator for the rest of her life instead of a man."

Andrea smiled. She was used to Beverly's frankness. "Your daughter is a beautiful, intelligent young woman. You must be so excited that she's graduating from Cornell next year."

"Yes, we are." Beverly beamed with pride. "I'll never be able to thank you enough for helping her when she first went to college in New York. She was so homesick."

"It was my pleasure," Andrea said, fondly remembering the shy young woman who was nothing like her gregarious mother. "I met her fiancé when I was in New York. I like him very much."

"Me, too," Beverly said, her eyes twinkling. "They haven't set a date yet, but we're already looking at wedding gowns. If you'd like the names of the shops, I'd be happy to give you a list."

Andrea didn't have to see Nicholas's face to know he probably wore a stunned expression. "Thank you. I'll let you know."

"Please do," Beverly said, then proceeded to introduce Nicholas and Andrea around the room.

Andrea already knew some of the other guests, or they knew of her through her aunt. She'd never had any difficulty meeting people, and she didn't tonight. She wouldn't have lasted a week in New York if she had. Beverly's daughter almost hadn't made it. But with all her timidness, she had managed to find a man to love, a man who would love her back.

Andrea was still looking.

With Nicholas by her side and Beverly's obvious approval, most of the guests responded warmly to Andrea. If the single women were less than enthusiastic to see her, she readily understood. She wasn't quite sure how she'd respond when the woman Nicholas was fated to marry showed up.

For only the second time in her life Andrea toyed with the idea of making a wish, a wish to hold back time. But she realized that the wish would be as futile as that first wish she'd asked for when she was nine.

She'd lost then, and she'd lose this time.

As the evening progressed, Nicholas could see that the plan was working. Andrea had been right. Once women thought he had the woman he'd wished for, they left him alone. In the hour and a half since their arrival, the number of women had thinned out to about ten.

You could actually move around the lavishly decorated gold-and-white living room or sit on one of the overstuffed white sofas, if you were so inclined. For himself, he leaned against the side of the black baby grand, nursing a glass of chardonnay, and watched Andrea.

He'd been doing that a lot tonight. He couldn't help himself. Something about her drew his gaze, again and again. And each time it did, he discovered something he hadn't noticed before. How delicate her hands looked holding the stem of a wineglass, how her soft auburn hair shone in the artificial light, how kissable the smooth column of her neck looked when she laughed.

Desire stirred. He wanted her in his bed. She protected him from other women, but who would protect her from him?

"You lucky dog, I don't blame you for staring. Wish I had seen her first."

Nicholas turned to see Samuel Ferrell, a surgical resident who worked part-time at the hospital. Nicholas didn't even try to suppress the spurt of jealousy. "Not if you want to use your hands to operate again."

Samuel chuckled, then tipped his glass. "Message received and understood, but if this wish thing doesn't work out, surely you won't begrudge me asking her out."

"What makes you think she'd go out with you?" *Arrogant twerp.*

"Women like doctors' bedside manners, if you catch my drift," he said, and strolled off to the buffet table.

Nicholas felt like going after him and pushing his big head in the punch bowl. If he so much as touched Andrea, he'd draw back a nub.

"Nicholas, why are you frowning?"

He looked down at Andrea, saw the concern in her face, tried to relax, and couldn't. "If you're ready, we can leave."

"Of course." She allowed him to lead her through the house to find their host and hostess. After thanking them, they said their good-byes to the other guests and left.

In Nicholas's car, Andrea kept sneaking secretive glances at him as he drove her home. He was angry. She didn't understand why. She'd thought he'd been pleased with the way things had gone. They hadn't had to say a word. People had just assumed they were a couple, that she was the woman he had wished for. They'd soon find out how wrong they were. Her hands clutched her shawl and drew it tighter around her shoulders.

"You're cold? You want me to turn the heat up?"

She shook her head. "No." *That* wasn't what she needed or wanted. She glanced out the window as he turned onto the narrow two-lane road leading to her house. Darkness surrounded them. She'd traveled this road thousands of times, but she'd never felt so alone or so lost.

Nicholas pulled into her driveway and parked. The twin porch lights on either side of the front door gave off a muted glow. Through the curtain in the living room, another light shone. Opening his door, he went around the car and helped her out.

Silently they walked up the porch steps. "Give me your key."

"I can do it," she said, trying and failing to insert the key the first time. Her hand shook so badly, it took three tries before the key slipped in. Twisting the key, she unlocked the door and stepped over the threshold.

When she turned, her gaze went no higher than the middle of his broad, white-shirted chest. "Good night and thank you."

"Aren't you going to look at me?"

It hurt too much. "I'm really tired."

"Regretting your decision already?"

Before Nicholas, she'd never been afraid to face the truth. Her chin jutted. Inch by inch her gaze climbed higher until their eyes met. The light cast his face in shadows. "Perhaps you're the one regretting your decision."

"Never." He brushed his knuckles down her cheek. Andrea was unable to control the tremor that raced through her. "You're cold. Go inside."

She shook her head. "Why were you angry?"

"We can talk about this later."

"I want to talk now."

A deep sigh drifted between them. Removing his jacket, he placed it around her shoulders. It enveloped her just as he wanted to. "You're going to be stubborn, I see."

She said nothing, just continued to stare up at him. He almost smiled. He hadn't noticed the stubborn streak before. But he wasn't about to admit the entire truth. "I'm not sure what's the matter. Maybe it's the holiday blues. I may be thirty-three, but this is the first time I won't spend Thanksgiving with my family. Since Mom and Dad are the oldest children and both their parents are gone, their sisters and brothers all come to our house. Mom and her two sisters are fabulous cooks. We stuff ourselves; then the men settle in for some serious football watching on TV."

"And the women clean up the kitchen, watch the children, admire the new babies, and catch up."

This time, he did smile. In his too-large jacket, she looked like a little girl playing dress-up. "Sounds as if you've been to a few family gatherings yourself."

"When I was younger. It's just the two of us now," she said.

Disquieted, he pulled the lapels of the coat closer together. "That's rough. I come from a big extended family."

"Auntie and I both have a lot of friends here," she told him. "In fact, many of them will probably drop by on Thanksgiving. Why don't you come for breakfast and stay for dinner?"

"I don't want to impose."

"You won't," she told him. "Please come. I'll fix your favorite dessert. What is it?"

You, whipped cream, and cherries. Nicholas blinked. He couldn't believe the thought had just popped into his head like that. He was definitely losing it. "Ah, whatever is fine. You'd better get inside. Good night."

"Wait." Slipping off his jacket, she handed it to him.

"Thanks." Firmly he pushed her inside, then closed the door.

Andrea stared at the door. She just didn't understand Nicholas. Sometimes he looked at her as if he'd like to gobble her up, then other times, like now, as if he couldn't get rid of her fast enough.

Men.

CHAPTER 5

The hospital's grapevine was alive and well.

By eleven the next morning Nicholas was able to move about the hospital without a woman in his path. There was a briskness to his walk that had been lacking. He was finally getting back on schedule and getting some work done. He didn't even hesitate to get on the elevator when he saw three female staff members already inside.

"Hello, Mr. Darling," said a curvy young woman in an abstract-print smock. "I think it's wonderful about you and Andrea. I had a chemistry class with her in high school. Tell her Nancy Logan said hello."

"Good morning. I'll tell her," Nicholas said, mulling over the fact that Nancy was the fifth woman to ask him to tell Andrea hello. He had no idea that many people in the hospital knew her.

"She was three years behind me," commented a lanky orderly, his hand wrapped around an IV pole. "I remember she was cute and kind of scrawny. Saw her the other day. She's filled out some since then."

"That's an understatement. She's gorgeous."

Nicholas turned to see who had spoken. Samuel Ferrell grinned back at him. *Impertinent twerp.* "A wise man doesn't need to be told the same thing twice."

The grin slid from Ferrell's thin face. The silence was so thick in the elevator, you could slice it. The doors slid open and no one moved as the two men stared at each other.

"I believe this is your floor, Mr. Darling," Nancy said, holding the door open for him.

"Thank you." This time Nicholas didn't have to worry about giggles as he exited, but there wasn't a shred of doubt in his mind that the story of his confrontation with Ferrell would be all over the hospital by the end of the day.

It took less than an hour.

Women thought it was romantic. Men thought it was manly. Nicholas just wondered why hadn't he kept his big mouth shut. Especially when he received a call from Beverly Hawkins, who told him point-blank not to worry about Ferrell. Andrea, in Beverly's opinion, was too intelligent to fall for Ferrell when she had Nicholas. She was just as down-to-earth and charming as the day she had left for New York six years ago.

Nicholas was trying to think of a polite way to end the conversation when Beverly dropped a bomb. "I guess now she'll forget about going back to New York and stay here."

"Andrea can work anywhere," he said, repeating what she'd told him and fighting the sudden unease he felt.

"Isn't that just like a man, to think his career is more important than a woman's?" Beverly scolded. "In New York she could make more contacts. In this day and age, women can have both a career and a marriage."

The word *marriage* was like a bucket of cold water over

him. But if he corrected her, the madness would start all over again.

"Well, I have to run. I'll see you at the hospital party on the twenty-fourth. Guess your ranking on the wish list has dropped since Andrea has grabbed you." Soft laughter echoed over the phone. "A parting word of advice on Andrea's engagement ring: Nothing warms a woman's heart like diamonds. Big ones."

With Beverly's last words ringing in his ears, Nicholas hung up the phone. He hadn't thought past getting women off his case. They expected him and Andrea to become engaged. When that didn't happen, where would that leave Andrea? An unpleasant picture of Samuel Ferrell popped into his mind.

Coming to his feet, Nicholas left his office. "I'm going out for lunch."

"You have an appointment in thirty minutes with Mrs. Ratcliffe, the head of food services," Michelle told him.

"Let her know I may be late and see if she wants to wait or reschedule," he said, never breaking his stride.

"But you're booked up through the end of the day," she protested.

"Then tell them all the same thing." Opening the door, he left.

It took Nicholas exactly nine minutes to reach Andrea's house. His frame of mind worsened with each second that ticked by. Seeing both cars in the garage, he took a chance that Andrea might be in back and went around the side of the house. His gaze immediately found her.

She was bent over a legal pad, sitting beneath the same giant maple tree she'd been under last week. Today her bulky sweater matched the purple wool scarf beside her. He'd bet anything Augusta had knitted both.

This time Andrea saw him well before he reached her. Her eyes widened. She placed the pad on the grass beside her.

He crouched in front of her, their knees almost touching. "Half the people in the hospital know you. Several asked me to tell you hello."

Not sure if it was an accusation or a statement, Andrea said nothing.

"What's going to happen when there's no wedding?"

That she did have an answer for. "There'll be a wedding; it simply won't be mine."

His eyes narrowed to slits. He obviously hadn't liked that answer. "Do you know a doctor by the name of Samuel Ferrell?"

Andrea frowned, trying to follow Nicholas's train of thought and failing. "Wasn't he at the party last night?"

Nicholas's expression turned cold. "He wants to take you out if we break up."

Since they weren't officially in a relationship, they could hardly break up, but with the fierce way Nicholas was watching her, Andrea didn't think it prudent to remind him of that fact. "What he wants is immaterial to me."

Nicholas wanted to haul her into his arms, taste her mouth, stake his claim. "You might as well know I warned him away from you." He'd never been possessive or jealous or irrational about a woman in his life. "Last night, then this morning in a hospital elevator. It'll probably be all over the town by tonight. It's already spread through the hospital."

She tried not to let it matter that it was all part of his plan. "My hero."

Fierce anger shot through him. "I'm not a hero. I don't want this to hurt you. I know you believe in your aunt, but I don't."

Her eyes filled with unbearable sadness. "You will."

He didn't want to pick a fight with her; he wanted to lay her down in the grass and love her until she cried out in sweet ecstasy. "I'd better get back and let you work on your sketches." He picked up the pad and noticed there was writing, not drawing, on the pages. "What's this?"

Grabbing it out of his hand, she flipped the pages closed. "My special project."

He recalled her mentioning a special project in his office. "What kind of project?"

"I'm writing a novel. A romance novel," she qualified, her chin jutting out defiantly.

He sat there absorbing the information, thinking of the woman who believed wishes weren't granted to her but didn't begrudge those to whom wishes were granted; a woman who sketched happiness for others but not for herself. A woman who dreamed.

His hand grazed her chin. "What's the hero like?"

Her mouth curved upward. "Braxton is an ex-operative. He's intelligent, masterful, and a loner. Fiercely private, he's fighting tooth and nail not to fall in love with Melissa, but he's a goner."

"Can I read it?" He was intensely interested in Andrea's take on love and romance. She deserved so much of both.

Her arms tightened. "Perhaps one day."

He reached out to stroke her hair. He couldn't help himself. If she was within reach, he wanted to touch her. "Does that mean you're sticking around and not going back to New York?"

She didn't bother asking him how he knew. In a small town,

gossip was the main source of entertainment. "I'll go back eventually, but I'm not sure when. Perhaps after the holidays."

The fierce look came back in his eyes. "Why can't you stay here and work?"

"In my business, contacts count. Auntie is on a fixed income. I'm the only one she has to depend on. I have to help," Andrea explained. "I mailed the illustrations Friday for the last book I had a contract for. Publishing houses slow down this time of year, but after the new year, things will pick up and I have to be there."

It made sense, but he didn't have to like it. He wanted her here . . . with him. "What if you sold your book?"

"I could stay here, but editors receive hundreds of submissions," she told him. "It might not sell."

"Do you believe in Braxton and Melissa?" he asked.

"Yes," she answered immediately.

"Then the book will sell." He pushed to his feet. "Don't doubt yourself, Andrea."

"I don't usually."

"Good. Get back to work. I'll see you tomorrow morning."

"Wear clothes you don't mind getting dirty. After dinner we're going in the woods to get the Christmas tree."

"Another tradition?"

"Yes."

He nodded, liking being included. Whistling, he put his hands in his pockets, and strode off.

Andrea leaned back against the tree trunk and watched Nicholas round the corner of the house. She'd have to be careful and not get caught up in the pretense of caring for him. Nicholas could steal a woman's heart.

Flipping the pad open, she began to write. Melissa had just dared Braxton to come skinny-dipping.

Thanksgiving morning, Nicholas drove into Andrea's driveway and a red haze of jealousy came over him. A giant of a man he'd never seen before was swinging Andrea around in his arms. Nicholas came out of his car like a shot. Andrea's squeals of delight propelled him across the yard.

"Put her down!"

The man, three inches taller and forty pounds heavier, stopped and stared down at him. Andrea gazed at him with wide, uncertain eyes. "Nicholas."

"I'm not going to say it again."

Pushing against the man's wide chest, Andrea scrambled out of his arms. "He wasn't hurting me, Nicholas. Travis is a friend of mine. I'm sorry if my silly cries gave you the wrong impression."

The man, who was built like a linebacker, smiled. "I don't think that's the problem."

"Of course it is," Andrea said, staring up at Nicholas.

Nicholas jerked his gaze to Andrea, then shoved his hand over his hair. What was wrong with him? He didn't want any man holding her for any reason. First thing Monday he was putting in the request for the MRI machine.

"Travis Gabriel," the man said, extending his hand. "Andrea and I go back to the third grade. I already know who you are."

The handshake was firm even if the man's lips were twitching. "Hello."

Andrea moistened her lips. "Breakfast is ready. Come on in."

Nicholas took Andrea's arm and started toward the house. He wasn't being possessive. He was being a gentleman.

They were barely on the porch before a black Lexus SUV pulled up and parked behind his car. With a shout of joy, Andrea ran to meet the two men and one woman scrambling out. Travis was two steps ahead of her. They laughed and hugged and jumped up and down like children.

Nicholas wasn't prepared when they all turned to look at him. Only Andrea smiled. He could tell when he was being sized up. He could handle it. There wasn't anything about him that Andrea would have to be ashamed of.

He stepped off the porch and met them on the sidewalk with a friendly smile. Andrea made the introductions of the rest of the Fab Five of Jubilee High School, as she laughingly called them, who now lived all over the country but got together every Thanksgiving as they had since high school. Their parents, who still lived in Jubilee, had come to expect it and, in fact, would drop by themselves later on.

In the kitchen, Andrea's friends greeted Augusta with the same enthusiasm. The oak table had been extended to seat eight. Nicholas made sure he sat next to Andrea. Travis, a college history professor in Atlanta, might be all right; the jury was still out on John Williams, a photojournalist in D.C., and Clint Mack, a headhunter for a large corporation in Miami. The other woman, Elaine Bennett, a vivacious brunette, was a magazine fashion editor in San Francisco.

As soon as they'd finished breakfast and cleaned up the kitchen, they all set out to find a Christmas tree. Once again, Nicholas positioned himself by Andrea's side.

"It's just not right."

"Too skinny."

"Too lopsided."

Andrea's reasons varied as she ruled out tree after tree and tried to find the perfect Christmas tree in the acreage behind her house. The other men groaned, Elaine teased her, but if Andrea wanted the perfect tree, then that was exactly what Nicholas would see that she got. "We'll keep searching," he always said.

Each time, she smiled at him as if he were all that she could hope for in a man. Inexplicably, he wanted to stick out his chest. An hour and a half into their search, they finally found the tree.

"That's it!" Andrea said, staring at the plump, seven-foot fir, shaped like an inverted cone.

"Give me the ax, Travis." Holding out his hand, Nicholas turned to the man standing next to him.

Travis's grip tightened on the wooden handle. "Perhaps you should let me do it."

"Maybe you should," Andrea suggested, worry in her face. "He's done it before."

Nicholas's hand remained extended. "I may not have chopped down a tree, but I've chopped plenty of wood."

Travis handed him the ax and a pair of gloves. After a couple of swings, Nicholas's body remembered the motion; his mind, the technique. Several minutes later the tree toppled, to the delighted laughter of Andrea and the good-natured jibes from Travis that he could have done it faster.

Nicholas didn't care; all he cared about was the pride in Andrea's face. Putting the ax on his shoulder, he caught her hand, leaving the other men to load the tree on the rolling cart they'd brought.

Andrea couldn't get her heart to settle down. Every time Nicholas looked at her it would go out of control. She tried to tell herself he was just playing a part, but her body wasn't listening. This morning he'd been ready to fight Travis to protect her. He'd cut down the Christmas tree for her. He'd chosen her first for his team when they played tag football. It had been her idea to download the digital pictures John took to Nicholas's parents, but he had asked that a picture of *her* be sent to his computer.

It was too romantic. Even if it was pretend, she felt giddy with delight. He was the perfect prince.

"Since Mrs. Augusta has gone to bed, are you going to jump Nick on the couch or by the Christmas tree?" Elaine asked, a wide grin on her beautiful face.

Andrea laughed, but her heart went wild again. She'd walked her friends to the door. Nicholas waited in the living room where they'd put the Christmas tree. "Ladies do not jump men."

Elaine sent Travis a speculative look. "There's always an exception to the rule."

Travis grinned. "A man would count himself lucky if he were that exception."

Andrea didn't know if Travis and Elaine were finally going to act upon the attraction that had always been between them or keep on dancing around it. She loved them both and wanted the best for them.

"Maybe it'll be me," John chimed up.

"Or me," Clint said.

"Or none of you," Elaine said with her usual style. She hugged Andrea. "My plane leaves tomorrow afternoon. I'll call when I get back."

"I thought you'd stay over the weekend," Travis said with a frown.

"Work," she said succinctly. "Good night, Andrea. Get back in there, and for what it's worth, I think you hit pay dirt."

"Thank you." She trusted her friends, but she'd decided not to tell them she and Nicholas were just pretending. She didn't want them to think ill of him.

"I think Nick's a little stiff," John said, then clicked the camera around his neck when Andrea's expression turned mutinous.

She laughed. "If you show that picture to anyone, I'll have your head."

"It would rattle, because nothing is in it." Clint laughed.

"Come on, children," Elaine said, grabbing both men and going down the steps to her parents' car.

Travis stared longingly after her before turning to Andrea. "Be happy, Andrea, and if you ever need a big brother, you know you have three."

Andrea hugged him. "If you ever need someone to talk to about you-know-what, call." She now knew what it was like to care for someone and not be sure how he felt.

"Maybe one day." After another brief hug, he went to his car parked on the other side of Nicholas's and drove off.

Going inside, Andrea cut off the porch lights, took a deep breath, and slowly walked to the living room. At first, she didn't see him. The only light came from the hundreds of twinkling star-shaped lights decorating the tree. Her mother had bought them the year before Andrea was born. "Nicholas?"

He emerged out of the deep shadows near the couch. Andrea felt a chill race through her. For some reason he reminded her again of a large cat stalking his prey. He walked unhurried, his body loose yet poised to act if his intended prey tried to escape. She shivered again. Would she flee or remain?

He didn't stop until only a wisp of air separated them. She sensed his intention, the need pulsing through him. His hand lifted. Her breath caught, held. Then, his fingers traced her lower lip.

Her knees wobbled. "N-Nicholas?"

She swallowed. She couldn't gather her thoughts. His hand moved to her cheek, the curve of her ear.

"I like it." His hand trailed down to the hollow of her throat. "I've wondered what my name would sound like on your lips when need rushes and bums through your blood like sweet fire."

His hand continued down to the rounded curve of her breast. "Tonight I intend to find out. I've thought of little else all afternoon. If you have any objections, you have three seconds to voice them."

Voice. What voice? Her mind was numb, her body trembling with want of him.

"Time's up." His head lowered.

CHAPTER 6

The first brush of his lips shattered her; the second buckled her knees. Automatically her arms lifted, her hands clutching fistfuls of his shirt. His mouth was tender one moment, his tongue boldly erotic the next. He wasn't asking permission now; he was taking what he wanted.

Andrea pressed her body against his, heard him groan. Fierce pleasure swept through her that she could affect him this way.

Then as if part of him recognized that she wasn't going to flee, that she burned with the same wild desire that possessed him, his hold gentled; his mouth sipped, teased, tantalized, rewarded.

"Nicholas."

Her ragged whimper sank into him. This was what he wanted. He wanted to fill her thoughts as much as he wanted to fill her body. Her small hands now clung around his neck; her body eagerly, if inexpertly, tried to match the erotic rhythm of his hips.

Her eagerness, her inexperience, her trust in him did what

he hadn't expected. Tearing his mouth away, he held her fiercely against him. He couldn't take from her with no thought of the consequences. He held her until their breathing settled.

Sensing she wasn't going to be the first to speak, he tipped her face up. "I want you more than I've ever wanted any other woman."

She bit her lip. "I-I shouldn't have let you kiss me."

Nicholas didn't bother answering such a useless statement; he just took her mouth again, letting the truth sink in that her body hungered for his as much as his hungered for hers. A vague memory of his wishing something like that for her stirred on the fringes of his mind, but the sweet lure of her mouth was too strong.

A long time later, he ended the kiss and pulled her securely against him. The top of her head barely came to the middle of his chest. He felt both protective and powerful with her in his arms. "How about a movie tomorrow night?"

"I'm not sure it's wise to keep seeing each other."

He could argue, but he'd always found reasoning worked better with intelligent people. "There's no reason we can't continue to see each other. We haven't done anything to be ashamed of. People do more on first dates."

"I don't."

He'd already figured as much. "Everyone will be suspicious if we aren't affectionate. We're just getting used to each other."

She was silent so long he began to worry. His father always said if a woman was silent, a man was in trouble. He thought fast. "How's the writing coming with Braxton and Melissa?"

Her head lifted, surprise shining in her dark eyes. "You remembered their names?"

He started to kiss her nose, then thought better of it. "Of course I did," he said, then went on to tell her exactly what she'd told him about the hero and heroine of the book she was writing.

"They're at an impasse. Melissa had to put herself in danger to rescue him, and Braxton didn't like it. They're out of immediate danger, but they aren't speaking to each other."

Nicholas was determined not to end up like Braxton. "He's only angry because she put herself in danger for his sake."

"She knows that, but she doesn't like his macho double standard. If the situations had been reversed, he would have rescued her."

"That's the way it's supposed to be," Nicholas said emphatically.

"Men," Andrea said, and it wasn't a compliment.

Laughing, he stepped back before he kissed her again. "Now I'll have to read the book to see how he gets back in her good graces. In the meantime, I'd better go." He picked up his jacket from the arm of the green velvet sofa, then went to the front door and opened it. "What time should I pick you up for the movie?"

She glanced away. "Maybe I should stay home and work on my book."

"It'll be fun, and I promise to be on my best behavior," he cajoled. She was not getting away. There was no wish woman. He raised the ante. "You did promise to help."

Her head lifted, but she crossed her arms defensively over her chest. "I'll check the newspaper and call you."

"I'll expect to hear from you, then. Good night." He gave her a brotherly peck on the cheek, then strolled to his car, whistling.

A ndrea was trapped between wanting to keep her word and wanting a man who would never be hers. More than once she'd caught Aunt Augusta looking at her strangely. She didn't blame her aunt. Andrea had left out the soda in the biscuits, broken a glass doing the breakfast dishes, turned on the washing machine without adding detergent.

"You troubled, child?" her aunt finally asked when they were making the grocery list.

Andrea's hand clenched on the yellow ceramic top of the mushroom canister containing sugar. "A little, I guess."

Out of the corner of her eye, she saw Aunt Augusta nod her gray head. "You were always sweet and caring. Worried about everyone before yourself. That's why you attract people. When you were in high school this house was always full of your friends. They sense you're for real."

Not daring to face her aunt, Andrea checked the next canister and scribbled "flour" on the growing list. "You always see and think the best in me."

"And I'm right," Augusta said. "I think you forget that you deserve happiness just as much as the next person."

Finally, Andrea turned, her expression filled with anguish. "But suppose what I want affects another person's happiness?"

Augusta's gaze was steady. "What will be will be. Neither you nor I can change that no matter how much we might want to. To worry about it is useless. So stop worrying and live life like I've always taught you." She opened the refrigerator. "Add eggs, milk, butter, sour cream, whipped cream. We're outta so much, and the stores are probably picked bare from Thanksgiving. You want to go shopping this afternoon or wait until in the morning?"

"In the morning. Nicholas and I are going to the movies this afternoon. The feature starts at five-thirty," she said, trying to keep her voice light.

"Mighty early to go to a movie," Augusta said, rummaging in the refrigerator.

"I want to get back and work on *A Risk Worth Taking*." And it would be light enough when they returned so Nicholas wouldn't attempt to kiss her good night.

Augusta closed the refrigerator door. "Always liked that title. Says a lot about life and those two in your book. They're lucky that they've found someone worth risking their hearts for. Some people go through life and never do. My prayer is that you'll be brave enough to risk it all, that you'll dare to grab your dream."

"It may not be possible," Andrea whispered.

"You'll never know until you try."

All through the romantic comedy at the only movie theater in Jubilee, her aunt's words kept running through Andrea's head. Her aunt loved her. She wouldn't want her to fall in love with a man who could never be hers, but that was exactly what Andrea was doing, tumbling and falling deeper with every second that ticked by.

There was no stopping her fall, just as there was no way to alter what was to be. Could she be as brave as Melissa, to risk it all for love? But whereas Melissa would have a lifetime with Braxton, Andrea would have a few brief weeks, if that.

She couldn't very well depend on Nicholas to stop trying to entice her. Clearly, he was a man who went after what he wanted, and since he didn't believe in her aunt's prophecy, he felt no compunction in tempting Andrea every time the opportunity presented itself. It was up to her to keep their relationship platonic. But how could she do that when she wanted to gobble him up like a chocolate bar?

"Hungry?"

Startled, Andrea turned to Nicholas in the seat beside her. He wore a lazy grin that made her want to lick her lips, then lick him. "W-what?"

"I know the plot is predictable, the actors wooden, but you're not even looking at the screen, so I thought you might want to leave and go get something to eat," Nicholas explained.

"You'd have to be looking at me to know that," she told him.

He grinned. "Guilty."

She couldn't help the smile that formed on her face. "You're incorrigible."

"My mother would call you a smart woman."

Her smile never wavered. She'd never meet his mother. "Did they like the pictures John sent?"

"*Shhhh.*"

"Sorry," they both whispered. The holiday season, combined with all the schools being out, meant the theater was crowded.

"Let's get out of here," he whispered. Her hand in his, they went into the lobby, then burst into laughter.

A man who made her laugh couldn't be that bad for her. And she'd never been a coward. Suddenly she was ravenous. "I'd like a box of popcorn, a hot dog, and a Pepsi, please."

He steered her to the counter. "I thought I'd get out of this with just the movie."

"Not a chance." She bit into the hot dog as soon as she squirted it with mustard and sweet relish. "Delicious. Want some?"

His eyes on her, he bit into the wiener and bun. "You're right. Delicious."

She remembered him tasting her, her tasting him. Her hands trembled a bit. Her insides were full of butterflies, but she wasn't afraid any longer. As her aunt had always said, what will be will be. "There's a park nearby, if you want to walk there."

"It's cold. We'll drive." Pushing open the glass door of the theater for her, he followed.

"Hot dogs can be messy," she said.

Opening the passenger door of his car, he helped her in, then handed her the box of popcorn he was holding. "So can a head cold."

"Ha. Ha. Very funny."

"I thought so." He closed the door.

By the time he'd gotten inside and started the motor, she'd propped the popcorn between her arm and the seat and placed the Pepsi in the drink holder. "You didn't want anything to eat?"

"I thought we'd share."

The idea pleased her. "The park is two blocks away on the left."

When they arrived at the park, Nicholas insisted they stay in the car. Twisting toward him in the seat, she offered the box of popcorn. "You never answered me about the pictures."

"Mom loved them." He grabbed a handful of the buttered popcorn. "My brother teased me about cutting down the tree for you. He thought I was trying to show off."

Andrea sipped the cola. "Were you?"

He grinned. "What do you think?"

She grinned back. "The tree is beautiful."

"Mom asked about my tree. I told her I hadn't had time to get one." He finished off the hot dog. "I probably won't have one this year."

The straw stopped midway to her mouth. Her eyes rounded. "You have to have a tree."

He shrugged, digging into the popcorn and trying to keep a straight face. Her compassionate heart was leading her exactly where he wanted her: alone with him. "Maybe if I find the time."

"Do you want to look for one on our property or get one from the tree lot?"

There was no reason to be coy. "Tree lot is fine."

She reached for her seat belt. "We'd better go, or all the good ones will be taken."

"Now?"

"Now."

Nicholas soon found out that Andrea was as particular about his tree as she had been about hers. After three tree lots, he was willing to try a fourth until she started making noises about going in search of a tree by herself the next day. He chose the next tree he came to.

"Nicholas, you can't be serious!" Andrea cried. "It's barely three feet and it's lopsided."

"It'll do," he said, picking up the scrawny tree by the crown and carrying it to the cashier. "A few decorations will make all the difference."

"You want it flocked?" the young attendant asked, popping

his gum and nodding his head to the up-tempo beat of "White Christmas." "We got pink, blue, or white."

Andrea shuddered. "It looks pitiful enough."

"We'll pass." Grasping Andrea by the arm, Nicholas went to his car and put the tree in the trunk. Straightening, he saw Andrea, her arms folded. "What?"

"I've been thinking."

The only thing worse than a silent woman, Nicholas's father had said, was a thinking woman. "You have?"

"Your quick decision to buy that tree wouldn't have anything to do with my offering to cut you a tree tomorrow, would it?" she asked silkily.

Nicholas read the writing on the wall. "How long was Braxton in the doghouse for acting macho?"

"Two days."

"Care to tell me how he got out?"

Her composure faltered. Her arms fell to her sides. "Ah, Melissa got tired of his sulkiness and took matters into her own hands."

"What did she do?"

"You'll have to read the book," she said primly.

Nicholas opened the door and she slipped inside. "Just tell me one thing. Did he get over his sulks?"

Andrea smiled impishly. "Oh, yes."

It was close to 10:00 P.M. when Nicholas pulled up in her driveway. "Would you like to come in?" she asked after she'd opened the front door.

"I'd better get the tree home and out of the trunk."

She made a face. "I doubt anything will make it look better, but we have plenty of tree decorations in the attic. You're welcome to come over tomorrow and go through them."

"Thanks, but some of the staff are decorating the children's wing of the hospital and I volunteered," he told her.

Her expressive face saddened. "How terrible for a child to be in the hospital for Christmas."

"Yeah. We've set up a little store for them to purchase gifts for their parents with their smiles, so hopefully that will help."

"What a unique idea. Who thought of it?"

He shuffled his feet. "I guess I did."

She smiled up at him. "The first time I saw you, I knew you were a wonderful man."

His knuckles grazed her cheek. "The first time I saw you, my mind went totally blank."

Her heart drummed in her chest. "It—it did?"

"I thought you were the most stunning woman I'd ever seen. I still do." His hand continued the mesmerizing, body-stirring motion.

"Th-thank you."

His knuckles rimmed her chin. "If you're not busy tomorrow afternoon, we could use all the volunteers we could get."

Andrea tried to gather her thoughts. "I'll be there."

"Maybe you could go through the decorations for me. Then afterward, we could decorate the tree together." He'd traded the tips of his fingers for his knuckles.

"A-all right."

"Great. Good night."

"Good night, Nicholas."

He bounded off the porch and climbed inside his car. Going

inside, she closed the door. He hadn't kissed her. He'd been a perfect gentleman, and if he did the same thing tomorrow, she might be tempted to jump him as Elaine had suggested. Laughing at her own temerity, she checked on her aunt, then went to bed, and dreamed of Nicholas.

CHAPTER 7

The pediatric wing of Memorial Hospital was filled with the happy laughter of children. Every child who could possibly participate in decorating did so. The hallways were turned into varied scenes of the North Pole, from the elves making toys to Santa hitching up his reindeer.

In the atrium stood a twelve-foot Douglas fir. Scattered over the branches were colorful metallic glass ball ornaments, each personalized with the name of a hospitalized child. And to ensure that Santa Claus received their requests on time, a special delivery mailbox, wrapped in red and white satin ribbon, sat nearby for the nightly run to the North Pole.

The adults took as much pleasure in the transformation as the children. Many of the parents had come to visit and stayed to help. It wasn't long before the person—Nicholas Darling—who had initiated the project was singled out and thanked repeatedly. Each time, he'd say it was only his idea, and he couldn't have made it a reality without the generous donations of so many of the volunteers. Andrea watched the scene over and over again and felt her heart swell with pride. Nicholas was a caring, thoughtful man.

"You think he'll give you a ring Christmas Eve, or Christmas morning?"

Andrea turned to see Priscilla Campos, a friend from high school who now was a charge nurse on a surgical floor of the hospital. Three other female employees of the hospital were with her. All waited anxiously for an answer.

Andrea's happiness vanished. There'd be no ring on Christmas Eve or any other day. "I try not to think about it," she answered truthfully.

Priscilla, a leggy brunette, sighed dramatically. "If he were mine, that's all I'd think about."

"That's not all I'd think about," said Voncile Hale, a nurse with the sleek curves of a cover girl. They all howled with laughter.

"You ready to go, Andrea?"

The women's attention centered on Nicholas. He didn't seem to notice. His entire focus was on Andrea. She felt the melting softness, the tingling of her body. Whether it was real or he was pretending, he affected her as no other man ever had. "If you are."

"I'm ready." His hand closed possessively around her waist. Only then did he turn to the other women. "Ladies, thanks again for coming. You made the children very happy."

"We were glad to help," Priscilla said. "This is much better than the usual crummy decorations at the nurses' station. I guess the children were wishing too."

Nicholas's expression didn't change at the mention of the word *wishing*. "Perhaps. Good night."

"Good-bye," they chorused, their expression speaking volumes to Andrea.

Blushing, Andrea said good-bye, then walked with Nicholas to the elevator. He hit the down button.

"You want to grab a bite to eat or tackle the tree first?"

"The tree." Weak as she was, she wanted to know as soon as possible if this time he'd kiss her.

Her palms were damp when she pulled up behind Nicholas's car in his driveway. For the first time, they'd be completely alone. Her aunt had a meeting with the women's auxiliary of the church, then afterward they were having potluck at Auntie's house, so Andrea didn't have to worry about her aunt driving at night or being alone. She'd just have to worry about her feelings for Nicholas. She wanted to be with him, touching, laughing, sharing. She wanted to do all the things people in love did.

While she was still trying to calm her nerves, he got out of his car, then came back and opened her door. "This is it," he said, indicating the ranch-style home in a quiet residential neighborhood. "Are those the decorations in the backseat?"

She wiped her damp palms on her gray wool slacks. "Yes."

He handed her a ring of keys and picked up the box. "I usually go through the garage. You open the back door and I'll follow."

Gripping the keys, Andrea went through the tidy two-car garage and opened the door, then held it for Nicholas. He brushed by her. She closed the door with a hand that wasn't quite steady. When she turned, he was watching her.

"You don't have to be afraid I'll jump you."

She wanted to say something urbane and sophisticated to let him know she was worried that he wouldn't, but the words wouldn't come. "I trust you."

He scowled. "Well, don't. Didn't you learn anything in New York? You're too gorgeous to trust any man."

He'd said it again. He thought she was gorgeous. Her insides went as gooey as cotton candy on a warm summer day.

"If you don't stop looking at me like that, the tree won't get decorated for a long time, if at all," he said, his voice husky.

A delicious little tingle raced over her. "Auntie will probably ask me how it went."

"Thought so." Turning, he went through the kitchen. In the living room, he knelt with the box in front of him, then reached out a hand to Andrea. "Come on and tell me the story behind what you've brought."

Placing her trembling hand in his, she felt the strength and the zip of awareness that leaped from his fingertips to hers. Swallowing, she knelt beside him and reached inside the box. Many of these Christmas decorations dated back over seventy years. Whether store-bought or hand-made, each carried a special story.

Unwrapping the thick tissue paper, she picked up the crystal icicle ornament. A rainbow of colors glinted in her hand. "Grandpa Radford walked five miles through a sudden ice storm to reach his wife. He had a feeling she needed him and he was right. She was in labor with their first child. He delivered the baby boy himself. It was a week before Christmas. He gave his wife the ornament to signify that he'd always be there for her and their children. Each Christmas he added another ornament."

"What about this?" Nicholas asked, unwrapping several miniature figures.

"My great-grandpa Will carved those for his five children because they were too poor to buy real ones."

"I thought he was the town's blacksmith?" Nicholas asked, marveling at the details of the three horses and two dolls. The dolls wore gingham dresses and their feet had been painted black to appear as though they wore boots.

"He was, but the town was poor. They paid with produce or other goods." She picked up the foot-high doll and ran her finger over the face. "The story goes that the children loved these. They could carry their gift wherever they went."

Nicholas couldn't imagine a child today accepting a carving for the real thing. His cousin's children wanted the real thing and lots of it. Each Christmas there was a hot new toy. His thumb grazed over a horse's mane. "Did the children ever get their real horse and dolls?"

Andrea smiled warmly. "They did."

"Good." He picked up the next carefully wrapped bundle. Inside were strands of star-shaped lights. He was momentarily speechless. "These belonged to your mother. She bought them after she and your father wished upon a shooting star for a child. You were that child." He'd never forget the sparkle of tears in Andrea's eyes when she'd unwrapped the lights at her house on Thanksgiving. Travis had whispered the story to him.

There were no tears now, just a sadness about her that tore at his heart. "Mama bought all the store had. She wanted to make sure there would still be lights when I had a child of my own."

A knot formed in his throat. "Honey." Setting the lights out of harm's way, he pulled her to him. "She sounds like a beautiful, caring woman."

"She was. So was Daddy," Andrea said softly. "The first Christmas without them was so painful. I went up into the attic and got the lights. I wished so hard that it was all a mistake. That it was a dream and I'd wake up. Auntie found me there."

His arms tightened around her. "You were so young to have so much taken from you."

She rubbed her cheek against his shirted chest. "But I have wonderful memories no one can ever take away, and I had Auntie and Uncle Richard. He's gone, too, but Auntie and I still laugh over the fish yarns he used to tell us about the one that got away." She laughed. "He once claimed he had to throw a catfish out of his fishing boat because it was so big the boat started sinking."

Nicholas laughed, himself. "Sounds like my dad when he's talking about his golf game."

"Your family sounds nice."

"They'd adore you," he said.

Shadows came over her face again. Pushing away from him, she picked up the lights. "It's getting late; we'd better get the tree finished."

Helpless, Nicholas watched her kneel, then carefully wind the lights around the scrawny branches of the tree. He wanted so much for her to be happy. She deserved no less. It wasn't right that she wasn't. "You're sure you want me to have the lights?"

"They're meant to be enjoyed, and to remind you that wishes do come true," she said softly.

He wanted to argue with her that there was no wish woman out there waiting for him to fall in love with, but Andrea seemed so sad, so vulnerable. She'd had so much taken from her and yet she still went out of her way to help others. It angered him all over again to think that her wishes didn't count. That he didn't believe in wishes didn't seem to matter. Andrea did. "I hope you gave Melissa some of your qualities."

Her hands paused on reaching for the next set of lights. "She is a bit stubborn."

Nicholas shook his head, then began stringing the lights himself. "You're a pushover." He talked over her sputtering. "But you're loving, generous, compassionate, intelligent."

She picked up an icicle. "That's a backhanded compliment if I ever heard one, but Melissa is all that and more."

Nodding briskly, Nicholas spread the red felt skirt that had been a cousin's poodle skirt in the sixties. "You're sure Braxton is the man for her?"

"Unknowingly, Melissa witnessed a hit. Bad guys are coming out of the woodwork, trying to kill her," she told him as she hung icicles. "Braxton is the only man tough enough, smart enough, to ensure that she sees another sunrise. They're both strong and independent. Each can give to the other what they've secretly longed for all their lives."

Nicholas glanced up, about to place the last wooden carving beneath the tree. "What's that?"

"Unconditional love that'll last a lifetime and beyond."

Nicholas studied the assurance in Andrea's face, the absolute conviction, for a long time. Then he placed the wooden doll beside the other carvings. Two weeks ago, he would have laughed at such a statement, but somehow he couldn't with Andrea. "My parents have that kind of love, and so apparently did yours. I'm not sure that it exists anymore. My brother, Ronald, falls in love every other week."

"Perhaps because he hasn't met the right woman or, if he has, he isn't ready to take the next step. Loving a person makes you vulnerable." She began gathering up the tissue paper. "In *A Risk Worth Taking*, the dangers are emotional as well as physical."

"My point exactly. Falling in love is dangerous."

"Living with no hope of love is one of the saddest things I can imagine." She picked up the box and stood before he could help her. "The tree is finished. I have to go. Good night, Nicholas."

Shocked, he scrambled to his feet. "I thought we were going out to dinner?"

"Perhaps some other time." She started from the room.

He caught her arms and saw the pain in her dark eyes and cursed himself. He'd caused that. "You can't leave until you see how the tree looks. Won't Mrs. Augusta ask?"

"All right." Her fingers gripped the corner of the box as she faced the tree.

"Let me take the box, and if the lights need any adjustment, you'd do a better job than I could." He breathed easier as he took the box from her, then set it by the light switch and cut off the light.

He didn't even glance toward the tree. His entire concentration was on Andrea standing in the soft glow of lights that her mother had bought while thinking of her. He went to stand just behind her. "I have a confession to make."

"What?" she said, a whispered strain of sound.

"I got you over here under false pretenses. I fully planned to buy a tree and decorate it. I played on your goodness, but if I'd known it would make you so sad, I wouldn't have done it." His hand rested lightly on her shoulder; he felt the shudder that swept though her. "Please believe me when I tell you that it never entered my mind that you'd bring your mother's lights. Forgive me."

Andrea momentarily closed her eyes, absorbing the heat seeping through her sweater from Nicholas's strong hand, from his powerful body next to hers. "That's not the reason."

He stepped in front of her. "Then what is?"

How could she explain her jumbled feelings when she was still trying to understand them herself? She wanted him to find love, to be happy, but she wanted that woman to be her. But he didn't even believe in love or happily ever after.

"Andrea?" He lifted her chin. "Tell me how I can help."

For the moment there was only one way. "Kiss me."

He took her in his arms, his mouth brushing across hers, letting the heat, the anticipation, the hunger build. When his mouth finally took possession of hers, both were trembling. With a whimper of pure, unadulterated need, Andrea joined in the kiss, experiencing once again the passion that burned fiercely within her for this man.

It was a long time before he ended the kiss and pulled her to him. Their fractured breathing sounded loud in the room. "You'll never know how much I wanted to do that." His mouth brushed against the top of her head. "I wasn't sure how much longer I could keep my hands off you."

She refused to listen to the little voice that warned he'd never be hers. In his arms she could only think of him; out of his arms she only longed to be there once again. "But did you have to choose such a pitiful tree in order to get me over here?"

He gave her another quick kiss, then turned so they both faced the little tree in the bay window. "I kind of like it."

After a moment she said, "Me, too."

He palmed her forehead. "You don't feel like you have a fever," he joked.

She laughed. "I just remembered a cartoon I watched as a child about misfit toys and how nobody wanted them. It made me feel so sad. If you hadn't bought the tree, it might have stayed in the lot. Now, it's almost beautiful with the star-shaped lights sparkling off the glass icicles." And she liked the idea of them sharing the decorations. It made her feel connected to him.

"Will wonders never cease? A woman who admits when she's wrong," Nicholas teased.

"That's because it so seldom happens," she said with a lift of her brow.

He chuckled, hugging her to him. "It's going to be very interesting getting to know you better."

"You can count on it," Andrea said, hugging him back. *What will be will be.* "What should we do next?"

Make love to each other until we're too weak to move.

Before the thought had completely formed, he knew he wouldn't follow through with the rest of his reason for getting her to his house. Not with them standing in the glow of years of family tradition where intimacy meant love and lifelong commitment. Not with Andrea staring up at him with such complete trust.

Anyone could see she longed for the same thing in her own life. He wasn't ready for that type of commitment. He wasn't sure if he'd ever be. She'd been denied too much for him to carelessly take more. He wouldn't take her dream. "Why don't we go outside and see how the tree looks through the window, then go out to dinner?"

"I'd like that."

CHAPTER 8

In the past, Nicholas never had any difficulty remaining focused. Like his father, he was very detail-oriented. At least he had been until he'd met Andrea. In the three weeks since Thanksgiving, they'd seen each other almost every day. He'd catch himself thinking about her instead of working. *Like now.*

Twisting in his seat in his office, Nicholas leaned closer to the computer monitor as if that would help his concentration. He'd been working on a report for three hours, a report that usually took one hour to do. But it was difficult to think about operating costs when he'd much rather be thinking about Andrea or, better yet, being with her. But that was creating its own problem.

He scrubbed his face. He wanted her so badly he ached. He couldn't hide his need from her, and although he knew she wasn't experienced and still thought there was another woman out there for him, she never pulled back. That kind of trust and caring made his body ache and his spirit smile.

He lifted his face to the ceiling. "Spirit smile," he muttered. What kind of thing was that for a man to say? His phone rang and he pounced on it, ready for any distraction. "Yes?"

"Mr. Darling, you're needed on Pedi South," Michelle told him.

Nicholas frowned. "I don't have a meeting, do I?"

"No, but I think you should go up there."

Nicholas transferred the phone to his left hand and began hitting keys with his right. "Michelle, I'm in the middle of the report—"

"Andrea is up there."

He shot up from his chair before he realized that if she'd been hurt, she wouldn't be on the pediatric floor. "Why? What's going on?"

"I guess you won't find out, since you're so busy with the report. Sorry to disturb you."

Nicholas held a dead phone. In a matter of seconds he was standing before Michelle, his hands planted firmly on her desk. "Talk."

"You'll understand when you get there." Michelle placed the calendar she kept for him by his hands. "Your next appointment isn't for another hour."

How much he wanted to go didn't surprise him. But if he saw Andrea, he'd experience the same churning need that kept him awake at night. Andrea or her aunt might be fooled, but not the hospital staff. "I really need to finish that report," he said, with little conviction in his voice.

"Wouldn't you rather see Andrea?" Michelle asked.

He started to ask how she knew Andrea was in the hospital, then recalled that Michelle had an open pipeline to all the gossip in the hospital. Women no longer bothered him, but many of them were acquainted with Andrea. "I'll be on Pedi South if you need me."

All the way to the floor, he kept telling himself that he was simply going to say hello. It would appear strange if he didn't. She was probably reading one of the books she'd illustrated to the children.

With that thought in mind he wasn't surprised when, without asking, he was directed by several staff members to the atrium at the end of the hall. Entering the sunshine-filled room, he immediately spotted Andrea. She didn't have a book; she had a sketch pad.

Sitting in front of the lit Christmas tree was a little girl of about five in a wheelchair. She was precious, with huge chocolate eyes and a smile that was as bright as the sparkling lights behind her. One arm was wrapped securely around a bedraggled doll; the other was connected to an IV. As Andrea's hand moved swiftly across the page, she chatted with the child.

"She came to read, but when one of the nurses mentioned that Andrea drew the pictures in the books, the children wanted their pictures drawn," said Nurse Cipriano from beside Nicholas. "She's been at it for almost three hours. I called Michelle. I thought Andrea should take a break."

"What's wrong with the little girl?"

"Juvenile diabetes," Nurse Cipriano said. "Barnarda is one of the lucky ones. She'll be home for Christmas. But for those who can't leave even on a pass, you've helped. So has Andrea. The children want the sketches to give to their parents."

He watched Andrea leave her chair with the pad, then kneel beside the child to show her the drawing. The child's eyes rounded. With a squeal of delight, she wrapped her free arm around Andrea's neck. Andrea gently hugged her back.

The nurse sniffed. "You've got a good woman there, Mr. Darling."

"I know." He walked over and hunkered down. "Hello, Barnarda, Andrea."

Andrea looked at Nicholas, inches from her, and accepted that he'd always make her heart ache a little bit. "Hello, Nicholas. Barnarda, meet Mr. Darling; he helps run the hospital."

"You want to see my picture?" the little girl asked, already turning it around. "Andrea drew it, just like I asked."

Nicholas looked at the picture of smiling Barnarda in a tree swing, her doll in her lap. "It's beautiful."

The little girl nodded, then turned to Andrea, a frown stealing over her plump face. "You won't forget, will you?"

"No, sweetheart." Andrea brushed her hand over the child's curly hair. "I'll have it framed and get it back to you."

"Time to go, Barnarda." Nurse Cipriano came up and grasped the handles of the wheelchair.

"Bye, Andrea." The child's face scrunched up as she looked at Nicholas; then she smiled. "Good-bye, Mr. Man."

Nicholas smiled. "Good-bye." He helped Andrea to her feet as the nurse rolled the child away. "You've made a lot of sick children happy. Thank you."

"Christmas is a time for children, a time for dreams and wishes to come true," she said without thought. Then she went still, expecting to see irritation replace his smile as it always did when the word *wish* was mentioned.

His expression didn't change, but his eyes did. They narrowed and burned with an intensity that caused her to shiver.

He stepped closer until they touched from chest to knees. His other hand caught her arm. "Guess what I dream about?"

She didn't have to guess. Too many mornings she'd awakened restless and aching. Her lips parted.

"There you are!"

The irritating voice broke the spell. Andrea jumped. Nicholas cursed, then wanted to curse again when he saw Ferrell. Despite the interested eyes of the two staff members who'd just brought a group of children to the atrium, Nicholas slid his arm around Andrea, anchoring her to his side.

"Yes," Nicholas said in a clipped voice.

The other man's eyes stayed on Andrea. "I wanted to ask if you needed any more volunteers."

"No."

"Perhaps I could help you, Andrea," Ferrell said with a winning smile. "I've heard you plan to have all the pictures framed. I'd be happy to help you financially and with anything else you might need."

"I—"

"She won't need your help, Ferrell," Nicholas said. "Now, if you'll excuse us, we're about to go to lunch."

Ferrell's face hardened. "Why don't you let Andrea decide if she needs my help or not?"

Nicholas had the urge to punch Ferrell in the nose for even daring to say Andrea's name. "Tell him."

Andrea was caught between being flattered and wanting to hit Nicholas over the head with her sketch pad for acting like a Neanderthal. "If I don't, are you going to drag me off by the hair?"

Ferrell hooted. "She told you."

Nicholas's body stiffened. His arm fell from around her waist. "My mistake."

"We can discuss everything over lunch, then dinner tonight," Ferrell suggested smoothly.

She would have to be stupid to think that's all he had in mind. "Thank you for your offer of a financial contribution, Dr. Ferrell. Since Nicholas is the unofficial chairman, you can give him the check. If I need any additional help, I'm sure Nicholas will be there to assist me." She slid her arm through his rigid one. "Please excuse us. As Nicholas said, we were about to go to lunch."

She could have been walking beside a mannequin. Nicholas was stiff and unsmiling as they went down the hall, then boarded the elevator. She punched 1 for the parking lot. He punched 2. Hospital employees in the enclosure took one look at Nicholas's face, then busied themselves elsewhere.

The elevator doors slid open on 2. She didn't even think of disregarding the firm pressure of his hand urging her off. At Michelle's questioning look, Andrea sent a wan smile. He didn't stop until he was inside his office.

She took consolation that he hadn't slammed the door and was preparing to state her case when his mouth crashed down on hers. The kiss was hot and greedy, flaring to life the second their lips touched. There was also need and desperation.

Andrea dived into the kiss, giving, reassuring. Whatever it was he needed from her, she'd gladly give. Eagerly she leaned into him, heard his hoarse groan of pleasure. Boldly, his hands cupped her hips against his hard arousal. Her tongue stroked his as he stroked her.

The world tilted. By the time she realized he'd picked her up, she was flat on her back on the leather sofa in his office, his hard body above her. Uncertainty swept through her. "Nicholas?"

His head came up, his eyes dark and intense for a long moment; then he shut his eyes and sat up, his face in his hands. Andrea didn't move for a long time, then tentatively touched his tense shoulder. He flinched.

She drew her hand back. She wanted to comfort him but didn't know how. "Nicholas?"

"I'm sorry. I don't know what came over me." He glanced over his shoulder at her propped up on one elbow, her hair mussed, her lips swollen from his kisses, and wanted to drag her back in his arms. He surged to his feet. "I have no excuse."

"Since I was eagerly participating, I don't expect any." She slid her legs over the leather cushion and sat upright.

His hands clenched and unclenched by his sides. "You have every right to see whoever you want."

"Not if your plan is going to work." Coming to her feet, she went to stand in front of him. "I spoke up for myself, so there won't be any doubt."

Her answer didn't appease him. What would happen once the need for the charade was over? His gut twisted.

Not wanting to think about it, he bent to pick her sketch pad up from the floor, then handed it to her. "Getting these framed will cost a lot of money. Why don't you ask the hospital auxiliary to help you?"

"I've already spoken with Mrs. Ricks, the president, and she's agreed to help." Andrea tucked the tablet beneath her arm. "You ready to feed me so I can go back upstairs and finish?"

Frowning, he rezipped her sweater-coat, then fingered her hair. She looked like a woman who'd been thoroughly kissed and had enjoyed herself immensely. While it gratified him, and he didn't care what people said about him, he didn't want her to be the topic of hospital gossip. "Maybe you should go into the bathroom and freshen up."

She handed him the pad, then went into the room he'd indicated to apply lipstick and comb her hair. "How do I look?" she asked when she came out.

"Tempting." He grabbed her arm. "Let's get out of here before I have to apologize all over again."

Nicholas barely touched his meat loaf. If one person came over to their table in the hospital cafeteria to say hello to Andrea or mention the sketches, fifteen came. She never seemed to mind that her hamburger was getting cold, her strawberry malt getting warm. She was heaped with praise and hugs. Almost every person who stopped by asked her to give their regards to her aunt. Clearly, both women were loved and respected in Jubilee.

That irrefutable fact caused Nicholas a bit of uneasiness. How would the townspeople react when there wasn't an engagement? Christmas was a little over a week away. Not even his impetuous brother would become engaged to a woman he'd never met before in such a short time.

Hours later Nicholas was still mulling over the situation when he knocked on Andrea's door. He didn't have an answer, but he was going to make darn sure people knew he thought she was special.

"Nicholas, come in," Andrea said as she opened the door. Her eyes and face lit up at the sight of him.

"Get your coat and come outside," he said. Andrea started out of the door, but he blocked her path. "Coat and gloves first. Your scarf, too."

"Andrea, do as your guest says," Aunt Augusta told her. "Good evening, Nicholas. You want to come inside?"

"No, thank you. I'll just wait here for Andrea."

"I'll be back in a minute." She rushed down the hall.

Nicholas shifted restlessly. He liked Augusta, but lately he got the feeling she saw right through him. Considering what he'd done with Andrea and what he'd like to do *to* her, he guessed Augusta had a right to make him nervous. "Nice weather we're having."

"Very nice," she replied.

"Think we'll have a white Christmas?"

"A little snow Christmas Eve, but it won't stick or stop a man in love from doing what has to be done."

Nicholas blinked and snapped his attention back to her. "What?"

Augusta simply smiled, then stepped back for Andrea, who was putting on her gloves as she raced down the hall. "Have fun and tell Larry to drive carefully."

Nicholas's mouth literally dropped open, but then Andrea was there and he couldn't ask her aunt how she'd known who was outside.

"I'm ready. What's up?"

Mentally shaking himself, Nicholas led her onto the porch. "I'd thought we'd view the Christmas lights around town the old-fashioned way."

Andrea followed the direction of his gaze and squealed with delight. Grabbing his hand, she raced toward the horse-drawn open carriage that Larry Adair rented out for weddings and other special occasions.

Helping Andrea inside, Nicholas climbed up and sat beside

her, still puzzled until he saw what he'd forgotten. From the living room you could see the road. Obviously, Augusta had been looking out the window and had seen them pull up. Chiding himself for his overactive imagination, Nicholas tucked the blanket around Andrea's knees. "Let's go, Larry, and Mrs. Augusta said to tell you to drive carefully."

"Sure enough, Mr. Darling. Mrs. Augusta might do good with her gift, but that might change if a man harms Miss Andrea."

Laughing softly, Andrea shook her head. "Mr. Adair, shame on you. You know Auntie has never harmed a soul."

"That don't mean she won't," Larry said with an emphatic nod of his black top hat.

The disquiet Nicholas had experienced earlier returned. Frowning, he glanced toward the living room window. Then Andrea snuggled closer and laid her head on his shoulder. Curving his arms around her shoulders, he forgot everything but how good it felt for her to be in his arms again.

Barely three days later, he regretted that lapse.

Five days before Christmas, Nicholas knocked on Andrea's door and received no answer. He'd seen her earlier when she and a couple of volunteers had delivered the children's framed and wrapped portraits. The staff on the floor, Andrea, and the two women volunteers had all cried.

He knocked again. Since both cars were in the garage, he had a pretty good idea of where he'd find Andrea. He came off the porch.

Rounding the corner of the house, he saw her beneath the

huge maple tree, but she was neither writing nor sketching. She was crying. His heart in his throat, he raced to her. "What's the matter? What is it?"

Andrea sniffed. "I just finished *A Risk Worth Taking*. Braxton finally learned that no risk is too great to keep the woman he loves by his side. They made it, Nicholas."

He bent to kiss the tears away from her eyes, her cheeks, the corner of her mouth, then her mouth. They ended up stretched out on the grass. He had just enough presence of mind to keep his hand from wandering. "Congratulations."

"Thank you."

"What are you two celebrating?" Augusta said from less than five feet away.

Nicholas shot to his feet, dragging Andrea with him. He opened his mouth to apologize, then noticed Augusta was smiling. It was the same smile he'd seen when she granted him his wish. He began to tremble.

"No," he whispered. "It can't be."

"Your wish has come true, Nicholas," Augusta told him.

A whimper of pain came from Andrea. She closed her eyes. She'd lost him.

Nicholas grabbed both of Andrea's arms. Black eyes blazed. "Did you know?" he shouted.

"Know what?" she questioned, frowning.

His mouth tightened into a thin line before he said, "That you're my wish woman."

CHAPTER 9

can't be," Andrea said, regret in her voice. She looked at her aunt. "Tell him."

"Perhaps we should go inside and discuss this," Augusta said calmly.

"We'll discuss it now." Nicholas stepped away from Andrea. "All I want to know is, were you in on this? Did you know?"

Andrea glanced from her aunt to Nicholas, the enormity of what was going on finally sinking in. She was to be Nicholas's. She swayed. Nicholas reached out to steady her, but when she reached toward him, he stepped back. His cold gaze sliced through her.

"I didn't know." She spoke to her aunt: "Is . . . is it true?"

Augusta smiled. "Didn't I tell you what will be will be?"

Andrea shook her head. "I . . . I thought you meant his wish."

Her aunt laid her hand gently on Andrea's arm. "And your unspoken wish. When the dream came to me of you and Nicholas together, I wept with happiness. After all these years of having the gift, I'd finally be able to bring happiness to a member of my own family."

The women hugged each other. "Oh, Auntie! I can't believe it." Smiling, Andrea turned to Nicholas. His face remained cold.

Then she remembered he didn't believe in love, didn't want it. Tears sparkled in her eyes.

"Ma'am, you really pulled one over on me," he said tightly. "I was a fool not to realize that you'd never condone Andrea going out with me if you thought there was another woman out there for me. But your little plan failed."

Augusta silently studied him for a long moment. "You mean you don't care about my niece? That you wouldn't do anything to keep her from the slightest harm? That you wouldn't put her needs before your own?"

Nicholas's eyes widened. Her words were too close to things he'd thought and felt. "You keep forgetting. I wished for my brother, not me."

"Then," she said with a nod. "But how about when you were growing up? When you were a little boy in Akron? Before your friends started having marital problems?" she asked.

He ignored the chill that raced over him, refusing to believe. Andrea had told Augusta he was from Akron. She just had a lucky guess about the rest. "I'm leaving."

Augusta wasn't finished with him. "Once a wish is granted, I'm not allowed to interfere. But I should tell you that if you keep on running from the truth and refusing to believe, it may be taken away from you."

Andrea gasped. Nicholas's knees almost buckled. "Nothing will happen to Andrea."

Augusta shook her head. "Andrea will find happiness. If not with you, then with another. Is that what you want?"

For Nicholas, even the wind stopped blowing. It was as if nature and time stood still, listening, waiting for him to speak. He wanted to scoff at Augusta's words, but couldn't. Neither could he look at Andrea. Just the thought of any man touching her enraged him, but there was no such thing as a person being able to grant wishes or see the future. Turning, he walked away.

Behind him, Andrea wept in her aunt's arms. "Auntie, what am I going to do? I love him so."

"I'm afraid there's nothing you can do. Nicholas has to decide."

Brushing away tears, Andrea lifted her head. "What if he can't?"

"He'll lose, and so, my precious darling, will you."

The hospital's grapevine was running true to form. Less than two days after Nicholas stopped seeing Andrea, his name was back on the wish list. But women weren't chasing after him as they had before. In fact, people in general left him alone. That was fine with him. He needed to get things in shape before he went to Philadelphia for the holidays. There was nothing to keep him in Jubilee. He was flying out early Christmas morning. But first he had to attend the Christmas Eve party at the hospital.

Straightening his tie, he jerked his jacket from the bed and headed out the door, reminding himself that he needed to ask the housekeeper to take down the tree. It wasn't cowardly not to do it himself; he simply didn't have time.

Are you just going to give up?" Elaine asked, sitting beside Andrea in the middle of her living room floor.

"If he's what you want, go after him. Or I could beat him up for you," Travis offered.

"I'll help," said Clint.

"Me, too," agreed John.

Andrea blinked away the tears that were never far since Nicholas had walked out of her life. "I told you, he has to make the decision on his own."

"Pleeazze." Elaine waved her slender, manicured hand. "Since when has a man been able to come to a decision without the help of a woman?"

Her comment garnered the expected howls of disagreement from the men. Travis was the loudest. "Since when has a woman been able to come to a decision, period?"

He and Elaine went nose to nose, then lip to lip. Elaine slipped her arm around his neck and deepened the kiss.

Andrea sniffed. She couldn't be happier for her friends. Tears rolled down her cheek.

"Stop that! You're making Andrea cry," Clint said, snatching a tissue from the box on the coffee table.

"I'm sorry," Andrea said. "Don't mind me."

"You want us to go and beat him up?" John asked.

"I don't think that would help, fellas." Elaine sat down beside her again. "You really love him, don't you?"

"More than I ever thought possible."

"Then why are you sitting here?" Coming to her feet, Elaine pulled Andrea up. "When we get through with you, Nick will be drooling."

"But will he accept his wish?"

"There's a sure way to find out."

The Bluebonnet Ballroom of the hotel was jumping. People in the medical profession worked hard and partied harder.

They, better than most, knew how fragile life could be. The only person not having a good time was Nicholas. Arms folded, he sat in the back of the festive room in gold and white. Unlike the many people on the parquet dance floor doing the Electric Slide, the live music of the band didn't move him at all.

He'd planned on putting in an obligatory appearance, then leaving. Beverly Hawkins had insisted he stay. He was fully prepared to ignore her request until her husband and the other board members started talking about it being good for morale. He'd give it another five minutes; then he was—

His arms unfolded. He was unaware of coming to his feet.

Andrea stared hungrily at Nicholas, but when she started toward him, he sat back down. Her hands clenched inside the deep burgundy velvet cloak that matched her long dress. He looked as miserable as she felt. "I never wanted him to be unhappy."

None of her friends said anything, just stepped closer, giving her moral and emotional support. Andrea didn't notice them or that she and Nicholas had become the center of attention. If his caring for her made him that unhappy, she didn't want it for him.

She went to the table where Delores, Eula, and Rachel were selling wish tickets. "May I buy one?"

"I'm sorry, Andrea, but it's for hospital employees only," Delores said, her regret obvious.

"Can't an exception be made?" Elaine asked. "This is important to her."

Beverly Hawkins strolled up to the table, bringing her husband with her. "I'd like to purchase some tickets. How many do you think I'll need, Andrea?"

"I have to buy them myself," she said.

"Sell her the tickets," Bob Hawkins said. "After what she did for the children, I can't see anyone objecting. But if they do, send them to me."

"Yes, sir. How many?" Delores picked up the pad of printed tickets.

"All of them," Andrea said. "I intend to win."

Nicholas had tried to act as if he didn't care that Andrea was there, but he couldn't take his eyes off her. When she'd stopped at the table where the women were selling the wish registration tickets, he couldn't quite believe it. Andrea hadn't made a wish since her parents died.

He knew that with bone-chilling certainty. Then what was she wishing for? *Me.* He came out of his chair to cross the room. People parted. All except her friends. "Move out of the way."

"It's all right." Andrea turned the pad she'd been writing on over.

Nicholas glanced at the back of the pad, then at her. "It won't do you any good. Even if they pull my name, I don't believe in wishes."

"I know, but you'll be free." Getting up, she went to the table and gave Delores the tickets. She didn't even glance at him as she went to the other side of the room. Her friends gathered around her.

Nicholas heard the drumroll, then a call for silence. He stared at Andrea and felt unease scuttle down his spine. Out of nowhere he heard Mrs. Augusta's voice: *If you keep on running from the truth, refusing to believe, it may be taken away from you.*

That was nonsense. A person couldn't grant wishes.

"This is the moment we've all waited for." Delores spun the metal drum. "The winning ticket will receive half of the money made through sales to make their wish come true, and the remaining half will go to charity. Good luck." She stopped the tumble of papers. "Mr. Hawkins will draw."

Bob Hawkins reached inside. Nicholas watched tears roll down Andrea's cheek, saw her mouth *Good-bye*. It clicked all at once. She hadn't tried to trap him. Her wish had been to set him free.

Even as Nicholas shook his head in denial, he heard Bob Hawkins speak: "Well, I'll be. The winning ticket belongs to Nicholas Darling."

The more she swiped, the more tears fell. Nicholas was lost to her forever. Curled up on the sofa, she didn't move when she heard an impatient knock on the front door. "Please tell them I just want to be alone." As soon as Elaine had stopped her parents' car, Andrea had gotten out and forbidden them to follow. It had started to snow and she didn't want them on the roads.

"Andrea."

Her head came up. Nicholas stood in the doorway, snow-flakes sprinkled over his black topcoat. "Don't cry. Please don't cry. It took me a long time, but I love you. I love you."

She leaped from the couch. He caught her, lifting her against his wide chest. "I love you. I love you," he repeated over and over.

"But what did you wish for?" she asked.

He drew the winning ticket out of his pocket and handed it

to her. "That you'd be able to stay in Jubilee, and that you'd find a man who'd love you through all time."

Her eyes misted again, this time with happiness. "Nicholas."

He drew her into his arms again. "I bought the ticket on impulse after we started going out. I admired you so and wanted you to be happy, even if I wasn't that man."

She grinned up at him. "Did you really?"

"Yes . . . after I broke him into little pieces."

She kissed him. "My hero."

"Finally. Like Braxton, I learned no risk is too great to keep the woman you love by your side. We'll have our happily ever after. Will you marry me?"

"Yes, oh, yes."

In the hallway, Augusta smiled, remembering the dream she'd had the night before. Nicholas and Andrea were decorating their Christmas tree in this very house with the added tradition of snowflake ornaments while their four happy children helped.

On the coffee table were several published books by Andrea. Among them was a hardcover copy of *A Risk Worth Taking*. Nicholas and Andrea had taken a risk and had been rewarded with a lifetime of happiness.

And it had all started with a wish.

DONNA HILL began her career in 1987 writing short stories for *Confession Magazines.* Since that time she has more than one hundred published titles to her credit since her first novel was released in 1990 and is considered one of the early pioneers of the African American romance genre. Three of her novels have been adapted for television. She has been featured in *Essence,* the New York *Daily News, USA Today, Today's Black Woman,* and *Black Enterprise,* among many others. She has received numerous awards for her body of work—which crosses several genres—including the Career Achievement Award; the Trailblazer Award, of which she was the first recipient; the Zora Neale Hurston Literary Award; and the Gold Pen Award, among others, as well as commendations for her community service. As an editor she has packaged several highly successful novels and anthologies, two of which were nominated for awards. Donna is a graduate of Goddard College with an MFA in creative writing and is currently in pursuit of her doctor of arts in English pedagogy and technology. She is an assistant professor of professional writing at Medgar Evers College and lives in Brooklyn, New York, with her family. Her most recent novel, *Confessions in B-Flat,* received a starred review from *Publishers Weekly.* She can be found at donnaohill.com.

FRANCIS RAY (1944–2013) is the *New York Times* and *USA Today* bestselling author of the Grayson novels, the Falcon books, the Taggart Brothers, and *Twice the Temptation,* among many other books. Her novel *Incognito* was made into a movie aired on BET. A native Texan, she was a graduate of Texas Woman's University and had a degree in nursing. Besides a writer, she was a school nurse practitioner with the Dallas Independent School District. She lived in Dallas. "Francis Ray is, without a doubt, one of the Queens of Romance" (*Romance Review*).